THE ARMAGEDDON Strain

Book One of The Countdown

A NOVEL BY
SHARON K. GILBERT

W
WHITAKER
HOUSE

deepercalling

This novel is a work of fiction. References to real events, organizations, or places are used in a fictional context. Any resemblances to actual persons, living or dead, is entirely coincidental.

THE ARMAGEDDON STRAIN
Book One of The Countdown

All inquiries regarding this publication and Sharon K. Gilbert may be made to:
www.mytharc.com
e-mail: sharon@mytharc.com or derek@mytharc.com

ISBN-13: 978-0-88368-810-6
ISBN-10: 0-88368-810-7
Printed in the United States of America
© 2004, 2005 by Sharon K. Gilbert

1030 Hunt Valley Circle
New Kensington, PA 15068
website: www.whitakerhouse.com

www.deepercalling.com

Library of Congress Cataloging-in-Publication Data

Gilbert, Sharon K., 1952–
The Armageddon strain / Sharon K. Gilbert.
p. cm. — (The countdown series ; bk. 1)
ISBN-10: 0-88368-810-7 (trade pbk. : alk. paper)
ISBN-13: 978-0-88368-810-6 (trade pbk. : alk. paper)
1. Influenza—Fiction. 2. End of the world—Fiction. 3. Women physicians—Fiction. 4. Scientists—Death—Fiction. I. Title.
PS3607.I42325A89 2005
813'.6—dc22   2004027639

1 2 3 4 5 6 7 8 9 10 11 12 13 **ɯ** 14 13 12 11 10 09 08 07 06 05

DEDICATION

TO MY LOVING PARENTS, WHO IMPARTED TO ME THEIR CURIOUS NATURES, THEIR INNATE JOY AT BEING ALIVE, AND A DEEP FAITH IN THE LOVE OF GOD.

TO MOM, FOR GIVING ME A LOVE OF READING AND STORYTELLING, AND TO DAD, FOR HIS UNSHAKEABLE BELIEF IN MY CHILDHOOD DREAMS. THANK YOU BOTH FOR IMPRINTING UPON MY LIFE A LITTLE BIT OF YOUR OWN REMARKABLE SELVES.

Finally, my brethren, be strong in the Lord, and in the power of his might. Put on the whole armour of God, that ye may be able to stand against the wiles of the devil. For we wrestle not against flesh and blood, but against principalities, against powers, against the rulers of the darkness of this world, against spiritual wickedness in high places.
—Ephesians 6:10–12 KJV

And I heard a great voice out of the temple saying to the seven angels, Go your ways, and pour out the vials of the wrath of God upon the earth. And the first went, and poured out his vial upon the earth; and there fell a noisome and grievous sore upon the men which had the mark of the beast, and upon them which worshipped his image.
—Revelation 16:1–2 KJV

PROLOGUE

The final plague began on April 1st, a fitting and ironic begin-ning to an end, a day of fools and folly, a day when all but a handful of humans across the global village smiled into mirrors, broke bread with friends and family, sang lullabies to sleepy-eyed children, or turned on the evening news. Little did they know that the glory days of bread and circuses would soon be at an end, and that their glit-tering boxes of light and shadow would soon spit out lies to bury the terrible seeds that six men now sowed in a New Mexico desert.

"Can you hear me?" called a short man to his much taller companion. The pair was joined by four more men emerging from two shiny black cars. Each of them wore a ghostly white Hazmat suit and filtered mask.

"Is that the farm over there?" called the taller to the first man.

The short man nodded. "Rick! See that first shed—the one with the open door? I think that's where we need to start. Can you hear me?"

Rick Albertson nodded. He looked like a fat, white worm in the hot jumpsuit. Sweat already poured down his cheeks, and he wiped at his brow, his gloved hand clicking against the heavy plastic of the face shield. "Curse it all! Why couldn't we get the techs to do this?"

The short man patted his taller, heavier colleague on the shoulder sympathetically. "It's for the best, Rick. You, me, and the others, we might not be field ops, but we understand this stuff better than the techs ever could. Half an hour, and we'll be back in our cars and looking forward to a round of beers. How's that sound?"

"Like it's half an hour too long to wait," the white worm replied, his gray marble eyes searching the dusty farm for signs of life. "OK, let's do this. Three teams, right? Two each. Who do you want me to work with, Arnie?"

Dr. Arnold Smith pointed to the other four men, indicating a thin blob of white with a small tank attached to a sling on his back. "Why don't you go with Pete over there. Hey, Pete! You and Rick take that first shed. Look for signs of life first, then start spraying. Charlie, you and Tom take that second shed. Sam and I will take the house for now. We'll all meet up in the barn. Got it?"

"I don't like this wind, Arnie," came a mellow voice in Smith's ear.

"I hear that, Tommy, but we don't have much choice in the matter. The orders are to disperse the solution. Look, this is just a test farm. The folks in weather approved this morning's run, so let's get it over with. Everyone set? Let's rock and roll."

The six men fanned out in pairs, two to a battered chicken shed on the northwest end of the test farm; two to the second chicken shed, slightly longer in length but equally weathered and rotting; two to a spindly building known as the house, an empty shell filled with magazines, ancient furniture, and a rusting sink.

A dry wind etched fine lines into their face masks, and the mid-morning sun felt hot enough to melt flesh. A recent rash of solar flares had kicked up the temperatures in the New Mexican desert, and today's afternoon high would easily hit 115 degrees. Ridiculous for early April.

Dr. Tom Foil followed his team leader, a molecular biologist and longtime friend named Charles Hilliard, to the second shed. The pair looked like aliens in the strange landscape, and Hilliard laughed as they stepped into the abandoned building.

"We look like a couple of moon men, Tommy. Say, is that a chicken? I thought this place was supposed to be empty."

Inside, in the far right corner sat a scrawny white bird, stubbornly squatting upon a nest of six eggs.

"Ah, shoot! This isn't supposed to happen! Goble said he checked this place out. Arnie, you there? We got a brooding chicken in here!"

Smith answered from his position inside the crumbling house. "Chicken? Are you serious? Check it. It's got to be dead."

"He says check it," Foil said to Hilliard. "He doesn't believe me."

Hilliard shrugged and stooped next to the chicken, wincing as his seventy-one-year-old knees complained. "Hey there, Henrietta. You alive or not?"

The hen squawked, scratched at Charlie's shield, and began racing around the dusty floorboards, feigning a wing injury to keep the intruders from her precious nest.

"That's an affirmative," Hilliard laughed. "She's got four pretty whites and two browns. What do you say? We could take these home and introduce them to Irish potatoes and a rasher of bacon."

"Negative," Smith called back, not the least bit amused. "Take nothing, touch nothing. Leave the hen. She's not going to last in this climate anyway. Just spray the area so we can say we did it. When we come back in two weeks to collect samples, she'll be dead, even if we find that 456 can't survive in the arid conditions of the desert. Copy that?"

"Yeah, sure, I copy," Hilliard replied, not bothering to conceal his frustration. "Tommy, you ready? I want to get this over with and get back to the lab. I'm too old for this field stuff, especially in this kind of weather. Man, it's hot!"

Foil, ten years younger than Hilliard but feeling the heat, bit his lip. "The suits don't help, C. D. What's Arnie thinking, telling us to spray with this chicken in here? I'm not sure that's a good idea."

"I understand, Tommy, but Henrietta here isn't going to spread 456 to anyone or anything, not with the safety features we built into it. We'll lock the door behind us when we leave, and if 456 works at all, she'll be dead within a couple of days. If it doesn't work, she'll still be dead in a couple days, with the heat and all. Come on. Let's get it over with. My ticker's gonna short-circuit if we don't get back to air-conditioning soon."

Foil nodded, switched on the canister marked Sln. 456, and lifted the trigger sprayer from its holster. "Here goes," he said as his forefinger pulled on the plastic trigger.

A fine spray began to fill the air, and the chicken stopped her frenzied dance to stare for a moment. As if sensing the danger, the Rhode Island White scurried back to the meager nest and covered the six smooth eggs with her emaciated body.

Noticing the hen's bravery, Foil paused for a second, wishing he could snatch up the chicken and remove her and her eggs from harm's way. *Too late*, he thought. *She's already exposed.*

Biting his lower lip so hard he drew a thin trickle of blood, Foil reactivated the spray head and dispensed the remainder of the container. He watched the fine mist hang in the air, illuminated by the yellow fingers of the morning sun, and he suddenly realized what he and the other scientists from BioStrain had unleashed. *It's no good letting it bother you,* he thought to himself. *You can't unstop the bottle now. May God forgive us.*

The pair of scientists finished up their task, each emptying a canister of 456 into the shed. Small dust devils took up the aerosolized virus and carried it to freedom outside the rotting timbers. The Rhode Island White watched from her dark corner. Within seconds, the lethal virus had infiltrated her lungs and eyes, where it swiftly began compromising cell walls and weakening blood vessels. After only five minutes, the hen began to twitch, and bright blood poured from her black eyes and pale beak. Red life dripped onto the brown and white eggs, and the mother hen spat and coughed, her body racked by convulsions.

As they watched in horror, the two men stared at each other, dumbfounded, their pale faces reflecting their shock.

"Oh, my dear God! It isn't supposed to work this fast! What have we done?" shouted Tom. In his ear, he could hear Smith's reprimands, orders to act like a scientist instead of a child. Tom didn't care. "Charlie! It isn't supposed to react like this! What in heaven's name is in this canister?"

Charles Hilliard couldn't answer. His mouth had flown open, and his eyes glazed over with shock. As he regained his composure, he grabbed Tom Foil's arm and shouted. "We've been had, Tommy! This isn't what we've spent the last four years creating! It's that Grayson!"

As the chicken bled out, neither man noticed the pale iguana that had slipped into the shed, mouth open, tail held high. The lizard's cold eyes followed the men's white shapes, waiting until they had disappeared through the doorway. They barred the door and locked it with a steel padlock. Neither man saw the iguana steal toward the unguarded nest and take a brown egg into its jaws.

Once the lizard had gorged upon the bloody eggs, it crept back into the blazing desert, carrying Solution 456 in its own resistant veins, ready to infect a hungry condor that had been watching the iguana's movements since dawn.

As the two black company cars sped away toward the underground laboratories of BioStrain, the condor pounced, carrying the iguana back to its own clutch of hatchlings not far from the small village of Los Muertos, New Mexico.

The Armageddon Strain had been born.

CHAPTER 1

Six weeks later—Saturday

Maggie closed her eyes against the glare of a merciless afternoon sun. Despite the shade cast by the striped canvas awning that the funeral home had provided, she could feel her face burning.

She hadn't cried. Four days of hell had passed through her life, and she hadn't broken down—not even a whimper. *We're so sorry, but your father passed away twenty minutes ago. Would you like to speak with his nurse?*

How many times had she played those words over and over again in her brain until even the echo hurt? She should have been there—with him. She had failed her father in the final moments of his life, and she couldn't go back and fix it. Not now, not ever.

"At least it isn't raining," she heard her cousin Andrea whisper. Ninety degrees and near saturation humidity, insane weather for Indiana so early in the summer. It needed to rain. The skies weighed down upon them, ready to weep, yet not one drop of emotion. Not even a tear.

The preacher consoled the family quietly as he walked the line of folding chairs, addressing the mourners who sweated and fanned themselves in the heat. Maggie's mother smiled bravely. Her two sisters and twin brother shook the cleric's sweaty hand, each blinking away tears.

"Dr. Hilliard, I am truly sorry for your loss," he said as he reached Maggie.

Liar. He hadn't even known her father.

"It's actually Dr. Taylor," she corrected. *At least until my divorce is final.* "Thank you, Reverend. Your message was very, uh, comforting."

The minister withdrew his hand, a soft blob of thick, white flesh. He smiled, but the sentiment didn't quite reach his pale blue eyes, watering in the heat. "God's will be done."

Maggie shivered as the cleric passed by on his way to speak with the funeral home director. Carol Hilliard, Maggie's sixteen-year-old half-sister, nudged her impishly. "He's probably asking if they keep any snacks in the limo."

Maggie tried to laugh, but it came out as a pitiful squeak. "Let's go," she said softly, rising to join the others as they filed out of the makeshift tent. She didn't want to think of her dad this way. There had to be more than an empty ceremony at the end of a person's life. *Two dozen mourners, a stranger in a white suit, and a circus tent. Daddy would have been mortified.*

Then again, what did it matter to him now? Maggie could use a stiff drink.

"You're coming over, right?" Doug asked, shielding his eyes from the bright sun. "Angie's gone all out to welcome everybody. It'd mean a lot to her if you came, Mags."

Maggie forced a smile to a passing well-wisher, inwardly wincing at her brother's suggestion. He'd been married to Angela Wickert for eleven years. Doug's successful trucking business provided a gigantic house, which they shared with their three dogs. Angie was the perfect homemaker, decorating their home with painted birdhouses and sunny flowers. Maggie always felt choked there.

"I'd love to," she lied, figuring it was easier than going into long, painful explanations. She'd make an early exit and head back to Bloomington where she could bury her head in a pile of term papers from her lackluster summer school students. "I can't stay long though. Finals start Monday," she explained, noting Doug's disappointed look. " Is Connie coming?"

Constance Hilliard, Doug and Maggie's older sister, had been diagnosed with Alzheimer's years earlier and had been living with their mother in Madison. Connie's cheerful demeanor never changed, but doctors had promised little hope for remission. That didn't seem to matter to Alice Hilliard. She adored her oldest child, and the two had become a frequent sight on the downtown streets of Madison's historic district. The pair could be found strolling past the antique shops, both wearing bright smiles and carrying umbrellas, no matter what the weather.

"Connie will be there," Doug told her. "Maggie, you're welcome to stay the night. We have plenty of room. Think about it, OK?"

Maggie loved her brother dearly. He reminded her of their father, Dr. Charles Douglas Hilliard, scientist deluxe.

"I'll think about it. Let's get out of here. It's hot, and I'm roasting."

The pair headed toward the limo. Overhead, two helicopters circled, the size of birds. Maggie turned one last time to view the lonely, mahogany casket. Already, a digger had set about preparing the hydraulic equipment that would lower her father's remains into the precisely dug hole in the ground. Cold, dark, and deep. A slight breeze ruffled the awning, making a loud flapping sound, completely out of place in the still cemetary.

Maggie tilted her head upward, narrowing her eyes against the glare. Why helicopters? They seemed to be circling the cemetery like a brace of postmodern vultures. It couldn't be reporters. The death of one minor scientist wasn't very newsworthy.

"Must be a couple of birds from the old proving ground," Doug muttered. "Dad had a lot of friends there. Maybe it's a salute of some sort."

"Maybe," Maggie replied. "Funny that none of them showed up today. I suppose twenty-eight years of service doesn't warrant personal attendance."

"Come on, sis. Mom's waiting in the car with Connie. We'll talk more at the house."

The pair slid into the shiny black limousine, a funeral home "courtesy" that had only tacked on an additional three hundred dollars to the tab. Maybe she *would* stay at Doug's. The winding, hilly drive back to Bloomington wasn't much fun after dark. The older Maggie got, the less she liked driving at night.

As the limo pulled into the light Saturday afternoon traffic, Maggie felt hackles rising on the back of her neck. *He'll sleep in a cold hole tonight,* she thought, *with nothing more than a small white cross to mark his spot upon this earth.*

She'd need more than dinner and polite conversation to make it through this night without breaking down. She'd need at least a pint. And that would be just a start.

CHAPTER 2

Doug and Angie Hilliard lived comfortably in a meandering, tri-level modern with vaulted ceilings and a sunken family room. Five bedrooms, four baths, a multi-level deck, sauna, indoor pool, and European kitchen completed the perfect home that perched on a serene bluff overlooking the Ohio River. Maggie followed her brother into the family room, noting a heatless gas fire dancing in a creek stone fireplace. Only Angie would have a fire going in this heat.

"Hi, Mags," smiled Angela, hugging her sister-in-law tightly. "I'm so sorry about your dad. He was such a rare man. I wish I could have been at the cemetery, but Doug insisted I stay home. I'll tell you why in a bit." She eased past Maggie, holding out her small hands to Connie. "Hello, Connie, honey!"

Maggie glanced around the open space and longed for a corner to hide in. She'd been on the wagon for nearly three months, but this was killing her. She needed alcohol, and she needed it now.

"Drink, Maggie?" Doug asked from behind. "We've got iced tea, any kind of pop you can name, and a wonderful punch Angie's mother made. How about an orange soda? You used to love those."

"Put two fingers of vodka into it, and that'll be great," she answered, not bothering to hide her agony. "Sorry, Doug. Just kidding. Coke is fine."

Doug gave her a hug. "I'm really proud of you, sis."

"Where are the mutts?" she asked, looking around for the family's three dachshunds.

"We figured they'd be underfoot too much, so we boarded them in town. They'll be back by tomorrow afternoon, if you miss them, sis."

"That's just fine—they can stay right where they are. You know me and dogs."

"I sure do!" Doug laughed, recalling a Halloween night when a neighbor's German shepherd had thought the giggling ghost at his master's door needed to be taught a lesson. Maggie, the very surprised ghost, couldn't sit down for a week.

Maggie punched Doug lightly for laughing. "It wasn't funny, you big jerk! Now get me that Coke!"

Doug left for the kitchen, and Maggie looked around for a friendly face.

"Hey, Maggedy Ann."

Maggie turned toward the sound of her name to discover a tall, muscular man of about forty-five. His crinkly eyes of light blue sparkled, and his smile was as broad and honest as ever. "Andrew Ryder. Little Andy Pandy," she said with a genuine smile. "I thought you had moved to Washington."

Ryder nodded, walking her to a quiet corner. "I'm still there, but I'm not with the Justice Department any more. My new job is flexible enough to allow me to take a few weeks off to come back here for C. D.'s funeral. Gosh, I miss him, Maggie. Good man, your dad. Top of the line."

"He was the line, Andy. I hadn't realized you knew him that well. Dad and Mom were already divorced when you and I were dating, and he and wife number two—what was her name? Oh yeah, Penny—well, they were at White Sands by that time."

Ryder leaned back against the wall. His graceful movements reminded her of a cat. "We met a few times—once at Christmas when I gave you that Beatles album you'd been dying for, and you said you already had it. Remember?"

Maggie smiled for the first time in days. "I remember. *Yesterday and Today*. Dad mailed it to me a week before he got into town. He'd wrapped it up in a huge box with lots of paper and a bright blue bow. I really felt awful that I hadn't told you before Christmas, but I kept both of them. They're worth quite a bit now."

"Not as much as you, Maggedy Ann," Ryder said, smiling. "I would have given you the moon, if you'd asked for it, but I was glad you and your dad spent some quality time together. I know it was hard for you to be separated from him."

"More than I'd like to admit," she whispered tightly, her pent-up grief seeking release, but Doug's return interrupted the moment.

"A Coke in a tall glass and a cup of Angie's best coffee with the works for Major Ryder here."

"Major?" Maggie asked, wiping stubbornly at an escaped tear. "I thought you were a suit, Andy."

Ryder took the coffee and raised an eyebrow, unruffled. "Doug's teasing me. The major bit is a courtesy title. I guess it lends me an air of respectability when I'm on assignment. That's all. I'm still just a suit."

"He's a spooky suit, if you know what I mean," Doug said with a small laugh. "Hey, Maggie, be sure to make a moment for Angie. She wants to tell you our good news."

"I could use some good news," she replied, sipping the soft drink. "Is she still in the kitchen?"

"Nope. She went upstairs with Mom. I think they're starting a hen party. You may as well join them. Andy's not going anywhere. He's promised to let me beat him in a round of Ping-Pong downstairs. You can have him back after I've given him a sound thrashing."

Maggie grinned. If memory served her right, Andrew Ryder had been Indiana State table tennis champ in '75 and '76. "OK, Dougie. See you in a bit." She shot a smile at Ryder and headed toward the master bedroom suite at the top of the back staircase.

"Ping-Pong?" Ryder asked after Maggie had left.

"I have a table in the basement," Doug replied, leading the way to the finished lower level. "And we can talk while we're down there. Dad sent me a lot of his papers before he died, so we can have a look. Maybe the documents you asked about are there."

Ryder finished his coffee. "OK, Doug, let's see what you've got. And take it easy on the major stuff. I'd hate it if your sister got the wrong idea about me."

"I wouldn't worry. She likes you, Andy. But she's torn up about Dad's death. It's hit her the hardest, even though she doesn't want to show it."

"Fair enough."

Upstairs, Maggie sat gently on the bed. She didn't want to disturb the double-stuffed, down-filled comforter, covered in a rose-patterned duvet with tiny button closures. The vast bedroom suite would hold Maggie's entire Bloomington apartment. Assistant professors didn't make much in the Medical Sciences department, but she'd finally finished her molecular biology doctorate—thanks to a rescheduled defense—so she'd been promised a boost to associate professor and a tenure track.

With the M.D. and a Ph.D. in physiology she'd earned back in 1984, and now a second Ph.D. in molecular biology, she could buy a real house once the divorce from Jackson was final. Then she could look forward to spending her entire life in academia, and she would finally move up from carving cadavers to lecturing graduate students about genetics and forensic pathology.

"So we decided to go with the chenille rather than the velvet," she overheard Angie saying in the background. "Anyway, now that we've finally finished redecorating the house, we have to redo one of the rooms. Can you believe it?" Her schoolgirl voice sounded even more giggly than usual.

Maggie's attention unwillingly turned toward the gaggle of women. All eyes were glued to Angela's bright, cherubic little face.

"Well? Why the redo?" Angie's mother insisted. "You've been hinting at something all day!"

The diminutive woman, so easily dwarfed by her husband's six-and-a-half foot height, suddenly seemed larger than life, and her voice sang with excitement. "We're pregnant!"

Screams of congratulations and laughter filled the air, and arms encircled Angela while female voices chattered, demanding to know when she had found out, what Doug had said, and when she was due.

"Doug and I are really excited about it. Isn't it wonderful, Maggie?"

Maggie offered Angela her best warm smile. "I'm delighted, sis. You and Doug have waited ages for this. Does your doctor feel good about it?"

"Maggie!" her mother scolded. "I'm not sure that's any of our business!"

Maggie rose and gave Angie a hug. "Sorry. I'm just being a realist. Forty is a tricky age for first babies. I just want to make sure you and this little one are all right."

"Don't start preaching genetics, Margaret Ann," her mother insisted. "Doug and Angie deserve a little happiness. God's finally blessed them, and we should all be thankful."

"It's okay, Mom," Angie said, putting on a wide smile. "I'm fine, and I really do value Maggie's expertise." Angie turned to Maggie, "Dr. Pryor says the baby has every chance of being perfectly normal. He did recommend an amniocentesis, just to be sure, but he's confident that Doug and I will be proud parents in a little less than six months."

Another round of congratulations ensued, and Maggie fell back a bit. She'd talk to Doug and insist on the amniocentesis. They'd waited this long to be parents; they deserved to know the exact state of their baby's health.

"Hey, Maggie!" cousin Andrea called from the doorway. "That guy from Washington is asking for you. You'd better get down there. Doug has broken out the old football movies!"

"Angie, we'll chat later, OK? I may be staying overnight, so we can talk in the morning over a cup of your best."

Angela beamed. "Tell Doug we'll all be down there in a little while."

Maggie left the room, her ears buzzing from female laughter. She had never really fit in at times like this. When Charlotte had been alive, she'd nearly managed it, but even then, Maggie's scientific mind made her a square peg. Since the accident, she had little stomach for talk of babies and miracles. Five years ago, her life had changed forever, and she could never go back. Just like she couldn't alter the fact that her father had gone to his eternal rest in a mahoghany box six feet underground. Was that all there was at the end of life?

Ever the outsider, Maggie related best to Doug. Maybe it was because they were twins, or maybe it was because Maggie felt alienated in small talk.

Tonight, she'd try to fit in, for Dad's sake.

Maggie had spent most of the evening watching old home movies of holiday gatherings and Doug's football games, some showing her dad, some not. They would all be without him now. She'd left during the Christmas 1968 movie, when her father had given her a blue bicycle and her mother had learned he'd been cheating on her. Some memories weren't meant to be relived.

Ryder had followed her up the stairs and out the south doors to the wide, hardwood deck that overlooked the river.

"It's beautiful here, isn't it?"

"It's home, that's what it is, Andy. I grew up on this river. Somehow calling it merely beautiful demeans it—you know, it's just not enough."

"I know what you mean. How are you really doing, Maggie? I know this is hard for you."

She felt his hand on her shoulder and nearly broke down. She stiffened against the flood of grief, tightening her lips to hold back a sob. "Thanks, Andy. Nothing's been easy since I was a kid. I should have been there."

"Been where? In New Mexico? Maggie, your mom told me that C. D. died in the hospital just hours after he was admitted. There's no way you could have flown there in time."

She choked the railing with both hands, her slender knuckles blanching white. "I should have known he was having heart problems. I should have! Dad and I were always close—always.

Even when he left, he didn't leave me. He promised he would never leave me. And what did I do? I snubbed him when he called me last year. I begged off when he asked me to join him for Thanksgiving, and I spent the entire time crying in front of the television. Then last week, he goes in with chest pains, and I should have known how it would end! I'm a doctor, for goodness' sake! I should have flown out as soon as I heard."

"Maggie, honey, you couldn't have foreseen how it would go. You didn't know."

"Oh, Andy, that's a bunch of crap! I should have been there! Dear God, it's like losing Charlotte all over again!" Her shoulders shook, and her body sagged with grief.

Ryder helped her to sit in a dark wicker loveseat. "I can get you a drink if you like. You know, a real one."

Her eyes glistened with unwept tears. "A drink?" For a second, she imagined gulping down the burning liquid, letting it settle into her veins, course through her system until it reached her brain. She would feel better almost instantly. The pain would dull to a deep throb, and she might be able to cope, but the momentary brightness would be followed by inevitable blackness. Alcohol had provided a convenient crutch for years, and she had no desire to return to that foggy world of dependency. She'd have to find other ways to cope.

"Iced tea is fine, Andy. Thanks anyway. Alcohol and I don't mix anymore."

He kissed her hand. "You are one special lady. Iced tea it is."

In a few moments, Ryder had returned with two teas. She had managed to compose herself, and he joined her on the wicker loveseat, nestling in close the way they had an age before, when they'd been young.

"Like old times, eh?"

"Old times are dead, Andy. Here's to some new ones."

"I'll drink to that, Maggie," he answered, clinking his glass to hers. "So what happened with you and good old Jackson Taylor, if you don't mind my asking. Your mom said he left you. He must be nuts." Ryder shook his head in exaggerated disbelief.

She laughed—a deep throaty laugh that she'd almost forgotten. For a few hours, she'd actually put aside thoughts of her pending divorce. Then her laughter was gone with a long sigh.

"Truth? I left Jackson emotionally when I hit the bottle, but he made it more permanent when he started seeing another woman. I guess you could say it was mutual, if you get my drift."

Thoughts of Charlotte swept into her brain, and she gulped the last of the tea, longing for something to dull the rising heartache. "So, how about you? I thought you were going to marry Debbie Schlager."

He shrugged. "She was a lovely woman. Or girl, I should say. Remember, she was four years behind us. She didn't want to move out of Madison. She lives here still, married to Roger Hardin."

Below, a river barge floated past, laden with long containers and dotted with boxes of various sizes and shapes. The river caressed it as it slowly moved the boat to its destination upriver. Time stopped on the Ohio. Maggie loved watching it, for its constancy filled her with hope.

"And you never married?" she asked, absentmindedly running a finger along the rim of her empty glass.

"Marriage and the government don't mix well. At least that's what I've been told. Although your dad pulled it off."

She laughed. "Yeah. Three times." She stood up, leaned on the railing. "So what is it you do in Washington?"

25

"Trying to change the subject? I can take a hint. Well, I could tell you what I do, but then I'd have to kill you."

She laughed softly, and he smiled, but there was coldness in his eyes. Noticing it, Maggie felt a slight chill and shivered visibly. "I'll keep that in mind," she replied, only half joking.

"I was kidding," he answered, the lifeless eyes becoming soft again. "I guess I'd better get back inside. Doug should be showing our senior year playoff game soon. Want to come? You don't want to miss that."

"You go on inside. I think I'm just going to enjoy the scenery for a bit."

Ryder hesitated for a minute then headed toward the doors. "All right." He started to go in, then turned back. "Listen, Maggie. I'm sorry for all you've been through. My bad manners haven't made it any better, but I'd really like to see you again, if you're interested. Here's my card. Call me, and I'll come running."

He handed her a stiff, white business card with no company name, just his own and a number in black copperplate. Major Andrew James Ryder, 812-555-1313.

"Local number, Andy? Not one in D.C.?"

"I'll be stationed here for a while. In fact, I have a meeting in Bloomington late next week. May I call you?"

"Sure. I'm in the book, or the campus switchboard can patch you through to my office. I spend most of my time at the medical school. We could have lunch."

"Good. Thanks, Maggie. If I don't see you again tonight before I leave, then I'll see you next week, but you can call me anytime, OK?"

"OK. Goodnight, Andy Pandy."

"'Night, Maggedy Ann."

26

He disappeared into the friendly lights on the other side of the French doors. Alone at last in the darkness, Maggie turned back toward the gray ribbon of water and finally began to cry.

CHAPTER 3

Nearly fifteen hundred miles from Madison in an underground laboratory far beneath the gleaming surface of the New Mexican desert, a man in a white coat typed furiously on a computer. Dr. Thomas Foil watched the clock nervously as he pounded the keys of a Macintosh laptop, sweat pouring down his high forehead. He'd nearly finished entering all the data, but he had to make sure the recipient understood all he had to say. He had very little time left, but he was determined to use it well.

He glanced up at the large clock that looked down on the main lab area of BioStrain. Only 3:10 on a ghastly night shift. He wondered if he might be the only person awake now in the small bunker. He certainly felt isolated and friendless. Wiping his brow with a disposable tissue, he licked his thin lips and continued.

Be sure to read through all of your father's papers. He'll have hidden the real ones, I'm sure. I'm sorry for what we've done. Your father tried to fight them. He was a good man, an honest man, and they killed him for it. I'm done for, too, if I don't get out of here. Don't try to find me. If I can, I'll disappear. If I can't, well, you can guess. Take care. Uncle Tommy

Foil hit the save button and sat back in relief. He'd encrypted the message in the usual way, and he'd protected the entire hard drive with a tough password. He prayed Maggie Taylor would figure a way to decipher it. She'd always been a smart cookie, just like her old man. She'd know what to do with the information. She'd have to.

The balding scientist closed the laptop and tucked it into a black leather messenger bag. Then he inserted the bag into a white liner box, fit that into a blue and white cardboard box, taped the box shut, and wrote an address with a black Sharpie. PROF. MARGARET TAYLOR. MEDICAL SCIENCES BLDG. INDIANA UNIVERSITY. BLOOMINGTON, IN 47401.

Foil removed several items from his metal desk, including a computer disk marked RESEARCH, and put the items into his coat pockets. He then grabbed the box with the laptop inside and headed out of the secured area, through the maze of white-lighted tunnels, and up a series of elevators. He checked out with the security guard by scanning his thumb and exited the building for the last time. Once outside, the scientist walked briskly to his Toyota, fighting the urge to look back, and drove to the nearest shipping station, still nearly twenty miles away. There, he deposited the prepaid box and drove toward Mexico.

His plan was to drive across the border, stay overnight in a cheap hotel, and charter a plane for South America. His plan hadn't been to die. But twelve minutes and thirty miles later, his car suddenly began to steer on its own. Foil tried desperately to regain control of the automobile, but a mysterious force now operated the green Toyota.

As the renegade car carried its terrified passenger into the path of an oncoming oil tanker, Foil had time for a prayer—his last. The sickening squeal of brakes and the smell of burning tires assaulted the air, but the truck driver couldn't stop in time. Foil closed his eyes, and his thin lips continued moving even after the small car slid beneath the jack-knifed tanker and his balding head separated from his lifeless body.

Three miles away, the hands that had taken control of the dead scientist's car relaxed.

"Nice work," a man's voice said, patting the controller's shoulder.

"Thank you, sir."

"See to the cleanup. Then make sure he didn't leave any trails."

"Yes, sir."

The superior left the steel-walled room and headed for his office. He'd have to report this. Make sure the usual sanitation took place. Foil also had to be replaced. Preferably with someone equally expendable.

CHAPTER 4

Sunday Morning

Maggie woke with a start, slathered in dachshund kisses. "What the...?" she croaked, bleary-eyed. "Doug! Call off the wiener patrol!"

Two dogs had jumped onto her bed, and the third lingered on the floor near her shoes, sniffing curiously. "Don't even think about it," she warned. She pushed back the two kissing machines and sat up.

"Are they bothering you?" called Doug from the hallway. His impish face appeared in the open doorway, and the three dogs rushed to frolick beneath his large feet.

"I thought they were at the kennel," Maggie replied, noticing how bright the window looked. "What time is it anyway?"

"After eleven. Angie picked them up early. She missed her babies."

Maggie stood up. She had worn a pair of her brother's pajamas to bed, and the long legs drooped past her feet. "Yeah, well, she'll change her tune once the human baby arrives. Larry, Moe, and Curly will become the forgotten kids."

"You're in a lovely mood," he said, crossing the room to open the curtains. Sunshine flooded into the guest suite, and the dogs raced toward the opening to bark at a squirrel perched on a nearby silver maple. "Bad dreams?"

Maggie counted to ten before backhanding her obnoxious twin. She'd had little sleep, but what she could remember consisted of nightmarish images of her father and Charlie, her precious Charlotte Danielle, both buried alive in a common grave.

"I don't dream," she lied. "Does Angie have any coffee left, or did you hog it all?"

"There's plenty. She made a fresh pot when Andy came."

He had her attention now. "Andy came by?" she repeated, hoping the tone sounded neutral.

"He's still here," Doug told her, giving her a light kiss to the cheek as he left. "Shuffle off your bad night and come on down. Angie made cinnamon rolls."

The delightfully sweet aroma of Angie's cinnamon rolls drew Maggie to the kitchen, where she found Ryder talking shop with Doug. Angie busied herself with washing dishes and keeping coffee mugs filled.

"Doug, you shouldn't make Angie wait on you hand and foot anymore," Maggie scolded her brother as she joined the conversation. "In fact, you should wait on her!"

Ryder stood as Maggie entered and offered a bright smile. "Morning, Maggedy Ann."

"Andy Pandy! What a surprise! I didn't know you were here," she laughed, winking at Doug. "How nice that the government gives you so much free time."

"It's pretty flexible," he replied, pouring her a cup of coffee. "Cream?"

"And two sugars," she said. "See, Doug? Major Ryder here knows how to treat a lady."

She took the coffee and sat opposite Ryder. "So what are we discussing this fine summer day?"

Doug handed her the Sunday *Indianapolis Star.* "That," he said, pointing to the headline. AVIAN FLU HITS NEBRASKA. 10,000 CHICKENS SLAUGHTERED. "Andy says it's even worse than the papers say."

Maggie sipped the coffee thoughtfully while skimming through the article. "It says here that the CDC thinks it might jump species. They're testing all the pigs in Nebraska, too. The price of sausage could go way up, Douglas. Better invest in pork futures."

"Already do, sis. No, seriously, I was just telling Andy how weird it is that some of Dad's papers refer to the discovery of some abrupt change in bird flu in China."

Maggie perked up. "Antigenic shift?"

All eyes stared, blinking.

"Antigenic shift. It's a sudden, dramatic change in the genetic makeup of the virus," she went on, realizing she'd lapsed into technical speak. "As opposed to a slow, gentle change, which is called antigenic drift."

"Drift? Shift?"

Maggie grinned. "Just think about drifting on a raft—it's slow. Shift—well, that's like a racecar. Fast."

Doug blinked. "Yeah, well, Dad went on to say that this new strain could be pretty nasty."

"He did? Where are Dad's papers anyway? I'd like to take a look at them. Maybe reproduce some of his work."

Doug looked at Ryder. "Sorry, Maggie. I gave them to the major here. Since Dad worked for the government, the papers technically belong to them."

"Dad didn't work for the government when he died, Doug. He left four years ago, remember? He worked for some private company in New Mexico. Gosh, what was the name of it?"

"Grayson Labs?" Ryder asked, folding the newspaper and setting it aside.

"Maybe," Doug said. "None of his papers had any letterhead or even a date. They were just notes, really, Maggie. I'm sorry, I should have asked you about them before handing them over. It never occurred to me that you'd be interested. Stupid of me, I know. I keep thinking of you as a teacher, but I guess you do research, too."

"It's okay," she said honestly. "Maybe Andy can copy them for me. Huh, Andy Pandy? Pretty please?"

Ryder wiped his mouth with a napkin and smiled. "Oh, it's possible. Remember I said I'd be in Bloomington this week. What do you say I call you on Friday?"

"That's perfect," she said. "Classes end on Thursday, so I'll have some free time. I'm not planning on teaching the rest of the summer since I'm switching to molecular biology and pathology classes in the fall. The school's given me the summer to write new lesson plans."

"Giving up life in the morgue, sis?"

"Probably not. Teaching pathology usually involves some lab work, but I'll be spending less time there."

"Could we talk about something lighter?" Angie asked from the sink. "All this talk about bodies and bird flu is a little much for such a beautiful day."

"You're right, honey," Doug said, rising and joining her. "Here, let me finish that. Why don't you call Mom and see if she wants to meet you and Maggie for lunch?"

"That sounds like fun," Angie said, looking to Maggie.

Maggie squirmed. "Angie, I'd love to, really I would, but I still have papers to grade in Bloomington. What if we plan to get together next weekend? Let me finish up this term, then I can relax for a while."

Though disappointed, Angie kept her constant smile. "Maybe we could make it a whole day. There's a concert on the river on Saturday. Would you like to come down on Friday?"

"I'll call you later this week," Maggie promised. "I'd better give Mom a call before I leave. Mind if I use your phone, Doug?"

"It'll cost you a quarter," he teased. "You can use the one in the den if you want some privacy."

Maggie took her cup and plate to the sink and gave Angie a quick hug. "Thanks for understanding, sis," she whispered, and then she headed toward the den in the basement.

Angie washed the last of the dishes while Doug dried. "She's really torn up, Doug. I think she wants to get back to Bloomington so she can be alone."

Ryder drained the last of the coffee and handed the empty carafe to Doug. "Doug, I know this is hard on all of you, but I think Maggie is still dealing with Charlotte's death. She mentioned her last night."

"It's been five years, Andy. She needs to get over it and move on with her life. Maybe this will push her to face it," Doug said, ignoring his wife's glare. "What? We're all thinking it! She needs to move on, and that includes moving on with her marriage. She should either let it go or fix it. Of course, I'm thinking Andy here would prefer the former. Right, Major?"

Ryder nodded thoughtfully, his eyes fixed on the interaction between husband and wife. "You two have certainly made your marriage work. What's your secret?"

Doug laughed and stacked the last of the plates. "Simple. I pay for the pants, and she wears 'em."

"Doug!" Angie shouted, slapping him playfully. "Seriously, Andy, if you're interested in Maggie, then don't push her. She needs some space. Doug may think five years is too long to grieve, but I think I can understand it. Especially now," she added, rubbing her belly thoughtfully. "This baby's barely made his presence known, but I've grown so attached. I can't imagine losing him. Anyway, that's how I feel."

Doug threw his arms around her and kissed her forehead. "You're a softy, and I love you for it."

"Mom says hi to everybody," Maggie said, returning from the basement. "Did I miss anything?"

"Nothing much," Ryder answered, standing. "I'd better go, Doug. Maggie, I'll call you on Friday."

Angie wiped her hands on a towel embroidered with sunflowers and removed her apron. "Can't you join us next weekend?" she asked with a nod toward Maggie.

"We'll see," the major promised. "Have a safe drive back, Maggedy Ann."

"That goes both ways, Major Andy Pandy," she said, following him to the door. "Does your superior officer know about that nickname? Maybe I should call him."

Ryder stepped out the door but looked back. "I don't have a superior, Maggie. You should know that. Have a great week, everyone!"

He kissed her hand and headed toward the concrete parking pad behind the house.

Maggie watched until his car disappeared and then closed the door. "It's going to be another hot day," she said thoughtfully.

Doug and Angie exchanged knowing glances, and Doug put an arm around his wife. "We'll see how hot it gets around here," he said with a laugh. "Come on, Mags. Stay for a little while. We don't have to go anywhere. It can be just the three of us."

"Four of us!" Angie corrected, pointing to her belly.

As if on cue, the three dachshunds suddenly bounded into the room, tails wagging and short legs scrambling on the kitchen tiles. "Make that seven!" Angie added, and they all laughed.

"All right, I'll stay another hour, if Doug lets me trounce him in chess."

"You're on!" he brightened, stepping around a wiggling wiener dog. "But plan on losing to the master," he warned. "Come on. I'll set up the board."

Maggie finally left her brother's house shortly after five that evening. She'd planned on leaving much earlier, but three chess matches and one movie later, she'd lost all track of time. Now as she maneuvered the hairpin turns of Brown County, she thought through the weekend, sorting out the bad and mentally storing the good.

Seeing Andy again was a welcome surprise. Maggie had even enjoyed a few moments when Charlotte's accidental death wasn't haunting her thoughts. No such reprieve now. Driving the route to Bloomington always brought back memories of former times when she, Jack, and Charlotte had covered this same stretch of road, en route to a play, a basketball game, or a weekend at the lake. However, such wonderful times had morphed into something less cheerful in Maggie's mind. Remembering Charlotte kept her heart alive, yet it also left her empty and ragged. Keeping busy helped.

As she followed a sweeping curve up a hill, Maggie thought of the week ahead. Four more days of classes and paperwork, then she'd be free to enjoy the summer until August. This would be her first vacation since she'd stopped drinking.

Charlotte's dead. And so is your dad.

This could be the longest summer of her life.

CHAPTER 5

Sunday Evening

urn that up louder, man," called a carrottopped beanpole from the kitchen. "It's more about that virus, I think."

Dave Hitchins rolled his bulk forward enough to turn the volume dial on an antiquated black-and-white TV set. "More chickens slaughtered. You're right, Pop. Bring me a Dew, will ya?"

Popeye Bailey joined Hitchins in what served as a living room/dining room/bedroom for the gangly student. "Here ya go," he said, handing his guest a cold Mountain Dew. "It's the last one. Scooch over, man."

Hitchins shifted right, causing the 1950s vinyl sofa to shudder. Bailey eased next to the bulky man he'd gotten to know during last year's Dungeon and Dragons marathons. "Barney should know about this stuff, Hitch. This is a government cover-up. Avian flu, my Aunt Sally! It's a secret test of some new weapon, and we'll be next!"

"Shut up!" Hitchins insisted, putting two orange fingers to his Doritos-stained lips. "Listen!"

Indianapolis news anchor Brian Hartman frowned seriously into the camera. "Although the virus has not yet been reported in Indiana, the state branch of the CDC has issued instructions for all citizens. Anyone finding a dead bird, especially a crow or raven, must report it to local authorities. Do not touch the dead animal. The statewide phone number for all incidents is 1-855-BIRD-FLU. That's 1-855-BIRD-FLU. Remember, the virus has not yet been reported in humans, but experts recommend extreme caution nonetheless. And now in a related story, we go to Jenna Dryden, reporting from the nation's capital."

The scene shifted to the exterior of the Capitol building in Washington. Twilight cast long shadows behind the slim reporter, but artificial lighting smoothed the nooks and crannies of her face into a perfect canvas. Her surgically trimmed nose perched daintily above pouty lips that spoke of a nationwide plan to battle the relentless avian virus.

"She's a honey," Hitchins drooled, reaching into his Doritos bag but finding it empty. "Got any more chips?"

"Shh," Bailey said.

Dryden blinked, her left eye irritated by something—maybe pollen. "Brian, I've just left a meeting with the Assistant HS Secretary, where he explained the role of Homeland Security in this war against nature. As most of our viewers know by now, the Centers for Disease Control has been under the all-inclusive umbrella of Homeland Security since day one, and Project BioShield, one of the President's recent innovations in the new biowar, is set to provide free vaccinations to every citizen as they become available."

Hartman adjusted his earpiece. "Did you say vaccinations, Jenna?"

Dryden nodded, her left eye tearing, causing her to blink madly. "That's right, Brian. Although it's a tragedy that so many farmers have had to lose expensive flocks to mandated slaughter, each case has provided another opportunity for the CDC to evaluate the virus. We were told that a vaccination has been in the works for months, and we can expect it to be available shortly. This vaccine will be administered to animals and humans, although the chemical content will probably differ between the two. Last time I looked, I didn't have feathers, Brian."

"And we're delighted you don't!" the anchor laughed. "Sounds like the government is keeping on top of the situation, Jenna. Thanks for the report."

"You're welcome, Brian."

Popeye Bailey leaned into the green plastic back of the couch that he'd inherited from the apartment's previous tenant. "Vaccine? Dude, Hitch! It's starting! Just like Barney said, man! They're gonna try to stick it to us—literally!"

Hitchins eyed the empty Doritos bag and hummed the theme to Star Wars. "Looks like we need to call a meeting," he said at last, standing and pulling his X-Files T-shirt down to cover an ample stomach. "Grab your cell phone, Pop. You dial and smile, and I'll drive."

Jenna Dryden rubbed at her irritated eye. "I have another live feed scheduled in about an hour, Bill. I have to see what the deal is with this contact first, but after that I'm going to try Grayson's office again. If that fails, I'll put in another call to Ryder. Andy owes me a favor after deserting me at the White House Christmas party. This itches like crazy!"

Bill Conners snapped the cover on his camera case and looked up. "Your left eye's really red, Jen. Maybe you should forget about the calls and see to it. You don't want one eye swollen shut when we go live."

Jenna rubbed at the eye, nodding. "Yeah. Okay. Meet me at my hotel in half an hour. I'm heading back there now to change contacts. I think this one has a rip in it or something."

Conners loaded the remainder of the equipment onto his dolly and hailed a cab. "Okay," he said as Jenna stepped into the waiting car without offering to share with Conners. "Want me to shoot some background footage of the Homeland Security offices?"

"Good idea," she said, gazing into a compact mirror. "See if you can catch any big name people in the shot. And if you can shoot that CDC doc, I'll kiss you."

"Pucker up," he laughed and slammed the cab door shut.

"The Hilton on Embassy Row," she said, picking up her cell phone and dialing. "Come on, Ryder. Answer."

A few seconds passed, which Dryden spent removing her lens and examining it for flaws. "Andy? Jenna here."

On the other end of the connection, Andrew Ryder smiled. He closed the file he'd been reading, a fat legal file marked Dr. Charles Hilliard, and leaned back into the soft embrace of a walnut-brown leather chair. "Jenna Dryden. Come crawling back, have we?"

"You wish," she spit back angrily, but immediately adjusted her tone to a softer, sexier one. "Look, Andy, let's just let the whole party matter drop, OK? I'm willing to let it go. Life's too short, you know?"

"Oh, I know all about life and its frailty," Ryder answered, taking a long sip of amber liquid. "What can I do for you, Jenna? Set up a meeting with someone high up?"

She smirked. Ryder bugged her, and he knew it, but she needed him, so she turned on the charm. "I need to talk with Grayson, if you can arrange it."

"Who? Grayson?"

"Don't play dumb with me, Ryder. I know you have connections to every bioweapon project in the free world. So you must know Rex Grayson."

Ryder grinned and gulped down the last of the Scotch. "And if I do?"

"Then I'd do just about anything it took to meet with him. I have a hunch about Chuck Hilliard's death, Andy. Do you know he's the twenty-seventh scientist to disappear or die recently?"

"Really? Why is that news, Jenna, my love? Scientists die, too. Mortal beings all die."

"Sure, sure, but not scientists who are all interconnected. I've been drawing diagrams, and they all cross at one central point, Ryder. Rex Grayson. Come on! I still have that slinky red number you like so much."

Ryder imagined the woman's trim figure in the form-fitting dress and leaned forward to pour a second shot of Scotch. "I'll hold you to that," he said, a low laugh rumbling through the wireless connection.

Jenna blinked, her intuitions itching worse than her eye. "OK," she answered at last, raw ambition overcoming her internal alarms. "I'm in Washington until tomorrow night."

"I'll leave first thing in the morning. We'll have breakfast together. Are you staying at the Hilton or the Hyatt?"

"Hilton. The Hyatt was booked."

"I'll be there at seven."

Jenna heard a click. Ryder had hung up.

"Hilton, Miss," the cab driver said as he parked. "That's twelve even."

Jenna paid the middle-eastern man then headed for her room on the eleventh floor, trying to dismiss the creepy smile he had given her. By tomorrow she'd have the phone number for Rex Grayson, and she'd be on her way to WNN. So long, Indianapolis! Hello, fame and fortune!

But she'd never get the chance.

By eight the next morning, she'd be dead.

CHAPTER 6

Monday

G ood morning, Dr. Taylor."
     Maggie smiled at the student. "Are you certain it's good, Mr. Halloran?"

"Absolutely! I spent the entire weekend studying."

"That's a refreshing change, Mr. Halloran. I'll look forward to grading your exam."

Halloran laughed and took one of twenty-eight seats in the small classroom. Within minutes, the room's wooden chairs filled with seventeen men and nine women ready to take the written portion of their final examination in first-year gross anatomy.

The first summer session of the intensive course had begun in mid-May and continued through mid-June, with marathon days that tested the determination of both student and teacher. Working on cadavers for six hours straight did not rank highly on most students' lists of summer fun. Everyone in the room felt he or she had earned a good grade just for putting up with the schedule.

Maggie spent the first half of the three-hour exam period quietly reading through a stack of term papers from the neurobiology class she taught at the Optometry School. Midway through, she asked her graduate assistant, Victor, to monitor the room while she stretched her legs.

The Med Sciences building seldom had visitors this time of year. In fact, it had very few students, except for a small cohort of medical students. Maggie loved the quiet. She walked down the tiled hallway, listening to the echo of her own footsteps, and decided to sit outside for a few minutes.

She headed down the well-worn marble steps and out the back door to a parking area that faced the back of the Chemistry Building. Maggie, who wore loose-fitting khakis and a polo shirt, sat down on the dusty concrete porch of the north entry. A gentle breeze fluttered posters and flyers that had been stapled to surrounding trees and light poles. Despite the number of students inside, she counted only seven cars.

Margaret really loved the college town. One of her favorite pastimes was watching the expressions of east coast visitors when they first arrived. Bloomington, Indiana—a tiny Midwestern burg with connections to the entire globe. In a typical week, a visitor here could attend a lecture by a politician and follow up with an evening's entertainment at the MAC with diverse headliners from opera singers to pop stars. Bloomington maintained a reputation as a provider of all things to all people at all times, and the town seldom failed to fulfill its promise.

Besides the amazing variety of politics and personages, Bloomington's scenery could inspire even the dullest soul to poetry. Area lakes, hills, and spectacular valleys offered water sports, hiking opportunities, and even seasonal downhill skiing. Few who came to the home of the Hoosiers left disappointed.

In the late 1970s, Maggie had come for an undergraduate degree in biology and stayed, partly because of her marriage to Jack Taylor, but mainly because of her love for the land.

As she breathed in the clear morning air, Maggie noticed a man who appeared out of place. Summer attire here meant shorts and tank tops, with khakis and polos for evening. This man wore a dark suit and white shirt. Even his tie appeared to be solid black.

Must be a Blues Brother, she thought with an internal giggle, but the stranger certainly didn't look like Jake or Elwood. He had to be a visitor. Maybe a businessman who'd dropped by to meet with his son or daughter.

"Can I help you?" she asked.

The stranger looked Maggie's way then changed direction to walk right toward her. "Maybe. I'm looking for the Medical Sciences building. I asked someone over there," he said, pointing toward Jordan Hall, "and he told me to walk this way, but I don't see any sign."

"We don't have one on this side. This is the back of the building, but you're right on the money. Are you meeting someone?"

He shook his head. "Not exactly. A friend of mine recommended I stop by to talk to one of the professors about my daughter. Would you happen to know if Dr. Taylor is here today?"

Maggie stood up and reached out her right hand. "You're talking to her. I have a class in the middle of an exam right now, but I could chat afterward."

The man's face brightened, which helped soften the severe attire. "Wonderful! I'm very happy to meet you, Dr. Taylor. I'm Henry Meier. Most of my friends call me Hank."

"Nice to meet you, Hank. If you don't mind waiting in my office, I'll finish up the class, then come by. Is your daughter one of my students?"

"No. She's a third year biochemistry premed at Eden College. I don't know if you keep up with the news, but Eden's had its share of crime lately, and I don't like my daughter living there. I'd actually prefer she attend medical school in Indy, but she likes the smaller towns better. I'm sorry. I'm going on and on. I can tell you the whole story later. You need to get back to your class. I really appreciate your making time for me."

"Nonsense, come on inside."

She led him into the building, and the rush of cool, conditioned air caressed both their faces. "I don't know what we'd do without this new cooling system. Boy, it's been hot for June, don't you think? Gigantic solar flares are to blame, at least that's what my buddy in astronomy keeps saying. My office is just up these stairs on the second floor. You said a friend recommended me. May I ask who to thank?"

"Andrew Ryder, actually. He said he went to school with you."

Maggie turned right down the second-floor hallway. "Funny. I just saw him this weekend at my dad's funeral. He didn't mention you."

"Oh, I am sorry, Dr. Taylor. I had no idea your father had just passed away. Are you sure this is a good time?"

"Absolutely. So how do you know Andy?"

"We once worked together on a—private project. I'm in a different line now. Pharmaceuticals, if you couldn't tell by the suit and tie. They're pretty strict about attire. Boring, but efficient, I guess."

Hank followed her to a tiny office at the southwest end of the hallway. The walls were lined with gray filing cabinets, faithfully labeled. A metal desk faced a large window that overlooked Third Street. On top of the desk, neat rows of wooden organizers held class papers, research project data, and correspondence. A red and white blotter from the Union Bookstore revealed a well-marked calendar. In the margins, Maggie's doodles decorated blank space with tiny cartoons.

"This is it, such as it is. I don't have a permanent guest chair, but you're welcome to sit at my desk. There are snack machines in the basement. Bathrooms are down the hall." She checked her watch. "It's ten now. I'll finish the exam by eleven or so and be back here by, say, eleven-fifteen. Make yourself at home, Hank. Feel free to turn on the radio."

"Thanks, Dr. Taylor."

"Call me Maggie," she answered, closing the door behind her and heading back up to the classroom on the third floor.

Now alone, Meier settled into the comfortable leather chair and surveyed the landscape of the large desk. Clearly, Taylor organized her life well, which made his job that much easier. Checking his watch, he began to search through the files.

By the time Maggie finished chatting with students, eleven-thirty had come and gone. In fact, it was nearly noon before she returned to her office. Opening the door, she found Hank Meier sitting quietly on a straight-back metal chair he'd found in the hallway.

"Sorry I took so long," she said. "Nearly everyone took right up to the last minute to finish. Maybe I made it too tough?" she laughed. "Nah!" She fell into the leather desk chair, which creaked happily at her weight. "So, Hank, tell me all about your daughter."

Meier watched her carefully, assessing the woman he'd been assigned to watch. "Well, like I said before, she's just starting her final year, but I'd really like to move her up here to Bloomington. I know she's set on going to medical school, and she has a 3.8 going in her major. Would it be possible for her to transfer here for her final year and then apply for med school either here or at Indy?"

"Sure. IU requires that the last thirty hours be completed here, but that's probably close to what she has left. We'll need to take a look at her transfer credits to make sure the coursework meets our standards. Since she's biochemistry, the evaluation would be up to the chemistry department."

Hank crossed his long legs. Despite the heat, he looked crisp and cool. "That would be wonderful. I just want her out of Eden right now."

"I've read some of what's going on there. I'm originally from Madison, which isn't far from Eden. Did they ever find those two kids who went missing in May?"

"One of them, a boy named Donny Alcorn. His girlfriend, Amy Horine, is still missing. Only a few days after his return, Donny died a horrible death, incinerated to near ash. The high school principal confessed to it, but no one feels safe there now. I don't know all the details, just what's been in the papers or what Becka tells me, but I've heard her mention UFOs, demons, some pretty awful stuff. I'm sure most of it's just sensationalism, but it keeps me up nights."

"Becka's lucky to have a dad who worries about her. How about setting up a time for me to meet your lovely daughter?"

Hank smiled, revealing deep dimples. "She is very pretty. I couldn't help noticing the photos on your desk. Looks like you have a very pretty daughter yourself."

Maggie touched the gold-framed trio of pictures that always kept her company. "Her name was Charlotte, named for my dad. She was thirteen in that picture. She died just one month after it was taken."

"Oh, I am sorry. An illness?"

"An accident," she answered, her eyes seeing something faraway, a moment from the past, forever frozen in her mind.

It was summer. Jack and I had just bought a new house. Jack had wanted a pool, but the house didn't have one. We argued about it for weeks. He won. We broke ground on the pool on June third. Three weeks later, Charlie was chasing the cat through the back yard. I never liked that cat. It had rained for three solid days, so all work on the pool had stopped. The cat skirted past the hole, but Charlie was barefooted, and she slipped in. The doctors called it a freak accident the way her neck snapped as soon as she hit. No pain. What a lie. The five years since have been nothing but pain.

Maggie's thoughts returned to the present, and she blinked the past away. "Even now, it will hit me when I least expect it, but I'm managing. At least I don't drink anymore. Sometimes, though, it hits between the eyes, like with those Eden kids you were talking about. It was all over the news for weeks. I watched for a while, but then I had to tune it out. It brought back too many awful memories."

"I can certainly understand that. You're a strong woman, Maggie. That's very clear. I mean, you just lost your dad, and here you are only a couple of days later, chatting about my problems. I admire your strength."

Maggie wiped an errant tear. She hated crying in front of anyone, especially strangers.

"Don't give me too much credit. My strength came from a bottle for years after Charlie died. I crawled inside a bottle of Jack Daniels and stayed there for a long time. In fact, I had to take a sabbatical from teaching because of it. Roamed around Europe for a while, drinking my way from country to country. My soon-to-be-ex, Jack, couldn't take it. I can't blame him. I wasn't the strong, stable Maggie he'd married. Before Charlie's death, I was supermom. After Charlie died,

Jack watched me crumble and hated me for it. It's funny, though. I still keep his lousy picture on my desk. Am I sick or what?"

"You're human, I guess. Jack's a handsome guy. Sorry about the marriage. I can relate. Traveling broke up Karen and me. My work used to take me all over the country at a moment's notice. Only in the last year has it settled into the central Indiana area. Mainly Indy, but sometimes Blooming-ton or Terre Haute. I like it."

Maggie took a bulletin and a transfer application from a drawer to her right and handed them to Hank. "I hope Becka likes it, too. Give these to her, and we can meet up," she said, checking the blotter calendar. "How about this Friday at ten? Can you make that? We need to move quickly to get her into the fall classes."

Hank took a PDA from his jacket pocket and checked his datebook. "That's perfect. I'll give you my card, just in case you need to reach me to reschedule." He handed her a white card from a silver case. The company name read BioStrain, Inc. Dr. Henry Meier.

"Dr. Meier? M.D.?"

"No. Ph.D. in communications. Cornell 1988. Our company pioneers ways to prevent disease. It's a great company."

Maggie placed the card in the back of her planner. "Maybe you can tell me all about it next time. For now, I hate to run off, but I'm meeting my ex for lunch. We're debating settlement issues. It won't be pretty."

"Then I'm happy to miss it. Been there, done that." He stood up. "I'll look forward to Friday," he said warmly. "I'll make sure Becka has all her papers in order. Have a good week, Maggie. And thanks for making time."

He shook her hand, his warm brown eyes sparkling.

Maggie nearly blushed, but she managed to keep her cool demeanor alive. "Not a problem. I'm happy to help. And I look forward to meeting Becka. Do you need directions back to your car?"

"No, I'm good. Thanks again, Maggie. So long."

"Bye," she said as he turned back down the hallway and out of sight.

Once he'd turned the corner, Hank pulled out the cell phone that had been vibrating in his pocket. He pushed talk and listened to the crisp English accent on the other end.

"Did you find it, Dr. Meier?"

Meier skipped down the stairs, nodding to a couple of coeds who flashed their best smiles to impress him. "It wasn't there, sir. I'm coming back on Friday. I'll get it then."

"I pray you do, Dr. Meier. Accidents can and do happen, as you're well aware."

Meier closed the connection and headed back into the bright sunshine of the south parking lot. Returning the phone to his pocket, he gazed back at the stone building where Maggie Taylor worked. Suddenly he wondered just how great his job really was.

CHAPTER 7

Nick's English Hut on Dunn and Grant had been Jackson Taylor's favorite place for lunch in Bloomington ever since he and Maggie had studied there back in the late 1970s and early '80s. Back then, Jack earned a stipend and research money toward his master's in physiology working as a graduate assistant in the Medical Sciences department. He'd completed his M.D. in Indianapolis the year before but wanted a research degree to expand his options beyond practicing.

Maggie Hilliard had been in her first year of medical school, and she'd fallen hard and fast for the tall GA her very first day in class, although she hadn't admitted it to him until their fifth wedding anniversary. After three months of platonic meetings and one month of whirlwind dating, Jackson proposed.

They married Christmas of 1981 at the Fellowship Baptist Church in Madison. Maggie's father had driven up from New Mexico and insisted on three dances that night, nearly drowning her with tears each time. The one spoiler for the nearly perfect night had been her father's unsuitably young date for the evening, Rachel Wellstone, later to become the third Mrs. Charles Douglas Hilliard.

True to form, Jack arrived late, but Maggie said nothing. She wanted to get through the painful process of cutting up their lives as quickly as possible. A well-tanned waiter showed them to a two-topper in the back, away from the crowd where they could talk.

"You look good, Mags," Jack began. She'd put on a few pounds since he'd last seen her, but the extra weight gave her a lovely, round look.

"You, too. Nick's never changes, does it?" she asked, choosing small talk to warm up to the main event. Boxing gloves optional.

"I'm glad you suggested it. It brings back some nice memories."

Their waiter returned with menus and drink suggestions. Jack ordered a Coke with lemon, Maggie a large iced tea.

"Iced tea?" he asked. "Still staying dry?"

There was not a hint of sarcasm there, but the statement ruffled her feathers anyway. "I manage most days. You know me. Booze and bones."

"I didn't mean it that way, Mags. Please. I'm really proud of you, you know. It can't have been easy for you to stop after almost five years of drowning your woes. Believe me, I'm in your cheering section."

He meant it, darn it. She wished he'd just yell. It would make this agony so much easier. "Sorry. Yeah, it's been hard, especially with Dad's death. By the way, thanks for not going to the funeral. I know you wanted to. It helped to go through it alone."

"How's your mom?"

"Actually, she's doing fine. I guess not seeing much of Dad for over thirty years made losing him easier. We're all doing pretty well, considering. Can we talk about something else?"

Jack smiled, and Maggie's heart flipped. It always did when Jack Taylor's bright smile lit up. Dark hair, gray eyes, and a killer smile. What woman could resist him? Jack had always reminded Maggie of Jeremy Brett, the man who'd played Sherlock Holmes for British television. She'd had a major crush on Brett when he played Freddy in the film version of *My Fair Lady*. That may have contributed to her instant crush. Who knows? It was over, that was the reality. Over and done.

"How's the practice?" she asked as the waiter brought their drinks.

"Better than ever. I've opened a second office, in fact." He paused to give the waiter his lunch order, medium rare sirloin and salad. Maggie considered the menu and finally chose a BLT with extra mayo and seasoned fries.

"Yes, I'm carb-loading," she joked after the waiter left. "I guess it takes the place of the booze. It gets me through the day, but the extra fifteen pounds has forced me to shop for new clothes."

Jack grinned, sipping his Coke. "It looks good on you. More Rosalind Russell, if you get my drift. And you have that sassy sparkle back in your eyes."

The comment caught her offguard. "Gee, thanks. I could say the same for you, except aren't we supposed to be dividing up the silverware?"

Jack nodded, sighing. "Yeah. Look, Mags, about that. I'm not in any hurry, unless you are. Can't we put this on hold for a while?"

"You're not in a hurry? What about your little honey?"

"There is no honey. Not now, and I regret that whole affair. Look, I'm really trying to turn it around, Mags. I know you're gonna laugh when I say this, but the only someone I'm seeing now is a counselor."

Maggie bit her lower lip, struggling to keep from pouring salt into an obviously open wound. "You're not going to blame me for your childhood, too, are you?" she asked, failing in her struggle. "Just pin the rap on me. I'm the poster child for martyr of the month."

"Margaret Ann, what is the matter with you?" he asked, his gray eyes widening. "Can't you stop wallowing in self-pity long enough to see how destructive this kind of thinking is? Darn it, I miss Charlie, too, but we have to go on with our lives! I just want us to try to recapture what we've lost. Is that so wrong?"

She leaned forward, ready to throw his cutting words right back into his handsome face, but her eyes fell upon a familiar figure, and she stopped cold. Of all the places the man might eat, he had to choose Nick's.

"Maggie?" Jack asked, her frozen silence alerting his radar. "What is it?"

"Nothing," she whispered, lowering her head to hide. "Nothing at all. Let's just eat, okay?"

"I would if I had some food," he answered. He reached for her hand. A big mistake.

"Well, hello, there! Small world!"

Maggie jerked her hand away so quickly she left marks on Jack's palm. Her head snapped up, and Jack beheld a rare, gleaming smile upon his estranged wife's lovely face. "Hi, there, yourself!"

Henry Meier stuck out a manicured hand toward Jack. "Name's Meier. Hank Meier. I'm sorry to interrupt your lunch. Dr. Taylor and I had a meeting earlier, and it struck me as serendipity to see her here, so I couldn't resist coming over."

Jack rose and shook the stranger's hand amiably. "Jack Taylor. Maggie's husband," he answered, verbally marking his territory.

"Oh. Sorry again. Well, good to meet you. Thanks again, Dr. Taylor."

"Maggie, remember?"

Meier's expression brightened, and he tipped an imaginary hat. "Maggie. Well, I'd better go to my own table. I look forward to our meeting on Friday."

Meier bowed with a grin and turned toward the lower floor, searching for his waiter.

"Nice guy," Jack grumbled.

"Yeah, he's pretty nice. Look, Jack, I'm sorry for the crab routine. Dad's death is still biting at my ankles. I'm not up to sparring just now. Do you mind if we do this another day?"

"I thought you wanted to rush the process," he said.

"I just want to get a good night's sleep."

Minutes later, their meals arrived, and they ate in awkward silence. Maggie did her best to ignore Meier, but she couldn't help thinking how strange the coincidence was—his coming to Nick's.

"Jackson, I'm sorry," she said at last. "What do you say we call it a truce for now?"

Taylor's face brightened. "Sure. I'm full anyway. We can leave if you like."

"Yeah. Walk me back to my car, OK?"

"OK."

As the pair threaded their way through the maze of tables, Maggie looked over her shoulder, just for a moment, and let her gaze linger on Hank Meier's angular face. Though he sat in shadow, she could imagine his dark eyes. *A man of shadows,* she thought to herself. *Shadows with a dash of mystery thrown in. Nothing like a bit of mystery to tempt a woman.*

Suddenly she shivered, and Jack pulled her close. "You cold in this heat?" he asked. "That'd be a first."

Maggie shook her head. "Just a funny feeling. You know, like someone walked on my grave."

As the couple left the restaurant, a man with a strong build and a military haircut watched silently from a park bench. Pretending to be reading, he made a notation in the margin of the book. Only moments later, Hank Meier exited the restaurant, and the man scratched another note in his book. Once Meier had driven away, the man opened a small satchel at his side, removed a cell phone, and punched in a series of numbers. "It's Yarber. You were right about Meier. He's shadowing Taylor. Should I move in?"

The voice on the other line gave a series of orders, which the muscular man wrote down faithfully. "Understood," he said at last. "I'll continue surveillance."

CHAPTER 8

Monday Afternoon

Bill Conners slid the wrapper off a piece of chewing gum. "That's all I know," he answered, his throat parched from three long hours of answering questions. "Can I go now? I need to call my station and let them know what's happened."

Detective Mike Russell closed his notebook. "OK. But don't leave Washington just yet."

Conners stood up and popped the stick of gum into his mouth. The last five hours had been a nightmare for the young cameraman. After wrapping up their final stand-up the night before, Conners had left Jenna in the Hilton lobby and walked back to his own room at the Wyndham. He'd spent several hours editing the video that he'd shot during the CDC briefing, then he'd uploaded samples to the station back in Indy via his in-room Internet hook-up.

He'd jerked awake at ten that morning, surprised that Jenna hadn't called to scold him for oversleeping. He'd tried to call her several times, both from his room and his cell, but no answer. Deciding she must have met with success concerning the Grayson story, he'd chosen to enjoy a leisurely shower and hot breakfast before knocking on her door at noon.

When she hadn't answered, he'd begun to suspect something might be wrong, so Conners had asked a nearby maid to check the room. Concerned that Jenna might have dumped him to snag all rights to the Grayson story, Conners waited in the hallway, poised for a fight, but the maid's sudden, piercing scream had scared away all remnants of anger.

Conners had rushed in to see why the woman had shrieked, and then he'd seen it. As the indescribable smell hit him, his first thought was of a barbeque fiasco two years before at his grandmother's house. The steaks had burned to a crisp. They'd looked a lot like this.

But nothing in Conners' twenty-five-year-old memory had ever smelled like this.

Little remained of what had once been Jenna Dryden, except for her right hand, still wearing a white gold wrist-watch, untouched by the fire that had consumed the rest of her body. A fine, powdery ash covered the white sheets of the queen-sized bed. Little else in the room showed any sign of fire, let alone exposure to heat, except for the television, which had melted slightly.

Just before throwing up, Conners noticed a bright splash of red in the gray ash. It was a fragment from the dress Jenna had shown him, the slinky number she'd planned to wear in her breakfast meeting with Andy Ryder.

"Are you going to arrest Ryder?" he asked the police detective.

Russell pocketed the small spiral notebook and shook his head. "Why should I? Major Ryder's not involved. In fact, he's still in Madison, Indiana. We sent a local sheriff's deputy to check on it. You want to tell me now why you made all that up about Miss Dryden meeting a government man?"

"I didn't make it up!" he protested, his raw throat cracking again. "Check her cell record! She called him last night! She told me so!"

"Already did," Russell said calmly. "According to the phone company, Miss Dryden only made one call last night. To you. Your cell records confirm it."

Conners blinked. His mind raced, and his throat went from dry to desert. "So, what are you saying?" he croaked. "That she—that she just—uh, spontaneously combusted?"

Russell looked to the two uniformed officers who'd originally answered the 911 call. "Pretty funny, Conners. I'll be sure to include that in my report," he said. "What I'm gonna do, Mr. Conners, is keep an eye on you. We don't take kindly to men cooking up young women in our town."

Conners gulped, swallowing the gum. "This can't be happening!"

"That's what they all say," Russell whispered into Conners' ear. "Right up to the last minute, when the executioner turns on the gas."

Andrew Ryder turned off his car's engine. The sign ahead said Eden, Indiana, Welcomes You! Ryder knew from his previous visits that the Mount Hermon Institute lay two miles further down this road, a right turn past the Dairy Queen, then east for a mile up the long curving hill that followed the Ohio River. He didn't want to be late for his meeting with Grayson and the others, but Ryder savored the quiet moments after a victory.

He imagined the scene in faraway Washington, D.C. The chaos that must now reign over the hotel staff as well as the police assigned to solve the case. They would never solve it, of course. Oh, they might arrest an innocent man, might prosecute him, perhaps even execute him, but they would never truly solve it.

Ryder laughed, a low throaty laugh, as he turned the key to his rental car and revved the engine. Small pleasures; how they made his day!

CHAPTER 9

Rosita Ibanez shook a faded Navajo blanket into the dry, bleached New Mexico air, coughing as a week's worth of sand and grit assaulted her already weakened lungs. Rosita squinted reflexively against the white heat of midday, and a rare tear, wasted bodily fluid, coursed slowly along the deep furrows of her sunburned face.

She licked her lips, tasting salt. Another long, miserable day in a dying desert. Another day closer to a three-by-six foot hole in the sand. She'd not felt well since the nurse from the county had come to inoculate her and the children. She'd meant to ask Dr. Tohe about it, because she trusted him, but she'd found only a sign saying he had gone out of town. She would have to talk to him when he returned. The headaches kept her awake at night, and her arm ached at the injection site. The children had fared better, despite Angelina's cold. Her husband had refused the injection, having no trust in the Anglo government.

She slapped at a fly, noticing only then that several of their chickens lay dead near the makeshift roost. Flies covered the carcasses. The sight made Rosita sick.

She folded the blanket into a small square and turned back toward the aluminum oven her husband called a trailer. Rosita called it a tin coffin.

"Hey, Rosie! Get in here quick!"

Rosita's unemployed husband, Gomez Ibanez, stood in the trailer's narrow doorway, shirtless and shoeless. His hair hadn't been combed, and he had a wild look to his face. His shouts pricked at her delicate ears like a crow's beak at a dead man's eyes.

"Rosita! Come here now!" he shouted again, his insistent bellow nearly drowning out the wail of a police car siren. Inside the cramped mobile home, three children huddled in front of a thirteen-inch, black-and-white television set, watching a police chase on a rerun of *Starsky and Hutch* beamed from Las Cruces, the only station the old TV set could still receive.

The smallest of the three, four-year-old Angelina, who had suffered from a weak heart since birth, jerked suddenly and began to cough up blood.

"Rosie! It's Angel! Come in here now!"

Rosita ran into the trailer, discarding the blanket as she rushed to the girl's side. "Angelina!" she cried as she dropped to her knees. "Bambina! Can you hear me?"

The girl looked up, wide, red-rimmed eyes asking what her lips could not. *Por qué, Mama? Why me? What is God doing?*

Rosita cradled the girl's chalky face in her etched hands, but the brief life that had shone in the questioning eyes flickered, then faded. Blood foamed from the child's small mouth, and a deep rattle shuddered through the tiny frame. The girl was dead.

"Angelina?" Gomez Ibanez asked his wife of thirteen years. "Rosie—what—God in heaven, is she—gone? She cannot be dead!"

"God! Oh, God, no!" Rosita screamed, falling onto the child's lifeless body. "She cannot be gone! Angelina! Wake up!"

The other children huddled close, touching their mother's shoulders. "God will heal her, won't He, Mama?" Miguel whispered, hugging her tightly. "You said God will make her well."

Rosita had no words of comfort for her living children. Already she had lost Jorge to this flu the nurse had spoken of, and now Angelina. The anguished mother's tears dripped slowly onto Angelina's swollen, purple cheeks.

"Rosie?"

"Dig a grave, Gomez. A little one. Beside Jorge's tiny spot, I think. Then dig another one for me."

The mother's eyes rolled into her head, and she fell backward, her body jerking with spasms. Horrified, the two remaining children began to scream, and their terrified father fell to his knees, crying out to a God he had often cursed.

Behind the grotesque ballet of death, a police car's siren wailed in sympathy from the flickering television screen, and a pair of red eyes peered out from the thirteen-inch world of light and shadow, eagerly watching the raw pain of the crumbling family. The spirit-creature behind the flaming eyes began to laugh.

CHAPTER 10

D r. Taylor, there's a package for you."
Some said that Ellen Trueblood had worked for the Medical Sciences department since the dawn of time, but everyone agreed that she alone kept it running. When Maggie had first arrived here as a student, she'd found the domineering department secretary forbidding to say the least, and now as a faculty member, she found her stern manner all the more intimidating.

"Thanks, Miss Trueblood. I'm about done for the day. Do you mind if I leave the mail until tomorrow?"

Trueblood twisted her mouth into a pursed pout. "It's best not to let these matters go, Dr. Taylor. *Carpe diem,* you know. Besides, my office isn't exactly equipped with a storage closet."

Maggie shrugged and did her best to charm the unmovable Trueblood with a conciliatory smile. "You're right. Is the package heavy?"

"About ten pounds. Even you could lift that, I think."

Maggie sighed. "OK. After this, I'm leaving for the day. And since I don't have a class until eleven, I may not be in first thing."

Trueblood's heavily made-up eyes narrowed reprovingly. "It's best to keep to the schedule, Dr. Taylor. Office hours are posted, after all."

"And my own hours sometimes have to come first, Miss Trueblood." The secretary handed her a fat FedEx box. "You're right. About ten pounds. Good thing I've been working out, huh? See you tomorrow afternoon."

"Faculty meeting at two," replied the aging spinster.

Maggie walked toward her own office, intending to stow the package inside until the following day, but she noticed a light under Sam Fountain's door. Remembering that she wanted to ask him about a mutual student, she hefted the package into the crook of her left arm and knocked on the oak door marked "Samuel F. Fountain, Ph.D., Anatomy and Physiology."

"Come in!"

Maggie pushed the unlocked door, which gave way to a cramped, twelve-by-twelve room that smelled like old shoes and formaldehyde. Fountain sat behind a two-year stack of journals, sharp eyes darting across the various headlines in that morning's Bloomington *Herald*. He wore a dull brown dress shirt over threadbare corduroys he'd bought twenty years before in his native Minnesota. A balding forehead wrinkled over a pair of rimless eyeglasses that he'd been assured made him look ten years younger.

"Hey, Maggie. Looks like that bird flu is spreading. Another three chicken farms bit the dust in Kansas, and Nebraska is reporting swine infections near some town called Loomis. It's jumped species, just like I said it would. You heading home?"

Taylor put down the package and tumbled into the only other chair in the cramped office. She kicked at an old McDonald's wrapper and let out a heavy sigh. "Not if you have a bottle of Scotch."

Fountain laughed, a musical giggle that sounded like a girl's but always endeared him to women. "Yah, sure, that's a good one!" he answered in a thick Minnesota accent. "But I know you don't really want to drink, so I'll be happy to pour us both some coffee. I could add a nice pair of steaks and some candlelight, but I'm betting you'd turn it down as usual."

Maggie liked Sam Fountain. His unobtrusive manner and high IQ made him pleasant company, but she couldn't imagine ever being more than friends.

"I could do the steaks, but let's skip the candlelight for now, Sammy. Besides, you wouldn't want to hear me bellyache about my day. I just wanted to ask you about Curt Halloran. Have you noticed anything unusual in his test scores lately?"

Fountain leaned forward in his metal-armed chair, plastic wheels squeaking on the tiled floor. "Like some unexpected high grades when he's always been a consistent C student. Yep, I've noticed. Sent your antenna up as well, eh?"

"Do you think he's been cheating off Emily Scott? I mean she's not the type to participate, but he is pretty darn charming. What kills me is that he could pull the grades on his own if he'd just get serious, but he lets his good looks do the work for him. I don't get it."

Fountain opened a side drawer and fished for something to satisfy a nagging sweet tooth. "Candy bar, Maggie?"

"No, thanks. Say, is there a faculty meeting tomorrow?"

"Oh, yah, you bet—at two, why?"

"I didn't get a memo." She stood, bending to retrieve the package. "I'd better get home, Sam. Maybe we can do the steak thing after the meeting tomorrow. I could even rent an old Cary Grant movie. No, wait, what's that one you said I should see? The one from 1939?"

Sam's sharp eyes twitched with excitement behind the thick lenses. "*Gaslight!* Although anything from 1939 is a safe bet. Best year ever in film. Best ever, but *Gaslight* is top of the pack. Oh, you can't do better. Bergman, Boyer, Cotton. You'll love it! I have it on DVD. I'll bring it. And don't worry, Maggie. I know it's just friendship. We'll have fun."

"Thanks, Sam. You're one of the good ones. I'd better run. Catch you tomorrow."

She left his office and headed down the west stairs to the parking lot. After loading the box and her briefcase into the back of her Santa Fe, Maggie pointed the silver SUV toward her temporary home at University Apartments.

The utilitarian nature of the small, second-story flat had appealed to Maggie when she had first left the home she and Jack had built together. She had left most of her possessions behind, except for a few clothes. She didn't care. Life in the furnished living room, kitchen, and bath had offered her solitude when she'd needed it most. And part of her felt she didn't deserve to live in a nice house if her daughter couldn't. Now, as she drove toward the cramped studio, Margaret thought again of handsome Jack and his kindness at lunch.

She parked the car and fought back tears. Thinking of Jack meant thinking of Charlotte, and Maggie couldn't bear that, not even after five years.

Solitude was all she had.

Solitude and guilt.

Locking the car door, Maggie dragged herself into the limestone building and up the marble stairs to the room she'd come to know so well. Keying herself in, she could smell a faint hint of lemon. Julie had been here.

Her neighbor, Julie Emerson, cleaned her apartment once a week in exchange for grocery money. The graduate student from Kentucky loved using lemon-scented solution, and the floors sparkled for days after Julie's visits. The fresh scent hit Maggie hard today, for it reminded her of a real home and real rooms. She longed for a family again, but she knew that was all in the past.

She had to look to the future and make teaching her life.

That's when she remembered the package. After turning on the television for background noise, Maggie turned her attention to the unexpected box. The return address read New Mexico, which meant the contents must be related to her father in some way. Most likely her dad's assistant had forwarded personal effects, although Maggie wondered why the package hadn't gone to Jack's place, since her father's address book would have undoubtedly listed the Columbus street home's number, not Maggie's office. No name on the label. That seemed odd, but she dismissed it.

Funny, she realized as she stared at the package, *I don't even know the name of the company Dad worked for the last four years of his life. Is it Grayson Labs? Nice daughter I was.*

Forcing all negative thoughts from her mind, Maggie grabbed a paring knife from the cramped kitchenette to slit the clear tape and then tore open one side. Inside, she found a smaller box and more tape. Maggie frowned and tackled the inner box as well as the opposite side of the outer case. It took several minutes and some muscle, but she finally freed the sturdy inner box and lifted it from the exterior shipping carton.

The inner box was clean and white with no writing to hint at the contents. Margaret lifted the tabs and lid, revealing clear bubble wrap around something black. Reaching inside, she removed the clear wrap, surprised to find a black leather messenger bag looking up at her. Her father's bag?

She opened the case and puzzled over the odd contents: a silver laptop with a yellow Post-It Note attached. A shaky hand had written, SORRY IT ISN'T MORE. Maggie removed the note and stashed it in her jeans pocket.

Why would her father's assistant send a computer? This made no sense. Maggie carried the unexpected gift to the lumpy structure that served as both couch and bed and settled the laptop onto her knees. She lifted the silvery lid, pressed the on button, and heard the throaty chime familiar to all Apple fans.

Maggie had cut her computer teeth on Apple back in the eighties. She and Jack had bought one of the first Macs, an SE II, spending nearly every spare moment bedazzled by the flickering screen. Since then, Margaret had owned or operated nearly a dozen Mac computers, some through the university, some in her own home. Her twin brother Doug had never understood her love for the Mac Operating System. He preferred PCs, as had their father. Why then would Charles Hilliard switch to a Mac so late in life?

As the boot-up sequence finished, a login screen appeared with her own name listed as the solitary user. A blank password screen stared at her with an annoying, blinking cursor that insisted she type in a word or phrase.

"Great," she muttered.

She puzzled over the screen, trying different passwords, but none worked.

The phone chose just that moment to ring.

Maggie stared at the receiver with dismay. She had few friends outside work, so this would either be a colleague or a student. She dreaded both.

"Hello?"

Breathing.

"Hello?"

"Is this Dr. Taylor?"

A man's voice. "Who is this?" she asked, not wanting to volunteer too much to an unknown caller. *Probably some telemarketer dying to help me pay off those high-interest credit cards.*

"It's Hank Meier. Remember me from this morning?"

Maggie smiled, relieved and intrigued all at once. "Who could forget you?" *I shouldn't have said that.* "I mean, well, you know what I mean. How are you, Hank?"

"Fine, and I'm still in town. I got your number from the campus operator. Forgive me for calling you at home, but I just hated to leave without taking a chance. I know this is going to sound forward, but I'd love to get to know you better. Are you up for some coffee? I'll buy."

"You said the magic word. You say coffee, I say where?"

"Great! There's a place called Barney's Café near the College Mall off Third Street. I always go there when I'm in town. They have dynamite coffee, and it's not generally crowded this time of day."

"Sounds good, Doc. Promise you'll throw in a caramel brownie, and I'm yours."

He laughed, a soft, warm, honest laugh. "I'll remember that. Meet me there in half an hour?"

"I'll be the one in red."

"I can't wait," he added and hung up.

Maggie replaced the beige receiver and considered her prior supper plans. "Bag the nachos," she said aloud. "And bag this mysterious computer, too, for now at least." She stashed the laptop and the packaging in the long storage closet where she kept her bicycle and winter clothes, changed into clean tan shorts, topped them with her favorite red T-shirt, and headed out the door.

CHAPTER 11

Barney's Café had opened up the previous fall under the esteemed management of a local celebrity named Barney Ison. A former basketball player and, more recently, a talk show host on a local radio station, Ison preached an interesting slant on patriotism, which had quickly grown into a bona fide movement. The Barneyites, as his devotees called themselves, loved to hang out at his coffee bar and exchange insights and conspiracy news while sipping Barney's private blend with a dollop of whipped cream.

Arriving first, Maggie found a small table near the windows, as far as possible from a small knot of Barneyites, and set down the canvas tote she'd brought to save the spot. Removing her wallet from the tote's cavernous interior, she stepped through a small group of locals and ordered a latté with double whipped cream and double sugar. While waiting, she listened to the Barneyites as they discussed the flu scare.

"I can't deny that bleeding out is a bad sign. The plague is one of the last signs for Armageddon. You know it. I know it. Man, we all know it! And don't tell me you think it's all coincidence. Sheesh! There are already seventy-three dead in

China, so forget what the CFR media's been spitting out about this not affecting humans. We're next, man. Just ask Barney. It's the big one. Game over."

The speaker, a burly man with a week's growth of black beard, gulped down the last of his coffee and set the mug onto a nearby bistro table. Two other men, one with sandy blond hair and glasses, the other a carrottopped wraith wearing a Lone Gunmen T-shirt, stared at their burly leader.

"Hitch, you're partly right," answered the wraith. "Me and Trick here have been reading between the lines. This flu bug has CIA written all over it, so it's not going to hit the U.S. like it has overseas. The spooks need us cattle, if you get my drift. This is just a way to scare us into taking their lousy vaccinations. The vaccine with the mind control serum in it."

Hitch, the burly man with the beard, shook his head. Maggie laughed inwardly, imagining a rattle. *A redneck former jock with a head full of memories and self-importance but no room for brains,* she thought to herself. She'd seen her share of them, but she had to admit that this one had a different edge to him. He didn't smack of football and fertilizer. He had the sharp look of intelligence with an edge of danger.

"Popeye, you're out to lunch, man," Hitch said, sitting at the bistro table. "Keep it down, though. Professor at two o'clock."

Maggie looked around. Seeing no other instructor, she nearly laughed out loud. The human bear meant her! Nice to be noticed, she thought as she paid for her coffee and returned to the table by the windows. Settling in, she sipped at the rich whipped cream topping, letting the smooth, warm liquid beneath trickle down her throat. *Why is it that hot coffee tastes best in summer?*

"Been waiting long?"

Maggie set down her mug and glanced up. Hank Meier had changed into a pair of soft blue jeans and a teal polo. His black hair and dark eyes favored a strong color near his face—a vast improvement over the afternoon's Men-in-Black look.

"Not too long," she answered. "I just live a hop and a skip away. Hope you don't mind that I already ordered. I had a long day."

"Me, too. Shall I get you something to go with your coffee?"

"If they have that elusive caramel brownie, then bring it on," she said with a wink.

"If they don't make it, I'll whip one up myself!"

Hank left a small plastic bag on his chair and headed for the counter. All three Barneyites watched the tall stranger as he passed by. Hitch nodded to his smaller friends.

"Spook," he whispered just loud enough for Maggie to make it out. "I've seen him a bunch of times in the dean's office. Illuminati specialist. Disinformation is my guess."

Maggie listened as she pretended to stare out the window. Outside, cars rushed to and fro on Third Street, and she could hear a faint thwup-thwup sound from overhead. Helicopter? Probably a news crew or a traffic copter. She remembered the two helicopters she'd seen over her father's funeral. And she'd seen two helicopters that morning over the Chemistry Building. *Bag those nutty thoughts, kiddo! It's just a coincidence! Next thing, you'll join up with these Barneyite kooks!*

"So, did I miss anything?" Meier asked as he returned with a tray. "You look lost in thought."

Margaret jerked her head back, away from her reverie and the world outside. "Sorry. I was ruminating. Is one of those brownies for me, or are you just a pig?"

76

"I've been called worse," Hank said, his dark eyes glittering in the overhead lights. "The big brownie with the caramel topping is all yours. I'm going for the smaller one with the hot fudge. Unless that's one of your personal indulgences."

"Oh, you don't know me well enough to ask about indulgences—at least not yet, Dr. Meier. By the way, did you know that you're a spook from some bunch called the Illuminati? Should I talk now or wait until you turn on the bright lights?"

Meier leaned in, shifting the plastic bag to a third chair. "I'm not sure you know me well enough to ask that," he said, smiling. "Now eat your brownie before I change my Illuminous mind."

Maggie shook her head and picked up her fork. Taking a bite, she sighed, her eyes nearly rolling into her head. "Heavenly! Oh, I needed this. Thanks, Mr. Suit."

"That's Dr. Suit, and you're most welcome," he said. Behind the pair, Hitch and his companions had begun to stare.

"We're being watched. Don't look, but those three guys behind you are taking notes. Does this always happen to you on first dates?"

"Date?" he echoed. "I'm honored, but I really don't want to press for more than you're willing to give. After all, we just met, and you said you're still in the process of a divorce. It's a touchy time."

The trio of Barneyites huddled behind Maggie and her newfound friend, and their hushed voices rattled into Maggie's ears with more power than a shout.

"I think they're still talking about you," she whispered to Meier. "You're pretty infamous, in a conspiracy sort of way. Somehow I almost wish you'd worn your spook suit and a pair of MIB sunglasses. I imagine they wish you had as well. If they only knew that you're just a harried pharmaceutical man! Really, though, if you're bothered, we can go somewhere else, Hank."

Meier started to reply, but a meaty hand tapped his shoulder. "You look out of place, Spook," the voice rasped.

Meier turned to greet his accuser. "Just having some coffee, friend. Would you like to join us?"

Dave Hitchins, called Hitch by the others, cleared his throat for effect. "You'd like that, wouldn't you, Spook? We've got our eyes on you and your kind. Don't think you can put us in a box like some of the scientists you've made disappear."

Meier kept cool, but Maggie jumped into the fray, claws extended. "Just who do you think you are? And what do you mean about scientists?"

Hitch leaned forward, and Maggie could smell beer beneath the java. "Ask your boyfriend. Twenty-eight so far and counting. Where's Andrea Kuryakin? And what about Michael Dory? And what really happened to Tommy Foil?"

Meier stood suddenly, his tall, muscular frame hovering over Hitch's round one. "I don't know what you're talking about, friend, but I'd rather not make a scene. I'd be happy to talk outside, if you like."

Maggie jumped up as well, her face white. "Did you say Tommy Foil?"

"This gentleman doesn't know what he's saying, Maggie."

Maggie pushed past Meier to confront Burly Beard herself. "Did you say Tommy Foil? Yes or no?"

"What's it to you, Mrs. Spook?" he asked, noticing his companions' snickering.

Maggie jumped into Hitch's face, ignoring the beer breath and punctuating her words with a finger to the chest. "I happen to know Dr. Foil. Do you? Just what are you talking about?"

Hitch's face paled, and he turned to his friends for support. "I—uh, well, I just mean his death. It was rather suspicious, you have to admit."

"Death? Tom Foil is dead? Since when? Where did you hear that?"

Meier took her elbow, trying to pry her away from Hitch.

Maggie tore her elbow away from Meier, tears filling her eyes. "Tell me who told you!" she demanded, voice cracking.

"It was on the news! Sheesh! WNN broadcast it this morning. Like Spooky here didn't know. You should have told your wife, Spook."

"I'm not his wife, you idiot! But if I were, I'd be proud of it! And as for you and your deadbeat, conspiracy friends, Mr. Hitch," she finished, using the name she'd heard the others use and startling all three, "you can tell all your little computer geek friends that Tommy Foil is not dead! If he were, I would know! He's my godfather, you moron!"

Meier stepped between them, taking Maggie's hand firmly and leading her toward the exit. "Come on," he said softly, casting a dark eye back toward the embarrassed trio. "We can take our coffee money to Sam's over at the Union. At least there they know how to treat a lady."

He picked up Maggie's tote and helped her outside and to her car. However, he left his plastic bag behind.

Once he and Maggie had left, the Barneyite trio followed the pair's movements from inside the café, their jaws slack and eyes wide.

"You guys get your brains from the Three Stooges bank?" Barney Ison asked as he emerged from the kitchen. "Boy oh boy, you sure know how to impress women, Hitch!"

"I didn't know she wasn't married to the guy," Burly Beard bit back, his eyes still on Meier and Maggie. "What did she say about Foil? That he was her godfather? Man, that doesn't make any sense! What do you think, Barney?"

All three men looked to their leader for answers. Ison dried his large hands on a cotton towel and mused. "First off, I got no problem with you callin' Mr. Suit there the CIA spook that he is. As to the lady, she looks familiar. I think I've seen her on campus or somethin'. If she's telling the truth, and I think she is 'cause she looked real surprised, then she might be the link we've been looking for. Popeye, you get the license plate?"

Carrottop nodded and put his ever-present mechanical pencil behind one ear. "Got it, and a description of the car. Silver Hyundai Santa Fe. I'll have the name for you in less than five." Popeye reached into his backpack and withdrew a laptop. Deftly, he lifted the lid, tapped a few keys, and located a server that would reverse-identify license plate numbers. Smiling broadly, he snapped the lid shut and leaned back. "Told you," he bragged moments later. "Margaret Taylor. Dr. Margaret Taylor, but it gets better."

Barney raised a dark eyebrow. "Well? Give!"

Popeye laughed and slapped the table. "She probably *is* Tommy Foil's goddaughter. I mean, it only makes sense. Her maiden name is the clue, my lads. Before she married Jackson Taylor, our raven-haired doctor was Margaret Hilliard. Sound familiar?"

"Hilliard? Oh man, you're kidding, right? Not Charles Hilliard? Tom Foil's partner?" Trick asked.

"The very same, gentlemen. The very same."

Ison and the two smaller men shared surprised looks, but Hitch had left the group momentarily. Making sure none of his friends noticed, he retrieved Meier's plastic bag, withdrew the contents, then tossed the empty bag into a trash receptacle.

Stepping back into the group's tight circle, he rejoined their conversation as if nothing had happened.

"What do you think, Hitch?" Ison asked.

"I think we need to find out more about the lady," he replied, patting his pocket. The others nodded in agreement, and Hitch followed them to the office, where they'd make plans with Ison, not one of them realizing that Dave Hitchins, their conspiracy buddy of six months, carried an extra thousand dollars in his pocket along with a note detailing his next assignment.

"Sorry about that mess," Meier said as he opened Maggie's driver door. "For some reason, I get that sort of attention now and then, but you shouldn't have to put up with it. And I'm really sorry that you had to hear about a friend's death that way."

Maggie stood next to the car, her feet refusing to move, her heart pounding like a hammer. "Tommy's dead? He's really dead? But how? Hank, I don't understand it. I mean, Dad just died, and now Uncle Tommy. Poor Pip. I'll have to call her."

"Pip?" he asked, his modulated voice revealing little emotion.

Maggie shook her head, trying to clear her thoughts, to push past the grief into a more controlled mode. "Pippa Anderson. She's Tommy's unofficial daughter. She's a sort of a missionary to a small Southwest Indian tribe in New Mexico. Tom sponsored her work, and they grew very close, like father and daughter. I met her last summer, when she came here to take a graduate course in anthropology. We had Tommy in common, so we spent a lot of time together. Unless she's changed her mind on modern conveniences, I don't think she has a phone, but I could send a telegram. Look, I'm not thinking very clearly right now. It's been a crazy day. Do you mind if I say goodnight?"

Hank's dark eyes grew somber, and he nodded. "Sure. I understand. Maggie, I had a good time, despite the Three Little Pigs in there."

Margaret laughed, her warm brown eyes crinkling at the edges. "Three Little Pigs? They're probably calling you the Big Bad Wolf right now, but they're wrong. Can we rain check for another night?"

"How about Friday? I'll be back in town with Rebecca then. Maybe you and I could show her around Bloomington."

"I'd like that. Goodnight, Hank. And thanks."

Maggie climbed into the Santa Fe, and Meier closed the door behind her. Waving as he walked away, he returned to his own car, a black Accord, and watched her drive toward the light at Third. Sitting alone, Meier picked up his cell phone and dialed.

An accented voice answered. "Grayson."

"It's Meier, sir. Do you know about a woman named Pippa Anderson?"

"Anderson, did you say? I don't believe so. Who is she?"

Meier opened his mouth, thought for a moment. He could still see the Santa Fe's taillights as it idled at the stoplight. Meier closed his eyes, took a breath, and then did something he never thought he'd do. He lied to his boss.

"It's a name that one of the locals mentioned. I'm not even sure she exists. That's the extent of my report for tonight."

"Nothing else?" questioned Grayson.

"If you mean the package, sir, I don't believe she has it. It must have gone elsewhere."

"This Anderson person?"

"No! I mean, no, Anderson is a dead end."

"Very well, Dr. Meier. Call me tomorrow." Grayson hung up without any further words, and the line grew quiet. Meier returned the phone to his pocket and slumped in the seat. He shouldn't have mentioned Anderson. Grayson hadn't become head of BioStrain without excellent instincts. He would check it out for sure. Meier could hide his own blunder by diminishing the value of the source, but he wondered why he'd lied.

The Santa Fe turned left, and the taillights disappeared. As he watched, Meier understood why he'd given Grayson a false report. Maggie Taylor.

Rex Grayson closed his cell phone and returned it to his pocket. "It appears our Dr. Meier might not be as loyal as we'd presumed," he told the circle of men and women who comprised a group known as The Watchers. "Ryder, you are the one who recommended him to us. Can we trust him?"

Ryder puffed on a thick Cuban cigar and nodded. "To the extent that anyone can be trusted," he replied, looking toward Apollo Bell. "For instance, Mr. Grayson, how far can we trust you?"

Grayson stopped breathing for an instant and gazed into Ryder's unblinking, chameleon eyes. He shook his head to clear it. Had Ryder's image flickered into something else for a moment? Had Bell's face shimmered?

Rex Grayson had grown up on the mean streets of London's east end. He'd clawed his way into banking, doing whatever it took to further his career, and eventually cheated and lied his way to the top of a billion-dollar empire. The men and women who comprised the shadowy group known only as The Watchers had offered him a hand up very early in his ruthless climb, and he owed them his life.

"Major Ryder, you have the world's intelligence services at your fingertips. You would know if I can be trusted with what you and the others here have given to me."

Andy laughed and tapped his cigar ash into a crystal ashtray, recalling his earlier encounter with Jenna Dryden. "Just remember that," he said. "And now, ladies and gentlemen, since we've finished up with the BioStrain portion of our agenda, I'm sure Mr. Grayson will allow us the privacy we require to address other matters."

A dark-haired woman entered the room and took Grayson's arm. "This way, Mr. Grayson," she said, her movements as smooth as ice.

"Thank you, Lilith," Grayson answered. He resisted the urge to look back one last time before the magnificent mahogany doors closed behind him, but he could have sworn the room had filled with the unmistakable smell of brimstone.

CHAPTER 12

Tuesday

Look, Mr. Conners, I appreciate your dilemma, but we have problems of our own down here. I'm up to my eyeballs covering this whole chicken flu thing. Besides, I can't imagine how anything going on in Las Cruces could possibly have a bearing on what killed your partner."

"Not what, who!" Conners replied, frustration getting the better of his temper. "Sorry, Mr. Levatino. Look, before she was killed, Jenna was working on a story about missing scientists and how they all worked for the same company at one time or another. The company is BioStrain. According to my research, BioStrain is located near Las Cruces. All I'm asking is that you check into it for me. Send me what you have."

"OK, OK. Give me a few days. I'll see what I can do." Frank Levatino hung up, his stomach rumbling. The new diet wasn't working, but his wife insisted he stay on it for the rest of the week. Low carbohydrates meant no sugar, and his hypoglycemia hated him for it.

"Who was that, Chief?"

Levatino rubbed his eyes, fighting back the pain that threatened to split his head in two. "Nate, you ever hear of BioStrain?"

Nate Beacham closed his eyes. Of all the people who worked at the *Sun Times*, Beacham meant the most to Frank. Not just because of Nate's photographic memory, but also because Nate had served in Vietnam with Levatino. The two men had known each other for forty-six years. They'd shared joys, new babies, graduations, and even a few painful funerals together.

"BioStrain," the small-framed man recalled as his amazing memory went to work. "Got it. A subsidiary of Grayson Labs out of London. Took out a bunch of patents beginning six years ago. They're supposed to have an installation somewhere in New Mexico."

Levatino stared. No matter how many times he witnessed Beacham's remarkable ability, the feat always amazed him. "You're not human!" he laughed, and the two shared grins.

"Why?" Nate asked, sitting on the edge of his boss's desk.

"Some kid out of Indianapolis is asking, that's why. Seems his partner, a reporter name of," he checked his notes, "Jenna Dryden is dead. Died sometime this morning, smoking in bed, it sounds like, at the Hilton in D.C. This kid—name's Bill Conners—believes a man named Andrew Ryder killed her, and that it's connected with this BioStrain and some missing scientists."

Nate's eyebrows shot up. "Missing or dead? Frank, remember I told you last week about the unlikely number of scientists who've died in the last few years? How a bunch of them worked together at one time or another?" Beacham's face relaxed, and his eyes closed again. "I can't recall BioStrain, but I know Grayson Labs is involved. It's mentioned in three of the bios."

Levatino slapped his friend's shoulder. "Then maybe you can help this kid. Me, I gotta have a can of Coke."

"Tina will spit nails if she finds out, Frank."

"Let her. It's better than having my head split open right now. Here's this kid's phone number. Give him a call, okay? I guess the D.C. police are hinting that the kid's to blame somehow, even though they got no proof. Fly on out there, if you want. It might make a nice change from the chicken flu headlines."

"Did you see the flu's jumped species?" Nate asked. "Up in Nebraska. That can't be good."

Lavatino's dark eyes blinked. "I wonder why I didn't read that on the wire. Where'd you see it?"

"Read it on the Internet."

Frank reached into his pocket for quarters. "It's a sad world when an honest newspaper can't keep up with the Internet. Maybe I oughta just buy that old potato farm Tina saw in Idaho. Spend my days fishin'. Forget about the flu, chickens, and companies I've never heard of."

"Sounds nice, Frank. Me and Amy'll be right behind you."

"Thanks, pal. Call me when you get to Indiana, OK?"

Nate nodded, heading for the door. "Sure thing, Chief. I'll swing by home, pack a bag, and be on my way."

Levatino checked the change in his hand. A dollar seventy-five. The machine charged fifty cents for a Coke. He'd have enough for a pack of Twinkies. "There is a God," he whispered and headed for the canteen.

"Well, Sam, that's all for me," Maggie said as she keyed herself into her office.

"Done already?" the sheepish professor asked. "How'd the final go over in neuro?"

"Let's just say the groan factor was pretty high. Almost as bad as that awful faculty meeting earlier! How many ways can a man say 'out of money'? So, how about you? Are you done for the day?"

Fountain left his office and walked across the hall to Maggie's door. "Yah. All done. Taught my last class this morning. I won't post final grades until Friday, and then I'm going to drive to Indianapolis for the weekend. There's a physiology symposium meeting at the Crowne Plaza. Want to go?"

Maggie fussed with a file drawer and looked up. "Huh? Oh, yeah. I think you mentioned that to me last week. Honestly, it does sound good, but I'll have to pass. I've booked a flight to Las Cruces for Saturday to see Pippa. You know. Tom Foil."

Sam's lower lip pushed out, and he repositioned his glasses. "Yeah, that's too bad about Tom. Well, it's a small meeting anyway. But that cell membrane meeting next month, you're going to that one, right? It's here in town."

Maggie had found a butter knife, which she kept for sandwiches, and had started prying at the stubborn drawer. "Sure. Abe Preston's speaking, isn't he? Sam, can you help me with this?"

"Yah, sure thing!" he said, bending down and examining the underside of the file drawer. "You're off the track. Drawer's too full, Maggie May. Time to move a few folders."

Maggie stood up. "Drat it all. OK. I can do that. Of course, it means asking for a bigger filing cabinet."

"You kidding? After the hour-long knuckle busting we just got over this year's spending?"

"Rats! I hate bureaucracy!" she exclaimed, waving the butter knife.

Sam laughed and took it from her. "Here, before you get violent, let me set this over here, safe and sound. What do you say we blow this Popsicle place, as you so often say, and make tonight an early movie night. Huh?"

Maggie's face had turned red, and she puffed from the small exertion. "What? Popsicle? Oh!" she realized, her face softening as she remembered their plans. "That's right. I'd forgotten, Sam. Sure. I'd like that. My place or yours?"

Fountain blushed. "Well, I suppose it'd better be yours. Mine's pretty messy. Or we could go to a theater, if you like."

"My place is fine. It'll be fun. You can look at some of the real estate magazines I've picked up and help me decide on a house."

"Okeydokey. I'll bring the movies. Six o'clock?"

She thought a moment, then nodded, offering her most dazzling smile. "That's perfect, Sam. See you then."

CHAPTER 13

Now turning to national news, police in St. Louis are still seeking information on the whereabouts of Raymond Wistern, a Missouri native who's wanted for questioning in a series of violent assaults on college coeds. Also in the news, authorities in Atlanta have closed the case on missing scientist Matthew Parker, whose car was reported abandoned at a north side convenient mart by an employee. Parker, who disappeared three weeks ago, is now believed to have fled the country, and the case is now in the hands of the FBI. Michigan farmers are wondering how many of their chickens will survive the latest round of influenza..."

Pippa Anderson turned off the radio. She'd heard all she could bear. Nothing but bad news anymore. The world had changed so much since she was a little girl. Too much. She glanced at the dusty television she'd brought with her when she'd moved to New Mexico. Maybe the old Sylvania radio would soon gather dust as well. Pippa preferred the quiet scenery and gentle birdsong of the world outside her front porch to the harsh images and cacophony that came through the airwaves. *Satan is the prince and power of the air,* she thought as she stepped outside. *Maybe that's why he has so much control of television and radio.*

As she stepped out into the cool evening, Pippa inhaled deeply. "Beautiful," she said aloud. The multihued, watercolor evening sky had mesmerized Pippa Anderson from her very first trip here as a high school senior back in 1980. Since then, she had earned a master's degree in sociology and devoted her life to studying and ministering to the three hundred locals who called Los Muertos home.

Dancing above the softer notes of fragrant poppies, lupines, and ghost flowers, Pippa could smell smoke in the distance. Her sharp eyes scanned the horizon, and she noticed a small fire burning atop one of the nearby mesas. The sight sent shivers down her spine. Since February, many of the people of Los Muertos had fallen under the sway of a pseudo-religious man who called himself Meektay, short for Mictlantecuhtli, after the Aztec Lord of the Dead. This unscrupulous fraud had enough knowledge of ancient religion to impress, but he mixed it with bits of Catholicism and Hopi, adding rules of his own making. Though only a few had followed him at first, he now held the hearts and souls of many of the locals in his greedy hands. Pippa had come to dread the man, though she still prayed for him at night. The fire on the mesa could only be part of one of Meektay's rituals meant to appease the angry gods.

As Pippa watched, she noticed a small cloud in the distance, dust that had been kicked up by a passing car on the only road that led into Los Muertos. Pippa's sharp blue eyes followed the oncoming car's progress, not the least bit surprised when the familiar outline of a jeep came into view.

Sitting in one of a pair of rockers she'd made herself, Pippa prepared to greet her longtime friend and comrade, Dr. Daniel Tohe, local "medicine man" and self-proclaimed mayor of Los Muertos. The olive green jeep, bought by Tohe at an army surplus auction in 1989, chugged to a halt ten feet from the concrete porch to Pippa's trailer.

"I didn't know you made house calls this far out!" Pippa called as the tall Navajo wrenched his long legs out of the driver's seat. The driver's door hadn't worked in years.

"I get my money where I can. You know us doctors." He whipped his hat in the air to remove the thick dust and stepped up on the porch. "Do you have any tea, Pip Anderson?"

Pippa laughed and jumped up from the rocker. "Where have you been?" she asked as she grabbed the doctor in a bear hug.

Tohe smiled, his dark face creased with dust. "Just got back from Santa Fe. Medical seminar. Sorry I didn't let you know, Pippa. If you had a telephone, I'd have called. I drove out here to tell you, but you weren't home. Didn't you get my note?"

Pippa gave the doctor a light kiss on the cheek. "Note? I guess not. Oh, Daniel, you're a mess! Better go inside and wash up."

Daniel Tohe followed the tall Nebraska-born woman inside and removed his boots. "I really am sorry if you were worried, Pippa. The meeting was called with very little notice. It was an emergency session of the state's chief medical men. A solid week of meetings and workshops."

"Emergency?" she repeated, taking an old crock from a white, 1952 Frigidaire and pouring two glasses of cold tea. "Health crisis? This chicken flu?"

"You been reading the papers, Pippa?" he asked, coming out of the bathroom, his face clean. "Thanks," he said, taking the tea. He followed her to the front porch, where both sat in the rockers.

"I keep up. I may not have much call for modern devices, but Robert Billand brings me the *Sun-Times* twice a week.

I know this bird flu has caused over a hundred thousand chickens to die. I also saw where an outbreak of Hantavirus left three dead over by Roswell."

Daniel sipped the cool drink, his eyes fixed on the fires atop Ford's Mesa. "It may not be Hanta, at least not according to the CDC. I talked with Rich Owens from upstate, and he says some of our local chicken farms have tested positive for the avian virus. Now that it's jumped to pigs in Nebraska, there's no telling what may happen. Humans might be next."

Pippa grew pale. "Daniel, you'd better talk to Sheriff Down about Gomez Ibanez and his family. Robert told me that they were sick and that two of the children were dead. Probably not related, but Robert said something about Meektay going over there to sweep the spirits of the dead from the corners."

"Two children? Oh, dear God. Which ones?"

Pippa shook her head. "Jorge and Angelina. Robert told me. Gomez buried them near his trailer."

"Didn't anyone examine the children? Sheriff Down knew I'd asked Tom Behrens to take calls for me while I was out of town. Tom could have driven out there."

"Robert didn't say anything about Dr. Behrens. I drove over there yesterday, but no one was there. In fact, the trailer looked abandoned. I spoke to Warren Down about it. He thinks Gomez took what family he had left back to Mexico."

"It's possible. Gomez never liked being here. Rosita, now she had potential. She used to work for me at the clinic. Remember?"

"I do," Pippa answered, touching his shoulder thoughtfully.

"I wish I'd been here," Tohe said, thoughtfully sipping his tea. "Jorge was just a few months old. And Angie had a congenital heart problem. I suppose they could have died from a common flu infection. Still, I should talk to Warren about letting me exhume the bodies to make sure. It could have been Hanta."

"Daniel, you know how the folks around here feel about grave desecration. Warren Down won't want to upset voters. This may be a small town, but it's his town, and he doesn't want to give it up."

"You're probably right, but he has to obey the law, too. The CDC says to report all suspicious cases. Is that Meektay up there?" he asked, pointing to the mesa. "Why doesn't Warren Down arrest him and help us all sleep better at night?"

Pippa rocked thoughtfully, smiling as Daniel's large, rough hand touched hers. "Meektay's got power, that's why. Warren's more worried about winning the next election than he is about ancient Aztec gods. You ever talk to Meektay?"

Daniel finished the tea and set down the cracked glass. "You need some new stemware," he said with a grin. "Offer's still open to pick out china patterns."

"You're evading the question."

"Nope. You are. Have been for five years. You gonna make me wait another five?"

"Maybe. What about Meektay?" she insisted, kissing his fingers before gathering both empty glasses and heading back to the tiny kitchen.

Daniel watched the distant fire dance high into the air, and he could make out writhing shadows around it, foolish dancers imitating ancient worshippers. "If Warren thinks Meektay has power now, just wait. If this flu virus begins to infect humans, people will panic. And panic drives otherwise rational folks to irrational means. A man will try some pretty crazy things to save his family."

"That's what scares me about him," Pippa answered from the kitchen.

"Oh, I nearly forgot," Tohe called through the screen door. "I got a telegram for you. Susie gave it to me when I got into town. She didn't want to wait until Robert's next trip out to send it."

Pippa returned with filled glasses, gave one to Tohe, and resumed rocking. "Thanks," she said, taking the wrinkled, white envelope. "Hey, it's from Indiana. Maggie Taylor. You remember me talking about her, don't you? She teaches at IU. We spent some good times together when I took that course there last summer."

Tohe closed his eyes, nearly falling asleep as weariness settled into his bones. "I think so."

"She says that..." Her voice trailed off. "Oh no! Oh no!" Her face had gone white, and tears filled her green eyes.

"Pip, honey, are you okay?" the doctor asked, jumping from his chair and squatting in front of her. "Pip?"

She looked up, tears tracking down her freckled cheeks. "Tommy's dead. Killed in a car crash. He's dead, Daniel. Dead. How could this happen?"

Tohe helped her to stand and held her close, letting his strong heartbeat aid hers. "We'll find out," he promised. "Does Maggie say anything else? Is there a funeral?"

Pippa shook her head. "No. I mean, I don't know. She doesn't say. She just says she wants to come out here on Saturday after her classes end. I need to call her. Daniel, would you drive me into town so I can use your phone?"

He kissed her forehead, his own eyes reflecting his pain at her anguish. "Of course. Why don't you plan on staying in town for a few days? I have a guest room, you know."

"That might be best," she whispered. "I'll pack a bag."

Nate Beacham wondered if he'd made the right choice in coming to Indianapolis. Since his arrival two hours earlier, he hadn't heard one coherent word from the man who had prompted his last-minute flight from Las Cruces. Bill Conners looked as if he hadn't slept recently. A man often described as a "long drink of water," Conners reminded Beacham of a cartoon Frank Sinatra, except his brown hair hadn't been washed or combed in days.

Wearing a rumpled blue shirt and tie over khaki pants, Conners had met Beacham at the Indianapolis International Airport and driven him to this small apartment in Speedway, where Beacham had watched the lanky cameraman pace back and forth while spewing forth a stream of colorful accusations against BioStrain and a man named Andy Ryder.

"Didn't you just say the D.C. police ruled Ryder out?" Beacham asked rhetorically. "Why do you insist on naming him as a suspect?"

Conners stopped pacing and stared, bug-eyed.

Is he on drugs? Beacham wondered.

"Look, Mr. Beacham, I know you think I'm really off my nut, but I'm telling you I'm on the right track here. Now, Jenna and I may not have been the best of buddies, but she knew her stuff, and if she believed twenty-eight dead scientists meant a conspiracy, then they do. And she named Ryder as the man who could get her into the inner circle of Grayson Labs and BioStrain. Why would she choose Ryder if he's not involved?"

"Twenty-nine."

"What? Huh?"

"Twenty-nine," Beacham repeated calmly. "As of this morning. A biochemist who worked on the human genome project in France. Dr. Michel Duflot. He was hit by a commuter train."

Conners wiped at his thick hair, struggling to maintain composure. "Hit? Hit? What kind of man is just hit by a train, for God's sake? Killed! Murdered! Dear Lord. You know what this means? It means they could target me, too. They killed Jenna, you can bet on that. Oh, yes. You can be sure of it!"

"Calm down, Bill," Nate spoke gently.

"Calm down! Calm down! Easy for you to say, you're not under suspicion. All they would have to do is arrest me, and I'm toast. Poor Jenna. Oh, God, you should have seen her."

He tumbled into a nearby chair, as though he couldn't hold himself up any longer. William Brandeis Conners, a young man who'd wanted only to make a difference in the world through photojournalism, had just collapsed into a boneless heap of fear. Nate's heart broke at the sight.

"Look, Bill. I can't make any guarantees. I have to fly back to Las Cruces tonight, but I promise to dig up all I can about BioStrain and this guy Ryder."

Conners glanced up, his hazel eyes filling with tears of relief. "I'm not usually like this," he said, then the weight of the last few days fell on him, and he broke down and began to cry.

CHAPTER 14

Maggie returned to her apartment by five. She'd decided to make the most of the evening by ordering a pizza from Mother Bear's, but another idea struck her, and she left the phone for the time being and headed back into the hallway.

Maggie knocked on Julie Emerson's door.

No answer. She knocked several more times, but there was still no answer, so she left a note. Returning to her own apartment, she put in a call to Mother Bear's and passed the time catching up on the evening news.

An Indianapolis station offered local and national news at five, so Maggie tuned in and started putting together a salad. Romaine, endive, tomato, green onion (after all, it wasn't a date), and cucumber. She'd let the mix stay cold in the fridge until later, when she'd add some bleu cheese crumbles, croutons, and a creamy bleu cheese dressing. In the background, she could hear a female anchor reading the news of the day.

"...with the burial taking place at Crown Hill Cemetery. Those who would like to send condolences to Jenna Dryden's family may do so by sending them right here to the station or to Marlowe's Funeral Home. Jenna, we all miss you.

"Here's a story that Jenna Dryden spent many weeks working on in Washington, one that concerns all of us: the rising number of influenza cases on chicken farms here in the Midwest. We've sent our own Brian Hartman to the Centers for Disease Control in Atlanta to find out more about what we've all come to know as the Avian Flu Epidemic. Brian."

Maggie stuffed the salad into the fridge and returned to the living room/bedroom area. She sat on the sofa and watched as an athletic man who couldn't be more than thirty interviewed a middle-aged doughboy with an expensive hairpiece. "Linda, this is Dr. Edgar Fouchet of the Centers for Disease Control office. Dr. Fouchet is head of the Influenza Division. Dr. Fouchet, what can you tell our listeners about these outbreaks of bird flu?"

The man peered uncomfortably into the bright lights and camera, adjusted his tie, and spoke evenly. "Well, avian influenza, that is, bird flu, is a member of the A virus family, which originates in wild birds. This can be spread through excrement and nasal secretions to other birds, such as chickens, ducks, and geese. The strain that is currently infecting Asian and American chicken populations is H5N1, which is a particularly infectious agent."

"So, if one chicken catches it, then they all catch it? Is that it, Doctor?"

"Usually that is true. That's why the entire flock must be slaughtered when even one chicken tests positive."

"You called it H5N..."

"H5N1," the doctor completed. "That describes the type of hemagglutinin and neuraminidase proteins on the viral coating. These coatings determine the pathway for infection. The CDC has finished sequencing the outbreak in Nebraska, which is the most worrisome at present."

The anchorman turned investigative reporter looked thoughtful and moved the mic closer to his target. "Why is that, Doctor?"

"Well, ordinarily avian influenza remains in the fowl population only, but in Nebraska, it has jumped species and infected swine."

Hartman mugged once more. "Swine? Pigs, right?"

"That's right, Brian, which means there is a slight possibility that humans could catch a version of this influenza. The chances are low, although precaution is necessary. Therefore, any dead animals must be reported to the state CDC."

"And what about the proposed vaccine program that we've all heard Washington talk about. Will that protect us?"

Fouchet looked directly into the camera and nodded. "The vaccine that is being developed is nearly complete, and it will most definitely protect you and your loved ones from the virus, should it become dangerous to humans."

"So we're okay?" the reporter asked with a dimpled smile.

"Yes, Brian. We're okay."

Maggie turned off the set and stared. She thought about what Doug had mentioned regarding their father's papers. Could a strain of influenza A mutate into a potent human hunter? Had it already happened in China? She prayed Doug had misread the notes. She'd never seen her father proven wrong once he'd postulated a theory.

Just this once, she prayed he was.

Daniel Tohe couldn't sleep. He'd only been back in Los Muertos for one day, and already he'd faced four deaths and the inscrutable wall of justice named Sheriff Down. Leaving Pippa asleep in his guest room, the doctor decided to take a walk.

Tohe's brightly painted adobe home sat about a mile out-side of Los Muertos on the edge of the Chihuahua Desert. He'd spent most of his life in such a place as this. Born in Chaco from an unlikely union between a Navajo lawyer and an Irish dancer, Daniel had endured endless teasing from his classmates. White Eyes, they called him, because of his star-tling clear blue eyes, inherited from his black-haired, azure-eyed mother, Maeve O'Connell Tohe.

Daniel's father, Robert Tohe, had met O'Connell during his years as a law student at Ohio State. The petite, pale-eyed dance student and the tall dark-skinned law student had made an unusual, though handsome couple, and their unique talents had opened the doors of opportunity in New York, London, and Los Angeles. However, Robert's heart belonged to his own people in New Mexico, and he longed to return to Chaco, where he could offer his skills to the impoverished and the broken. Leaving her career behind, Maeve had willingly fol-lowed her husband's dream.

Two years after settling in Chaco, the couple welcomed their first child, a girl named Roberta, followed three years later by a precocious son whom they named Daniel, after Maeve's father. Maeve's love of dancing never waned, and she opened a small theater and dance school, where she taught ballet to the natives, who in turn taught her traditional Navajo and Hopi dance.

As he walked now among the moonlit sands behind his home, Daniel gazed upon a thick stand of creosote bushes, alive with hungry grasshoppers, and thought of the Ibanez children. Daniel's childhood home life had been filled with love, art, and plenty, a stark contrast to the tin-walled despera-tion of Gomez Ibanez's children.

Tohe squatted near a tall cocklebur and picked up a handful of sand. He watched the warm sand slide through his fingers like a gleaming quartz waterfall, and he thought of time. Time had deserted Jorge and Angelina Ibanez, leaving them nothing more than a barren patch of sand in a heartless plain. Or so most would think. Ashes to ashes. Dust to dust. Daniel knew better.

He looked up into the glittering night sky and studied the majestic panorama above his head. "When I consider Your heavens, Lord," he said aloud, quoting a favorite psalm, "the work of Your fingers, the moon and the stars, which You have ordained, what is man, that You're mindful of him? In fact, Lord, what am I that You are mindful of me?"

Overhead, a shooting star split the heavens as it fell to earth somewhere in Mexico. Daniel smiled. "Thank You, Lord," he said, standing and wiping dust from his hands. "How excellent is Your name in all the earth!"

Maggie wondered why on earth she hadn't spent more time with Sam Fountain. After watching *Gaslight*, Sam had produced a DVD Trivial Pursuit game, which had left the two teachers laughing until midnight.

"Sam, I can't believe this evening's gone by so quickly, but we're gonna have to call it quits here."

Fountain nodded, stifling a yawn. "Yeah, I'm usually into my third Raquel Welch dream by this time of night."

A soft knock sounded at the door.

"Let's hope it's not Charles Boyer," he said to Maggie with a devilish twinkle in his eyes.

"Ooh, let's hope not!" she laughed, rising from the floor, where they'd settled to play the game. She opened the door.

"Hey, there! Come on in!" she said to the midnight visitor. "Julie Emerson, this is Professor Fountain, my cohort from across the Med Sci hallway. Sam, Julie's my next-door neighbor and all around good friend."

Sam sprang to his feet and grinned from ear to ear. The young woman radiated warmth, and her bright, hazel eyes sparkled despite the late hour. "It's a pleasure," he mumbled, offering his hand.

Julie's small hand fit neatly into Fountain's, and she offered a strong handshake. "It's a pleasure, Professor Fountain."

Maggie smiled, noting the sparks between the two like a steady current passing between two Tesla coils. "Julie's a grad student in the School of Music," she explained, wondering if Sam even heard her.

"I'll bet you're a soprano," Fountain remarked, hesitant to release her tiny hand.

"How'd you guess?" Julie asked, a single dimple showing just beneath her full mouth.

"Stature and build. You have a delicately made instrument," Sam said. "Oh, I mean, well, I'm sorry if I've been too bold. I should be going, Maggie," he added bashfully. He released Julie's hand and dashed for the doorway. "A pleasure to meet you, Miss Emerson."

"Likewise, Dr. Fountain. Maybe I'll see you around?"

"Oh, yah. That's very likely," he muttered, backing into the hall.

"Sam, don't you want your game and movie?" Maggie asked.

"I'll g-get them another time!" he stammered. "Better leave you ladies to t-talk! G'night!"

"Goodnight, Sam! See you tomorrow!" Maggie called to the retreating professor just before closing the door.

"Boy, you made quite an impression," she said, turning back to Emerson.

"Maybe. First impressions never seem to last when it comes to my love life. Anyway, I came over as soon as I got your note. Sorry I couldn't make it earlier. Auditions for the summer opera were tonight."

"How did it go?"

"I'll know tomorrow morning. So, were you and the professor having a special evening?" she asked impishly.

"Hardly. I left you that note thinking you might be able to make this evening seem less like a date and more like a friendly good time, but I clearly had Sam all wrong."

Julie grabbed a slice of leftover pizza. "What do you mean?"

"How can you ask that, after what I just witnessed? Sam forgot I even existed once you walked in! I believe my Minnesota pal has a crush on a certain soprano."

"We'll see," Jules said, clearly delighted with her conquest. "Well, I'm off to bed. Oh, I nearly forgot! I found this taped to your mailbox downstairs. Thought I'd bring it up."

Maggie took the small envelope and opened it. She read quietly, her face glowing.

"So? Who wrote it?" Jules asked, popping the last bite of pizza in her mouth.

Maggie smiled and shook her head. "Just someone I met yesterday."

"A guy?"

"A really nice guy," Maggie answered, the smile broadening into a positive grin.

"Give me that!" Jules exclaimed, snatching the note and reading it aloud. "'*Dear Maggie,*' oh a nice beginning! '*I'd like to apologize again for the way last night turned out.*' What about last night?" she insisted. "Never mind, you can tell me later. '*Let me make it up over lunch tomorrow. I'll come by at noon. Hank.'* Hank? You have a lot to tell me, don't you, Dr. Taylor?"

Maggie sighed happily and opened the fridge. "I'll pour the iced tea, you plump up the cushions on the sofa. This could take a while."

CHAPTER 15

Wednesday

Arnold Smith reached for his alarm clock, tapping the off button lightly. Trying not to wake his wife, Smith eased his size-ten feet onto the concrete floor of their bunker suite and stretched. Wednesday morning. Just four more days to wait, then on Monday, he and the other scientists could return to the abandoned chicken farm to check on the newest batch of Solution 456.

Martha, Smith's wife of twenty-four years, knew nothing of the project's details, only that her microbiologist husband headed up a group of like-minded men and women whose purpose was to find a cure for the flu.

Smith had never told her anything different.

Standing, Smith gazed at his wife's auburn hair and wished he could remain beside her, snuggling next to her warmth, pretending to know nothing of BioStrain and its deadly secrets. Settling for a light kiss to her cheek, Smith quickly showered, dressed, and closed the door to their bedroom, still carrying his shoes and socks.

The concrete floor, though painted a warm red, chilled his feet, so he sat down and wriggled into the white double-soled comfort socks and black loafers with gel inserts. After his typical breakfast of cereal with bananas, Smith left the bunker suite, still adjusting the blue and white badge that gave him access to Level Six.

"Morning, Dr. Smith," a fat security guard said with a bleak smile. Powdered sugar dusted the front of the man's uniform.

"All the donuts gone?" Smith asked with a grin. "Better see to that sugar on your shirt there, Max, before Mr. Grayson shows up."

"Mr. Grayson is coming here? Today?"

"Nine on the dot. That's what we were told anyway. Look sharp, Max. And next time, save me one of the jelly-filled, OK?"

"Sure, Doc," the guard answered, dusting the sugar from his shirt. "Say, is it true that we've all got a three-day weekend coming?"

"That's news to me," said Smith. "I'll check with Grayson. I'll put out a memo if he approves it. See you later, Max."

Smith whistled a Gilbert and Sullivan tune as he entered the elevator next to Max and pushed a gray button marked Level Four. As the car descended, Smith thought again of his beautiful wife, no doubt still asleep. Even after twenty-four years, he loved her more than life.

During those years, the couple had lost their only child to SIDS. Martha had grieved so much that she nearly took her own life, but some strange intuition had brought Arnie home early that day, and he had managed to stop her. The narrow escape had driven them both to rediscover their faith and to bond as a couple.

Martha had faithfully followed him through teaching at Stanford, two trips to Switzerland, several more to India and China, and now she'd stuck with him through his four years with BioStrain. Smith's handsome salary and frequent bonuses had paid off the couple's three mortgages, two cars, and half a dozen credit cards, while stuffing their bank account with plenty for Martha's shopping habit.

Even when BioStrain had called six weeks ago and insisted the couple leave their new, million-dollar house and take up residence in an underground bunker, Martha hadn't complained. "Just let Florence live here while we're gone," she'd said, referring to their maid. "She's a good woman, and she needs a place anyway." Good-hearted Martha.

Smith got off on Level Four and entered a decontamination chamber. As he waited, he waved to Jim Kuppler, the guard who managed the chamber. "Morning, Jim!" Smith called. "How's that back?"

"Still nagging me, Doc. Turn around, please."

Smith turned and faced away from Kuppler, still whistling. "Try that poultice my wife told you about. It helped me last winter when I pulled my right hamstring playing handball. Lost to Tom Foil twice in a row." At the mention of his dead colleague's name, Smith's face grew somber.

"Sorry about Dr. Foil," Kuppler said. "Reckon I missed the funeral while I was off sick."

"Yeah, thanks, Jim," Smith answered, knowing full well that Foil's remains had been cremated less than six hours after the accident. No funeral was ever held, just a five-minute memorial the next day.

"That's all!" Kuppler called as the decontamination procedure finished.

"See you tomorrow."

"Say, Doc, did you hear anything about us getting Monday off?"

"Not officially. There's a rumor that the labs will be closed for a long weekend. I'll send out a memo once I know.

Mr. Grayson should be along in about an hour. Let me know when he gets here, okay, Jim?"

"Sure thing, Doc."

Smith exited the chamber then followed the brightly lit corridor to another elevator and stopped at a security desk.

"Good morning, Dr. Smith," a female guard said cheerfully. "We get a nice long weekend, I hear. Word is, we all get three paid vacation days. Is that true?"

"Maybe that's one reason Grayson's showing up today," Smith replied, writing his name on a digital reader and letting the guard scan his thumb. "Did you change your hair color, Rhonda?"

"Thanks for noticing, Dr. Smith. Do you like it? My boyfriend does, but I'm not sure."

"I'm prejudiced. Redheads are my passion," he laughed, referring to Martha. "It looks good on you. You should stop by and ask Martha. She knows this stuff a lot better than me."

"Thanks, Dr. Smith. Go on through."

Smith smiled, headed into the blue elevator, and touched the button marked Level Five. As expected, the car stopped at what appeared to be the final level, where a human meat wagon in a blue and white BioStrain uniform waved.

"Hi, Doc! I'll buzz you on down." Mike Powers, a former fullback for Wisconsin, entered a series of symbols that changed each day. A computer responded, and the doors activated.

"Thanks, Mike!" Smith called as the doors shut and the car again descended, this time much further into the rock beneath Ford's Mesa. The hydraulic brakes engaged, and Smith enjoyed a soft stop, where a set of black doors opened to an area unseen by most of BioStrain's three hundred plus employees. Just twelve men and women had access to this area. Twelve plus one additional man—the head of Grayson Laboratories and its top-secret subsidiary, BioStrain—an enigmatic British businessman named Rex Grayson.

"Hey there, Arnie!" called a woman's voice from the open laboratory that filled Level Six. "I've been working on the problem we discussed last night, and I think I have an answer. After you catch up on e-mails, come on over to my bench, and I'll show you what I mean."

Arnie nodded. "That's great, Eve. I'll do that. Is Pete in yet?"

Sam Dotson glanced up from a computer bay near Arnie's office. "Peter's late again. Albertson was here until midnight, so expect him in late, too. What's this I hear about Grayson making a visit? Zeus descends!"

Smith slapped Dotson on the shoulder and waved to Eve Martin. "I'd like to see both of you for a briefing. Eve, can you stop for a minute?"

Martin nodded. "Sure. Be there in a sec."

Once inside his office, Smith sat at the metal desk he'd occupied for four years now and clicked the mouse connected to his G5 tower. Sensing the mouse's movement, a seventeen-inch flat panel monitor woke from sleep and greeted Smith with an alert for new mail.

"Here's the freshest coffee we have, Chief," Dotson said, taking a seat in one of several side chairs. "Eve's batching some data, but she's nearly done. Albertson just got off the chute, so he'll be here in a minute. Say, you look like hell."

Arnold looked at Dotson over the top of the monitor. "'Cause I've been there, old buddy. Thanks," he added, taking the steaming cup. "Once Wilder is here, we can get started. I don't want to have to say this twice."

Albertson and Martin joined Dotson, each sitting in a favorite chair, each holding a cup of the coffee Dotson had made earlier that morning. "Peter just came in," the woman said. "Is this about Grayson? I heard he was coming in today."

Smith looked up again, pleased to see Pete Wilder waving from the main lab area. "Come on in, Pete! Grab some brew first! This could take a while!"

Within minutes, the entire team of five scientists had gathered in Smith's office. Before starting, Smith came around the desk and sat on its edge. He had never liked management from a power chair. These people had given up their private lives for science, and they deserved more personal, humane leadership. They certainly deserved more than BioStrain would be giving them.

"Thanks for coming in," he began. "We're down to five, but up one since Evelyn joined us. I've never really given a formal welcome to you, Eve, but we're glad you're on the team. You'd have liked Chuck Hilliard. Shame you couldn't have come in as an addition to the team rather than a replacement. Still, we're honored to have you with us."

Eve nodded. "Thanks, Arnie. So what's up?"

Smith shifted positions and continued. "OK. We're at half-strength right now since six members of our original twelve have been moved back to China, but that doesn't mean we can't make this work. Eve, you came in the day after Tom Foil's memorial service. He and Chuck had been fine-tuning the sequencing for 456's new hemagglutinin sequence. You've picked up nicely on that progress, but we still need to see how vulnerable 456 is to weather and other local environmental pressure. Monday's data collection will make or break us. That's why Grayson is visiting with us today. I know he's under government pressure to produce a finished product, so I'm betting he'll insist we step up the schedule. Any problems with that?"

111

Wilder crossed his long legs and waved a Sharpie in the air. "Grayson is the money man, Arnie. He says code, we say which gene?"

"Yeah, well it's not going to be easy," Rick Albertson said from the doorway. "Why'd Grayson move the other six back to China anyway? That makes no sense. If he wants the project completed on time, he should have…"

"He should have what?" asked a new voice from just behind Albertson.

All eyes settled on a tall man in an Armani suit.

"Good morning, Mr. Grayson. Sorry I didn't meet you at the elevator. No one told me that you were on your way down. We were just having a progress meeting."

Grayson's eyes scanned each face, darting from feature to feature with practiced agility. The president and founder of BioStrain stood nearly six-three with broad shoulders and a long neck. He bore an uncanny resemblance to Alexander Godunov, but with an English accent.

"Good morning, all," he said at last, entering the office and moving to stand behind the desk. "Please, you all look as if you'd been caught smoking at school! Relax! I am not here to spy on you but to congratulate you, dear friends! Project 456 has succeeded far beyond BioStrain's wildest dreams!"

Wilder uncrossed his legs and leaned forward. "I'm Peter Wilder, Mr. Grayson. It's a pleasure to put a face to the voice on the phone, but are you saying what I think you're saying?"

"I'm saying congratulations, Dr. Wilder. Your completion bonuses will be in your mailboxes on Friday afternoon."

All five exchanged looks. Smith spoke for the group. "Please, don't misunderstand this, Mr. Grayson, but we're not finished. While we'd love the bonuses, we still have to evaluate the recombination factors and then the human response. That takes time and test subjects. It could be years away."

Grayson smiled, revealing perfect white teeth, and the room's temperature seemed to drop. "Days away, Dr. Smith. Days. The China team has succeeded in completing the last of the recombination problems as well as the human response, and we begin testing the biochip implant on Monday. You have until Friday afternoon to complete the preparations. Dr. Smith, I'll speak to you privately about the details. Once that's done, you may all take the weekend to breathe a bit of fresh air, so to speak. As to the support staff, they needn't return until Tuesday."

"Won't we need them, sir?" Smith asked, casting a sharp glance toward Wilder, who clearly didn't like what he was hearing.

Grayson shook his head and sat in Smith's chair. "No, no. Not on Monday. In fact, they'd get in the way. We will be entertaining some very high echelon investors on Monday, who wish to keep their identities private. Only you five need be here—you and the test subjects, of course."

"Test subjects?" Wilder interrupted. "Mr. Grayson, no matter what the team in China may have found, testing on humans is out until we confirm their data. You don't want this vaccine to kill anyone, and it could."

Grayson's smile sent a chill down Smith's spine, and he made a mental note to talk to Wilder. "Sir, Pete speaks for all of us," he explained, hoping to let Wilder off the hook. "We need small animal tests first, then we can move on to confirming the human tests conducted in China. We just want to maintain safety, sir."

"Of course you do, and so do I! But the conclusions we've drawn in China are so exciting—well, you'll see once you sift through the results. That's what you scientists do, right? Interpret data? Now, I must be going. Remember, everything must be ready for our VIPs by Friday afternoon. No one is to remain in the installation over the weekend. Is that clear?"

"Very clear, sir," Smith agreed unwillingly. He thought of Martha. She'd be thrilled to know they had an entire weekend free of the underground constraints and damp air. They could visit the house, maybe even take in a movie. But then what? What would Monday bring? And who were these VIPs Grayson was so worried about?

CHAPTER 16

Maggie tossed in her sleep, fighting against a nightmare that stole into her mind at least once a week. Charlie. She could see Charlie standing at the end of her bed, dripping with mud and water, her smooth skin a freakish white, her lips like chalk. She mouthed words, but no sound came out, only a few bubbles and blood. Her head tilted to one side on a broken neck. Behind Charlie, she could see a large, hideous figure with luminous, red eyes. The terrifying creature embraced her dead daughter in its scaly claws and hissed into Charlie's delicate ears.

"You're all mine now, Charlie," the Thing would say. Then it would look up at Maggie, its leathery tongue writhing as its words burned into her brain. "You're next, Maggedy Ann. You're next."

Maggie jerked as the phone jangled her awake. That same nightmare again. Her head throbbed. The bright morning sun pierced her eyes. The phone continued to jangle, insisting she answer it.

She turned in her sofa bed, two exposed springs jutting into her back, her brain groggy from the nightmare and a long night spent working with the computer she'd received on Monday.

Wearily, she picked up the receiver. "This better be good."

"I don't know how good it is," Jackson Taylor's mellow voice spoke. "It's about the divorce papers, Mags. Look, according to my attorney—hey, are you awake enough to absorb this?"

Maggie blinked, shaking off memories of the nightmare. "Yeah, yeah. Divorce papers. What about them?"

"I've asked that they be torn up."

Maggie sat for a few seconds, her mind racing ahead to the subject of strong coffee. "Divorce papers torn up, OK. Wait a minute. What did you say?"

"I don't want the divorce, Maggie. I don't think you do either, so I've asked Harv to put a stop to the process."

"Let me call you back," she said, starting to hang up.

"Wait! Maggie, please! Just listen for a minute!" Jackson insisted.

"I'm not ready for this, Jack. You didn't want to be married to me. I told you I needed to move out to get my head together, and you couldn't take it. You started the divorce action, now you suddenly decide you want to be married again. Hearts don't work like yo-yos, Jackson. I need to think about this. Give me a day or two, and we can talk again. I'm flying out to New Mexico Saturday morning, so I'll let you know before I leave, OK?"

"New Mexico? I thought you had plans at Doug's this weekend. Is Carol all right?"

Maggie thought about the funeral. She remembered Carol Hilliard's bleak, puffy features as she watched her father's remains being lowered into the ground. She'd forgotten all about her half-sister and her pain. Real nice, Maggie. Talk about being self-absorbed.

"Yeah. That's not why I'm going. I have to spend some time with Pip. Uncle Tommy's dead, Jack."

Silence for a minute. Maggie imagined Jackson's face in her mind. His analytical brain would be adding up the words of her news and weighing the evidence for whys and hows. "I'm sorry," he whispered, the simple commiseration surprising Maggie.

"Thanks. Jack, I'm not trying to minimize the importance of your offer to stop the proceedings, but I just can't deal with it right now. Can you understand that?"

"I can, but listen to me for a minute. I could go with you. Barry Carpenter can take my patients. He owes me a favor anyway. I'd really love to go with you. Pip's my friend, too."

Maggie winced. She really needed that coffee. "Let me think about it. I'll call you later this morning." She hung up, knowing that remaining on the line would only allow Jackson the time he needed to change her mind.

Feet on floor, Maggie stumbled to the kitchen and started the first brew of the day. Fifteen minutes and one cup later, she emerged from the shower, her dark wet hair wrapped in a white towel. The phone rang again.

"Jackson, I don't want to talk about this yet," she spoke without thinking, an edge to her words.

A sheepish voice answered. "Am I calling at a bad time?"

Hank Meier. "Sorry, Hank. Mea culpa. I thought you were Jackson. Long story, and my morning caffeine hasn't kicked in yet."

"Oh, I get that kind of reception all the time. I'm used to it. I just thought I'd better let you know that Rebecca's mom got wind of our plans to talk with you, and she's in a snit. I have to drive down to Eden to settle it. I wondered if you'd be interested in going with me?"

Maggie didn't know what to say. She'd only known Hank Meier for two days. Going with Hank would be the final nail in her marriage with Jackson, no matter how he felt at the moment. She knew Jack, and he'd never take her back if he thought she'd moved on.

Had she?

"Sorry, Hank. Honestly, that sounds like a nice trip, but I have a meeting this morning. I'm flying out to New Mexico on Saturday, so I might make a day trip down to Madison to see Mom and my brother and sister."

A moment of silence.

"Hank?"

"I'm still here. Just a little disappointed, but I understand. New Mexico? That's sudden. Is it to see your friend Pip?"

"Yeah. And I'll probably visit my half-sister while I'm there. Are we still on for Friday?"

"I'll know once I've talked to Karen. She's not happy about Rebecca's plans to change schools. Either way, I'll be in town. Is dinner still on for that night?"

Maggie smiled and thought of Hank's honest eyes. "I guess. Call me. I've gotta run."

"Sure. Call you tomorrow. Bye, Maggie."

"Bye."

Maggie hung up and headed for the kitchen where she refilled her dinosaur mug with strong Colombian and drowned it in half-and-half. By nine, she'd dressed and finished blow-drying her thick hair. Maggie checked her makeup in the mirror that hung from the back of the bathroom door. Her dark eyes needed lots of makeup to pop, and she'd done her best to accent them without looking like a clown. Her brother Doug had always thought it funny how Maggie could have such a logical mind but have such a need to be considered pretty.

She thought of Jackson as she combed her long hair into shape. He'd loved to brush her hair back in the early years of their marriage, when her hair had hung past her waist. Now

118

the shoulder-length tresses, with a few grays for character, usually spent the day in a ponytail. Hank Meier had changed all that. She had even started considering hair color. Wash those grays away!

"Maggie!" sang a voice from the hallway.

Maggie buckled her brown, braided belt that finished off her jeans and sleeveless chambray shirt. "Is that you, Julie?" she asked, opening the door.

"Hey, neighbor," Julie said. "You're starting your day later than usual. It's nearly ten! Just wanted to let you know that I can't make dinner tonight. I'll be rehearsing."

"You got in!" Maggie exclaimed, leading Julie into the main room of the small apartment. "Congrats, kiddo!"

"Is that fresh coffee?" Julie asked, grabbing an IU cup from the mug tree. "You're out of sugar."

"I know. The French vanilla creamer is in the fridge next to the half-and-half. Which role?"

Emerson sipped the coffee black and shrugged. "Chorus."

"Chorus? Come on! You had Clorinda down cold. Don't tell me they passed over you again!"

Julie sat near the window, cup in hand. "It's politics. You know that. Dr. Breen told me I should have gotten the part, would have gotten the part, except there's an exchange student from Italy who knows the chancellor. She has a stringy voice, but she's got the role. I got understudy, if that means anything."

"Sure it does," Maggie said with a wide smile. "Bloomington sidewalks are full of irregularities, my dear. You never know when a trim Italian ankle might turn."

Julie laughed. "It's anything but trim, but the thought's a nice one. Thanks, Maggie. So, have you figured out the password to that laptop yet?"

"Are you kidding? I've tried everything I can think of, but no dice. Do you know anyone who might be able to decipher it for me?"

Her neighbor took a sip of the coffee and nodded. "Mmmhmm. A friend, well not a friend really, more of an e-mail buddy. He calls himself Popeye. He works in one of the Mac labs. I can instant message him if you want."

Maggie frowned. "Popeye? Why does the name ring a bell?"

"Olive Oyl. Bluto. Wimpy?"

"No, silly, but it doesn't matter. Can you get him to work on it today or tomorrow? I'm flying to Las Cruces on Saturday morning, and I need the information before I leave."

"Short notice, but he can do it. There must be some way to bypass the login screen, otherwise Mac techs wouldn't be able to access a hard drive to repair it. Give me the laptop, and I'll give it to Pop. I'll call you with a progress report at your office later. OK?"

"OK."

"So, have you talked to that cute sales guy anymore?" Julie asked, her hazel eyes twinkling.

Maggie blushed, which surprised them both. "Maybe," she answered, touching her warm face. "Stop giggling!"

Julie drew a small hand across her lips. "Wiping the grin," she told Maggie, mockingly. "Sorry. He clearly likes you. Your marriage is over, right? Time to move on."

"I'm not sure."

"Huh?"

Maggie handed the computer to Julie and grabbed her tote bag and keys. "I'll explain later. What are you doing for lunch?"

"Let me think. I have to clean Mae Pierson's apartment at ten-thirty, and I don't have a rehearsal until four. I could meet you at Mother Bear's about twelve?"

"You read my mind. Save me a booth, and I'll tell you all about it. I have to run. Do you mind locking up?"

"Sure, I can do that. Mind if I finish your coffee?"

"Help yourself. See you at twelve, Jules."

Maggie donned a pair of sunglasses and headed down the tiled hallway toward the stairs. Julie tucked the laptop under her left arm and grabbed the coffeepot with the other, then left the apartment and entered her own. She poured the last of the coffee into her own carafe and put the computer into her backpack. Fishing Maggie's keys from a cigar box, she returned to her neighbor's door and was surprised to find a strange man standing in Maggie's living room.

"May I help you?" Julie asked, keeping the door open and mentally reviewing the lessons she'd learned in tae kwon do the previous fall.

"Where did Dr. Taylor go?" the man asked. He was medium height, cute, military look.

"Who are you?"

"I'm Major Donald Yarber. I need to speak with Dr. Taylor right away. Will she be back in a moment?"

Julie considered the possibilities. She could always scream if he tried anything. And he was cute. "Sure. Let's go into the hallway. I was just about to lock her door."

The major nodded and followed Julie into the hallway.

"No uniform, Major. Is that regulation?"

"Sometimes," he answered cryptically.

Julie thought for a moment and then looked toward her own open apartment. "Maggie will actually be gone for a while. I can give her a message if you like. If you'll give me your card, I can pass it on to her. I'm meeting her later today."

"I need to speak with her this morning, Miss."

"No card?"

Yarber reached into his breast pocket and withdrew a business card. "Here. This is very important, Miss. Please make sure Dr. Taylor gets it. If you talk to her, tell her I'll stop by her office no later than noon."

"Got it. Tell her you'll come by before twelve-hundred hours."

Yarber turned on his heels and snapped down the hallway, leaving only a faint scent of Old Spice behind. Julie smiled as she watched his neat form retreat. Once he'd disappeared around the corner, she checked the card.

Major Donald Yarber—DARPA.

Maggie shouldered her tote and inserted the university-issue key into the lock of her office.

"Someone came by asking for you," a voice called from the opposite side of the hallway.

"Morning, Sam. I thought you were done for the week."

Fountain leaned against the frame of his own door and waved to a passing student. "Yeah. Truthfully, I don't have much to do. A student's coming by around eleven to complain about his test score, but I thought it would be nice to catch up on journals. I didn't think you had any classes today. What brings you in?"

"Pretty much the same thing as you. Catching up on paperwork. I might head to Madison later for an overnighter, so I wanted to clear the deck." Maggie said as she pushed her door open. "What the...?"

Sam crossed the hall. "Problem?"

"Look!" Maggie shouted, pointing to her desk. The formerly neat desk now hosted a paper riot. File drawers stood open, folders covered the floor, even her desk chair stood on its side. "This is nuts! Who would have tossed my office? Good grief, Sam! Grades aren't even posted yet!"

"No, but most students know what they got on your last exam. I heard it set new standards in pain."

"High expectations, Sam. You know we have to keep raising the bar." She stepped into the room, picking up papers as she did so. Fountain followed like a puppy, handing her file folders and errant papers. "Maybe you should call campus police, Maggie."

"And alert Ellen Bloodhound? No thanks."

Fountain laughed and knelt down to gather up a number of pens. "Careful there! Watch your step! Bloodhound may be a pain, but seriously, Maggie, Old Lady Trueblood would be in the right if she stuck her nose in. She could probably tell you exactly who did it."

"Maybe. But I'm not sure I want to—wait a minute. This desk was locked! Look at this, Sam. Do you see any marks on the metal where it might have been jimmied?"

Fountain removed his thick glasses and peered at the metal carefully. "Not a one. Someone either had your key or you forgot to lock it."

"Never. I never forget to lock this desk."

"Did I miss a tornado?" asked a high-pitched voice from the hallway. "Cripes! I'm not sure about this filing system, Mags."

Taylor looked up from her place on the floor. "Jules! Did I forget something back home?"

"Nope. Hi, Dr. Fountain."

"Good morning, Miss Emerson." Fountain blushed as Julie offered a wide smile. The Kentucky-born voice major's curvy assets had no trouble getting the professor's attention.

"It's Julie, Dr. Fountain. Or Jules. Here, I can help with this. You'll ruin the knees of your jeans, Professor."

Fountain stood, and for a moment his shortsighted eyes locked with Emerson's. Julie, who barely reached five feet in height, smiled in a way that showed off her Shirley Temple dimple. Her ample soprano chest rose and fell as her cheeks flushed.

"I hate to break this up," Maggie interrupted, "but my office, folks! Help me finish before Bloodhound finds out."

"You don't have a dog in there, do you, Dr. Taylor?"

All three froze as Ellen Trueblood's long feet touched the paper-strewn floor.

"A bloodhound that you're paper-training?" the secretary continued, her sharp eyes fixed on Taylor.

Maggie felt three years old. "No, Miss Blood..., I mean, Miss Trueblood. Sorry. Someone broke into my office last night and ransacked the place. I'm not thinking straight."

Trueblood's stern demeanor softened, and she actually became sympathetic. "Oh my. That's terrible! I'll call Campus Security right away. They'll need to check for prints. Better leave it alone, all of you. You're contaminating a crime scene."

"Contaminating a crime scene?" Fountain repeated. "Why, Miss Trueblood, you must watch a lot of police television."

"Every night," she bragged. "I'll give Detective Hendricks a call. He'll want to take depositions from all of you. Even you, Miss Emerson."

Jules gulped. "I just stopped by to see Dr. Taylor."

"Your fingerprints are in there now. Don't you want to explain why?"

Maggie led her friends into the hallway and locked the door. "I can explain why, Julie, if you need to do something else. Come on, Sam, we can get some coffee while we wait for the coppers."

Trueblood nodded and headed back toward her office. Left unsupervised, all three sighed in relief.

"Wow, she is strict!" Julie laughed. "OK, I just stopped by to give you this," she said quickly, handing Yarber's card over to Maggie. "He came by to see you this morning and said he'd stop by your office. I gotta run. I'll see you at noon, OK? I instant-messaged Popeye, and he's promised to work on the problem this morning. If he can make it, should I bring him to lunch?"

"Yeah, that would be terrific!" Maggie said.

"All righty then. See you at noon, Mags. Nice to see you again, Dr. Fountain."

"You too, Miss Emerson."

"It's Julie!" she called over her shoulder.

"Oh yah! Yah! Julie. Julie. That's nice. Say, are you singing in the opera this summer?"

"Long story, Dr. Emerson. Ask Maggie."

"Okeydokey. Oh, and call me Sam!"

Julie turned to offer one last, brilliant smile before heading down the west stairs. "Sam. A nice strong name." She giggled at his boyish expression and left the two teachers to talk.

"She sure is nice," Sam said awkwardly. "OK. So, how about that coffee then?"

"Come on, Romeo. I'll buy."

CHAPTER 17

Pippa Anderson closed her menu and glanced at Daniel. "Look, Daniel, Donna's got fried rabbit on the menu."

Tohe looked up, his face blank. "Sorry, hon. You said what? Rabbits?"

Pippa laughed. "You've been far away, Medicine Man. Are you still thinking about the Ibanez family?"

Tohe nodded and folded the menu. "I guess I'm not hungry. I don't like this, Pippa. That makes four dead in only two weeks."

"Four? Who else besides the Ibanez children?"

"Granny Roberts. She had a heart attack. But then there was Jim White Calf. Man, I sure picked a fine time to leave town!"

"Jim's dead? I hadn't heard that either. That's awful! He was only, what, twenty-something?"

"Thirty-one, but still too young. His wife's a mess. I think I'll go on over to Warren's office and see if I can convince him to let me autopsy the Ibanez kids at least. I also want to autopsy White Calf, if Nancy will let me. I'm going to have to send a report to the CDC."

Pippa took his hand. "Let me help, Daniel. You know, Maggie can probably help, too, when she gets here on Saturday. Pathology is her thing."

"Really? I thought she taught anatomy."

"She ought to be working for the FBI or something—she's that good. It will be wonderful to see her again. You know, I'm not really hungry either. What do you say I go to Warren's with you? Hey, Susie! We changed our minds about breakfast. Mind if we come back later for lunch?"

Susie Thayer waved. "No problem. I've got two-meat stew for lunch. Rabbit and chicken."

"Sounds good," Pippa said as she and Tohe rose. "See you in a few hours. Save some of that stew for us."

Tohe nodded to the woman as he retrieved his battered hat from a brass hook near the door. "Sorry 'bout that, Susie."

"No problem, Doc."

Tohe and Pippa walked into the bright sunshine, where a knot of teens had gathered to kill time. One of the teens, a seventeen-year-old dropout named Ray Bindell, smoked a hand-rolled cigarette. As Tohe emerged from the canteen, Bindell raised his voice to make sure Tohe heard.

"White man's medicine, that's all it is! And it's gonna kill us all. That's what the whites want. But white men come, white men go. The Hopi will remain. The Ant people will remain. That's what Meektay says, and he's right! Only blood can cure! Only blood can appease!"

"You really believe that, Ray Bindell?" Tohe asked, entering the young men's circle. "Meektay's gonna lead you into hell."

"You oughta know, White Eyes."

"My eyes may be blue like my mother's, but my blood runs red just like my Navajo father's. And just like yours does, Ray.

127

You want to see your blood spill on the sand? Huh? You keep away from Meektay."

Bindell's eyes followed Tohe as the teen spit into the dust. "That's what we think of your advice, White Eyes. Right, men?" he asked the others, who began to dance and sing a song taught them by Meektay.

> *Down in a hole, in a rabbit hole*
> *Follow the White Man—hey, na ya!*
> *Down in the ground where the steel winds blow*
> *Die with the White Man—hey, na ya!*

As the song finished, Bindell stepped forward, clearly threatening Tohe. The doctor sighed and took a step toward the young man. Bindell faltered for a moment, then started toward Daniel. Suddenly, large arms pulled Bindell back.

"Do you want to go to jail today, Ray?" asked Los Muertos sheriff Warren Down. "I got two nice cells, big enough to accommodate all you boys."

"Sorry, Sheriff Warren," the youngest of the group said.

"That's a smart reply, Matt Thayer. You go tell your sister that I said you're to help her wash dishes today. You, too, Bindell."

Ray cast a long glance at Tohe, then he followed Matt into the canteen. Just before entering, he spit on the ground again. "Sorry, Sheriff Warren. Got dust in my mouth," Ray said, flicking the stub of his cigarette into the small pool of mud and spittle.

Warren started toward the defiant youth, but Tohe stopped him. "Going after him now won't help, Warren. Come on, I want to talk to you about getting permission to autopsy the Ibanez kids."

Inside the cantina, Susie Thayer, who had been watching the exchange, raised a dark eyebrow at her younger brother as he and Ray Bindell came inside. "You're lucky Sheriff Warren didn't slap you into one of his cells, Matt. It's a good thing Mom and Dad aren't here to see you. Why do you and Ray hang around that bunch? All they want is a free ride, and they'll blindly follow Meektay and his crazy teachings just to get it."

Ray Bindell cast a dark look toward Matt. "Matt's his own man. He don't need to listen to white eye talk."

Susie handed both boys a dishtowel. "White eye, huh? Have you noticed that my eyes are as brown as yours? Besides, you're not pure Indian, Ray Bindell. Your grandmother came from Minnesota, just like my father. What makes you so special?"

Bindell threw down the towel and grabbed a knife from a nearby butcher block. "This does!" he screamed. "Blood is mine if I want it."

Matt moved in front of his older sister. "Ray, have you gone nuts? Put that down! I'll tell Sheriff Warren, and you'll get that free ride Susie talked about—right up to Springer Boys School."

Bindell's dark eyes narrowed, and a low guttural sound rose from his curled lips. Susie stepped forward, but Matt stopped her. "Susie's right, Ray! You're nothing! Now get out, and keep away from my sister!"

Bindell sprang toward the siblings, raising his knife. Susie screamed, but Ray stopped short. Something on Matt's neck froze him in his tracks. The low guttural growl was replaced by a high-pitched wail, and Bindell threw the knife down and ran out the back doors.

Sheriff Down, Daniel, and Pippa burst into the front doors of the cantina, Down with his gun drawn. "Are you okay, Susie?" Tohe asked, rushing to her side. "Matt?"

The youth's thin body shook, but he looked up bravely. "He was going to kill us! I know he was! I don't know why he didn't!"

Susie pulled her brother close and kissed the top of his head. "I know this sounds crazy, Doc, but I think it was Matt's cross."

Every eye glanced down at the small gold cross Matt Thayer always wore, a gift from a dying mother to her only son, a gift he'd promised never to remove.

"Can it be?" Daniel asked, looking to Pippa. For a moment, no one spoke. Their eyes said it all. Ray Bindell's mad plans had been stopped by the symbol for Christ.

"I'd better see if I can find Bindell," Warren said authoritatively. "He can't have gone far, but I don't want him wandering our streets tonight."

"Thanks, Sheriff," Susie said, her voice trembling.

"Susie, you two shouldn't stay here alone tonight," Daniel said. "You and Matt come stay with me and Pippa tonight. I've got room."

Susie looked at Matt, who shook his head and held the cross tightly. "We'll be all right, Doc. God will look after us."

Several miles outside Los Muertos, atop Ford's Mesa, Meektay listened to the wind. He claimed to speak the language of the hawk and the owl and the ant. He claimed to have the keys to life and death, but he said that neither could be attained without blood. Although Daniel Tohe couldn't have known it, Meektay's animal guides had already told him of the confrontation with the boys outside the cantina. As he sat carving a bone, the strange prophet closed his eyes and remembered the strange journey that had brought him here to his destiny.

The man known as Meektay had actually been born on Halloween in Ames, Iowa, under the name Milford Johnson. Johnson had been too much for his single mother, and she soon left him with foster parents. Bounced from one home to another, the unloved boy grew into a hateful youth with little regard for authority and less for women.

At sixteen, he ran away from his last foster home—still nursing half a dozen welts on his back from his foster dad's studded belt—and headed for California, where he changed his name to Sundance in honor of his idol, Robert Redford. Naturally skilled at wood crafting, the teen collected driftwood and carved it into pleasing shapes, which he sold to beach merchants. The modest earnings kept him alive.

One day before his twentieth birthday, Johnson met a man who would forever change his life. Introducing himself as The Prophet, the charismatic itinerant led a great following of unwashed and unwanted from the beaches of southern California. The Prophet preached a bloody religion of sacrifice and anger that fed his followers' own dark emotions. Sundance, whom The Prophet renamed Meektay, soon became a favored disciple.

At the age of twenty-one, tall, beach-bronzed, blond, and exceedingly handsome, the former Iowa native succumbed to The Prophet's brand of mentoring, which included intimate nights that his mentor insisted would prepare the one now known as Meektay to take his place as a great leader to a dead people.

In the early '90s, The Prophet declared he would soon leave Earth and that Meektay would be called to a desert. Three days later, The Prophet amazed all his followers by literally disappearing in a blinding flash, leaving nothing but his clothes behind. Meektay took it as a sign to begin his own ministry, so he packed up those men and women who would follow and headed for Los Muertos. The place of the dead.

Now, Meektay, Lord of the Dead, commanded a greater following than even his predecessor, whom he claimed to see in dreams. Still tall and bronze, but older now and presumed wise, the hate-filled leader preached the same bloody religion as his mentor.

Opening his eyes, Meektay looked down at his hands. The bone he'd been carving was covered in crimson. He'd slipped and cut his palm without feeling it. Without flinching, he reached into a small leather pouch and removed a small, dried slice of peyote and slipped it into his mouth.

Feeling no pain, Meektay began to seek guidance on how to exact revenge on Matt Thayer, how to overcome the spirits that protected the boy and his sister. Soon, a familiar voice began to speak to him. The Prophet had returned.

CHAPTER 18

So, Dr. Taylor, you can't think of anyone who might have a grudge against you?"

Maggie's head ached. "For the last time, Detective, I can't think of anyone. I appreciate your zeal, but it's just a little mess to clean up. I'm sure if a student did this, he's sorry."

"He? You think it's a male student, then, eh, Doc?"

"I didn't say that, Detective. It's just an expression. It could have been a female student."

"So you've had trouble with some female then? What's her name? I'll check her out."

Fountain rolled his eyes. He and Maggie had spent the last hour answering a circle of such questions.

"I am really sorry to disappoint you, Detective Hendricks, but I know of no one, male or female, who might have wanted to pull a prank—and it's nothing more than a prank—like this. Can't we call it a day? I'm meeting someone for lunch," she checked her watch, "in twenty minutes."

"Just one more question, Dr. Taylor," the ambitious detective continued. "When you first entered the office, what caught your eye first?"

Maggie stared at the policeman. He had to be kidding.

"The mess," she said blandly.

"OK. That's all I need," Hendricks replied, closing his notebook. "The lab boys will process the prints they took and get back to you in a few days. I may need to talk to you further. You aren't going anywhere are you?"

"I may drive to Madison later today, and I'm flying to New Mexico on Saturday."

"Sorry. We can't allow that."

Maggie, who sat in Trueblood's office with Sam and the detective, jumped to her feet. "I can't leave town? What kind of nonsense is that?"

"It's police sense, Dr. Taylor, but if you insist on leaving, then make sure we have a way to reach you. That's all for now, I guess," he added, shooting a stern look at Maggie. "I'll make my report and get back to you in a day or two. Thanks for calling me, Miss Trueblood. It's always a pleasure."

Ellen Trueblood blushed. Hendricks buttoned his suit coat and followed Trueblood to the hallway. "Remember what I said, Dr. Taylor. Don't leave without giving me a heads-up."

Maggie nodded. "I wouldn't dream of it." She then turned to Sam Fountain, who'd waited with her patiently. "I'm off to Mother Bear's, Sam. Care to join me?" she asked, walking back into the hallway.

"You mean 'us,' don't you, Maggie? Nah. You and Miss Emerson have a nice gab. I think I'll just grab a sandwich. You still planning to drive down and see your mom?"

"Probably. Oh, I forgot to call this guy Jules told me about. Well, I'll just have to call him after lunch. I'll be back tomorrow, Sam. You have my cell phone number, don't you?"

Sam waved from his office door. "Right up here," he replied with a grin, pointing to his head. "Have fun. Be safe!"

"Be safe, he says," Maggie muttered to herself as she grabbed her totebag and headed toward the door. Ellen

Trueblood, who had apparently escorted Hendricks outside, was just coming back in but didn't appear to even notice Maggie. The woman's face glowed.

Maggie shook her head and suppressed a laugh. Ellen Trueblood, femme fatale.

Bill Conners had been driving for over two hours. He'd left his apartment in Speedway early that morning, intent on going into the television station, but without knowing why, he'd turned instead onto Interstate 65 and headed south. Though unfamiliar with southern Indiana, Conners maneuvered his Mazda through the maze of winding state roads as if on a beeline for somewhere, someplace he'd not yet realized consciously. He felt drawn, pulled by an unseen force.

Almost to the Kentucky state line, Conners noticed a truck stop on his right. Low on fuel, he pulled into the Gas n' Go. Conners parked next to Pump 3, shut off the engine, and wearily wrenched his long legs out of the car and onto the asphalt. He hadn't slept in two days, but he had no desire to rest—not yet. A bell dinged as he opened the door to the small store.

"Mornin', hon," called a slim woman with flaming red hair and a gold front tooth. "You've gotta pump your own if you need gas. Restroom's in the back past the video games." Next to her on the counter, a small color television scrolled pictures of dead chickens. "Ooh, don't that give you the willies! All them dead chickens. Poor old farmers, they're the ones takin' it in the shorts. I'll sure be glad when the government starts handin' out those vaccines. Buddy, I'll be first in line!"

Conners stared. *Vaccines? What vaccines? Why couldn't he think?*

"Is this—Madison, Indiana?" he asked.

"Nope. You took a wrong turn somewhere's hon. This here's Eden. Now you can still get there, but you'll have to backtrack a mite."

"Map?" he muttered.

"Sure. Come on over here, an' old Rosie'll draw one up fer ya."

"I need to get to Madison. There's a man there I have to see."

Rosie looked the stranger up and down, sticking out her tongue slightly. "Okay, but we'll need cash for the gas."

Conners blinked, eyelids scraping over dry corneas. He patted his pants pocket and sighed with relief upon locating his wallet. "I've got cash. Map?"

Rosie shrugged and began to sketch out the road to Madison.

Frank Levatino shoved the last bite of Twinkie into his mouth just as Nate Beacham knocked on his office door.

"Come in!" he mumbled through yellow cake and cream filling.

Beacham entered, saw his friend's face, and began to laugh. "You have Twinkie filling on your upper lip, Frank."

Levatino wiped his mouth with his hand and cleared his throat. "Thanks," he said dryly. "How's that Hanta story coming along?"

Beacham fell into the wood and vinyl chair opposite his old friend. "Not Hanta. And there are six people dead. It looks like this might be the bird flu branching out, and I'm not convinced it's natural, if you get my drift. Truth is, I'm about ready to head for that potato farm you mentioned and start stockpiling food."

Levatino sat forward. "Spill what you know."

136

"OK. After talking to that Conners kid in Indiana, I did some digging on BioStrain and Grayson Labs. Boy, Rex Grayson is one well-connected character. Although he was raised poor on London's east end, he's actually related in one way or another to an occult branch of Jesuits, the Templars, European Royalty, and seven U.S. presidents. He's reputed to be a thirty-second degree Mason, and his company was awarded the rights to develop and manufacture a vaccine for the avian flu, even though the product is untested in the field! That's nuts!"

Levatino leaned back in his chair, steepling his pudgy fingers thoughtfully. "Keep going. I know you have more, I can tell from that twitch in your face."

Nate nodded. "And how! The first reported case of this avian flu occurred on February fourth, right? I triple-checked it. Grayson Labs received a fat contract for an avian flu vaccine four years ago! Just six weeks after incorporating the company!"

"Nice to know our government is so prophetic. They hired a company to make a vaccine before the bug even got here?"

Beacham nodded. "Within days of getting the contract, Grayson had hired four dozen eminent biochemists, microbiologists, virologists, and statisticians. Top grade, top pay. He set up a prominent lab near Fort Detrick, Maryland. Three dozen of the scientists went to work there. The other dozen went underground, maybe literally. I located a former employee who claims the BioStrain division is somewhere in the desert outside Las Cruces."

Levatino sat forward, his chair creaking against the weight. "Let me see if I got this straight. Four years back, the government hires Grayson to brew up a vaccine for a germ we don't even have here yet. Grayson receives a truckload of taxpayer money, hires top eggheads, sets up one public lab and one secret one. Four years later, the bug hits China then here, and Homeland Security starts proclaiming we need a vaccine. Then, some fresh-faced reporter from Indiana gets wind of the scam, tries to set up a meeting, but she's found dead—toasted like a Fourth of July weenie. Your guy, this Conners fellow, is set up to take a fall if anyone gets too close. Now, Roswell gets a Hanta scare, only it's not Hanta. And you're tellin' me that the secret lab is somewhere underneath my feet?"

Nate nodded. "That's about the size of it."

"That's just super. I'm gonna need a truckload of Twinkies, Nate. Let's go shopping."

CHAPTER 19

Maggie walked into Mother Bear's Pizza at twelve on the dot, thankful for summer traffic. "May I help you?" asked a skinny waitress. She wore a black sleeveless hoodie and skintight jeans.

"Yeah, I'd like a booth. I'm meeting a friend."

"Sure," the girl said blandly and led Maggie to a polished pine booth halfway back. "You want anything while you wait?"

"Could I have a Pepsi and a basket of bread sticks?"

"Sure."

Maggie settled into the booth with her tote bag on the seat beside her. She should call her brother before driving to Madison. For all she knew, they might not even be home.

Fishing in the tote, she found her small combination PDA/cell phone and brought up Doug's name. Doug Hilliard's trucking business number began to ring.

"Hilliard Trucking," a young woman answered.

"Hi, Gina. This is Doug's sister, Maggie. Is he in?"

"Sure is, Dr. Taylor. He's meeting with someone in his office over lunch. I'll check and see if he can talk, OK?"

"Thanks, Gina."

The waitress returned with a red plastic glass filled with Pepsi and a straw. "Sticks'll be up in a minute."

"Thanks," Maggie said, covering the mouthpiece on the phone. The girl shrugged as she walked away.

"Dr. Taylor, I can put you through. Go ahead."

"Hello, Douglas speaking."

"Hey, Doug. Sorry to call you at work, but..."

"Hey, don't worry! Is everything all right? You're still coming down this weekend, right?"

Maggie saw an athletic man enter the restaurant and talk with the waitress. The man appeared out of place. "I can't, Doug. Remember me talking about Pippa Anderson?"

"Yeah, I remember Pippa. Didn't she come with you and Jackson one time? Summer, I think."

"Good memory, bro. I'm flying out to see her in New Mexico this weekend. You see, oh, Doug, I don't know how to say it, but Uncle Tommy died."

The man at the counter looked Maggie's way, and an odd feeling crept into her stomach.

"I know about that, Mags," her brother said sympathetically. "In fact, I'm talking to Andy Ryder right now. He came in for lunch and told me about it. Awful, isn't it? And so soon after Dad."

Maggie kept one eye on the stranger and another on the front door, looking for Julie. "Yeah. Tommy and Rita practically adopted Pip. Poor Rita. I should call her."

"I think Rita and Tom broke up, sis. Last year. She's living in—say, Andy, where's Rita Foil living now?" Maggie heard Ryder's resonant voice in the background. "She's moved to Montana. I guess her folks were from there. Do you want company? I can take off a few days."

"You shouldn't leave Angie, Doug. I'll be fine. Look, I might come down there today. Are you gonna be home?"

"You bet! Angie's home all afternoon, so come anytime. Can you stay awhile—at least 'til you leave for New Mexico?"

Again, Maggie heard Ryder—this time asking about her trip. "Doug?"

"Sorry, sis. Andy wanted to know about your New Mexico trip. He says he'd go, but he has meetings in Washington. He's in town tonight, though. I'll buy some steaks, and we'll do it up right. I'll be home around six. See you then."

"Can't wait, Doug. Bye." She hung up, keenly aware that the strange man now stood right next to her booth. Although he wore a light suit, she had no trouble imagining him in full military dress. His close-cropped blond hair screamed Marines.

"You must be Major Yarber," Maggie said, sticking out her right hand.

The man's handshake was powerful, but short. "Excellent guess, Dr. Taylor. Yes, I'm Don Yarber. I spoke with your office secretary, Miss Trueblood, and she told me where I might find you. I promise not to waste your time."

"I'll be sure to thank Ellen for sending you to me." Maggie forced a smile. "You don't strike me as someone who would waste anyone's time, least of all your own, Major. Please, sit down."

The waitress came back with the breadsticks and set them down. "So, is this it? Wanna order now?"

Yarber glanced up. "Just coffee for me. Black. No sugar."

"I'll wait until my other friend arrives," Maggie replied, glad she'd ordered breadsticks.

Yarber looked embarrassed. "You're meeting someone. I'm sorry."

"You met her this morning. Her name's Julie Emerson, and she's a good friend. I imagine we'll finish our talk before she gets here. Julie time is twenty minutes behind the rest of the world."

"Very well then."

The waitress came back with Yarber's coffee and two glasses of water. "Just wave when you're ready," she said, popping a wad of gum the size of Iowa and walking away.

"Wow, she can walk and chew gum. It boggles the mind," Maggie whispered.

Yarber failed to grin, not even the slightest twitch. "Dr. Taylor, are you aware that your father worked for us some years ago?"

Maggie swirled a breadstick in thick cheese sauce and shook her head. "By 'us,' I take it you mean DARPA. I know Dad worked at White Sands for years and years. Is that what you're talking about?"

"He worked for us part of that time, but even after he left White Sands, Dr. Hilliard maintained his connection to DARPA. I presume you know what our agency does, Dr. Taylor."

"Something with defense?"

"That's a simple way of putting it. DARPA stands for Defense Advanced Research Projects Agency. I work with the DSO, the Defense Sciences Office. Your father helped them to find ways to combat the biological terrorism that so many countries have sought to use against the United States. If it weren't for your father's discoveries, many American military men and women would have died as victims of biological warfare."

Maggie dropped the breadstick back into the basket and stared. "You're not kidding, are you? I knew my dad was

142

involved in some pretty hefty projects, but I had no idea—I mean, wow. But why are you telling me this now? After he's dead?"

Yarber leaned in, and the scent of Old Spice wafted past her nostrils. "I'm telling you this, Dr. Taylor, because at the time of your father's death, he was still working for the DSO as an operative inside a company called BioStrain."

The entire world closed in on Maggie at these words. Her ears filled with the sound of her own heartbeat, the alternative rock that had been playing softly in the background now rose to crashing decibels, her tongue felt thick, her vision blurred, and she felt her insides churning inside her.

BioStrain.

Hank Meier's company. Hank, who was a complete mystery to her. Hank, who entered her life right after her father's death. Hank, whom the Barneyites called Mr. Spook.

It couldn't be a coincidence. Her father works for BioStrain, then dies suddenly, and Hank Meier shows up and never mentions that he even knows about her dad.

She felt like throwing up.

"Are you feeling all right, Dr. Taylor?"

She could hear Yarber talking, going on and on, but her brain had trouble deciphering it. Just like a code.

Code. The computer.

"The computer!" she said out loud.

Yarber's head tilted. "Computer? I'm afraid I don't understand that reference, Dr. Taylor."

Maggie nearly choked. She'd said it out loud. What was happening to her? Had she grown so attached to Meier in only three days?

"I'm so sorry—uh, really I am, Major," she blabbered. "It's just my father—yes, my dad—well, he never once even hinted that he was involved with the military in such a covert manner. Really, it's a—shock."

"I can see that it is," he said suspiciously. "Dr. Taylor, what computer?"

Smart cookie, she thought, wondering if she'd said that aloud as well. "My computer—in my office. I was just wondering if whoever broke in tampered with the files."

"Broke in?"

She relaxed now. Although she hated getting the student responsible for the burglary in further trouble, she could use this to bait and switch Yarber until she figured out just who Meier really was. "My office was broken into last night. Didn't Miss Trueblood mention that?"

"No, ma'am, she didn't. Did the local police investigate?"

"Of course. Detective Hendricks is the investigator's name. He's at the campus police building on Jordan."

"I know the location. Was anything missing?"

"I couldn't tell. The place had been turned inside out, and Detective Hendricks locked me out for most of the morning. I'd planned to take inventory after my meeting with Julie. I could call you."

"I'll check in with Detective Hendricks, then I'll call you, Dr. Taylor. I'd better see to this right away. I understand you're flying to New Mexico on Saturday."

"How do you know that?" she asked, and then realized spying was this man's stock and trade. "Never mind."

"We intend to keep you safe, Dr. Taylor. I just want you to know that one of our men will also be on that flight. You will never be out of our sight."

"What do you mean, 'keep me safe'?"

"There's no reason for you to know that at this time. Suffice it to say that you're well protected."

"Protected from what?"

He rose and put on his hat. "Not what, Dr. Taylor. Who. I can't say more than that. I'll talk with you again before you leave."

He turned to go, stopped at the counter, paid both their tabs, then left without looking back.

Maggie stared for some time before taking a breath. Hank Meier had lied. Her father had been a spy. The government had her under its protection; she shouldn't worry because she was being followed.

"Baloney," she muttered.

"We don't have baloney. Do you want pepperoni?" the waitress answered as she stopped to clear away Yarber's cup and saucer. "Is your other friend still coming?"

Maggie stifled a laugh. "Yes, she'll be here. Could you put in an order for a large pizza with the works?"

"Sure. Salads?"

"Why not? Jules is always looking for a free meal," Maggie said in return, and she mentally began to go through all that she knew.

CHAPTER 20

Good afternoon, slaves! Welcome to the Barney Ison Show, coming to you from good old Gloomington, Indiana. I'm your host Barney Ison, and it's time to bite the bullet or die on one. I'd like to take a few minutes to remind our listeners of a little topic that's burned up some airtime the last, oh, three years or so. Connie? You in there?"

Connie Justman nodded from her chair inside the control booth. Ison loved to put her on the spot. She just wanted to answer the phones and send him digital clues about the callers via his terminal. She wished he'd leave her out of the on-air gags. After all, she was the producer, not the talent.

"That's good, that's good, because we're going to need all ten of those lovely fingers to keep the phones from crashing when I get started on this one. Ready, folks? Two words: Dead scientists. What's that? you say. Dead scientists? Gee, Barney, have you taken leave of your senses? Hey, scientists die every day, just like non-scientists. Taxi drivers die, beauticians die, plumbers die, pilots, soldiers, mothers, fathers, children, well you see where I'm going with this. But I, Barney Ison, have the audacity to make the deaths of a select group of people the subject of a talk show? Puh-lease! You must all think I've really lost it this time! But trust me on this one. In the last

146

three years alone, now I'm not counting anything before, but in just the last three years, twenty-nine scientists—that I *know* of—twenty-nine dedicated, educated, and probably medicated peekers into the unknowns of inner and outer space have died or disappeared. Did you hear me? Twenty-nine scientists are now gone, kaput, bye-bye, not here!

"Why does this alarm me? Well, fellow slaves, it had better alarm you, too, because each and every one of these scientists worked for—oh, yeah baby, here it is—our government. Uh huh. Let me tell you how they've died, folks. Plane crash—remember that small plane that went down in northern China about six months ago? Yep, three scientists on board, all had worked for the government. Six have died in unexplained auto accidents, the most recent of which was a man named Thomas Foil, who happened to lose his head when his car swerved into an oil tanker. Nope, he hadn't been drinking. And no autopsy was performed. In fact, inquiries have revealed that good Dr. Foil's head and body were cremated without any inquest or investigation. Not buying it? I got more. Just stick with me through the break, and I'll scare the heck out of you. Be right back."

Julie Emerson turned off the car radio and parked behind Mother Bear's. "Come on, Popeye. Maggie's inside. You tell her what you told me."

"Did you hear what I mean about Ison?" he asked as she locked the car. "He knows the truth, Jules. He has the eyes to see and the guts to talk about it."

"Yeah, yeah. Come on. Maggie's waiting."

The pair walked into Mother Bear's back entrance, scanned the tables, and then headed toward the front booths.

"Looking for me?" Maggie asked as they reached her.

"Hey, there!" Julie said, poking Popeye on the arm. "Sit. Stay."

"This is your friend?" Maggie asked, handing two plates to the newcomers. "I figured pizza all around would work. I've seen you before, haven't I?" she asked Popeye. "At Barney's Café, right?"

Popeye gawked at Taylor, his face turning as red as his hair. "Uh, could be. I mean, I go there now and then."

"What do you mean, Pop? You practically live there! He's been preaching about this Barney guy since I've known him. Anyway, Popeye Bailey, meet Maggie Taylor. Now, tell her about the computer."

"You got in?" Maggie asked, amazed. "Excellent! So what's the password?"

Popeye wiped pizza sauce from his mouth. "It's 'yesterday and today,' all run together into one word. Does that make any sense?"

Maggie thought of the Beatles album her father had so carefully wrapped for her years before and nodded. "Yeah, it does. So what's in there?"

Popeye slapped another slice of pizza onto his plate and began to cut it with the side of his fork. "Everything's encrypted. I opened the e-mail program to check the sent file. It's clean, except for one e-mail in the draft folder. Again, encrypted."

"Well then, what good is it?" she asked in frustration.

"Calm down, Doc," Julie said to her friend and neighbor. "Pop here removed the encryption. He's just freaked because he read the contents. He told me a little about it, but he won't tell me all of it. Claims it's a national security breach or something."

Popeye leaned forward, his eyes round and his words coming in a staccato punch. "This is serious, Jules! Look,

Dr. Taylor, I know you probably got the wrong impression of our group from Hitch the other night. I mean, he was really rude to you and that guy—you know, the one Hitch kept calling Mr. Spook. I don't know why he did that, but we have seen the guy on campus. He visits the Arts and Sciences Dean a lot. Anyway, Barney and the rest of us, including Trick, the other guy with us that night, well we just want to bring the evil into the light, you know. Like making a vampire face the dawn. Sunshine law and all that."

Maggie stared. Whoever had sent the laptop had gone to a great deal of trouble to make sure only she could read the precious information inside. Now, here she sat, dependent on someone who thought the Sunshine Law meant frying vampires on Sunday morning.

"Did you remove the encryption or not?"

Popeye peered over his glass of Mountain Dew and nodded. He sipped one last bit through the personal loop straw he'd brought then set it aside. "OK, let's get down to business." He opened his backpack and withdrew the TiBook. "Nice 'puter, by the way. Once we have all the info off, I can rewrite the drive so you can use it. It's primo! Honkin' hard drive, gig of ram, big bus."

"She doesn't need a bus, Homer. Just give her the computer so she can read the files!" Julie told him.

"Sorry," Popeye answered, passing the silver laptop across the table.

Maggie opened the computer and found the login screen there again. "Can I change the password, once I'm in?"

"Sure," Popeye said. "I'll show you how later."

"All right then. Let's see if it works." Maggie typed in the password, "yesterdayandtoday." The login screen disappeared and the computer began loading her desktop. Right away, she saw a yellow box that looked like a digital Post-It Note. The content was gibberish.

"It's still encrypted," she told Popeye.

"Sure. You don't want just anybody looking at that stuff! Believe me! No, I set up a macro to do the work. Just hit that little apple button by the space bar and F8."

"Command-F8? Believe it or not, I do know something about Macs, Popeye. In fact, I started using Mac computers before you were even born. I've just never used OS X—hey! It worked!"

The nonsense letters and symbols had transformed into four lines of text that read: "Maggie, I know you can figure this out. Sorry I couldn't write more. E-mail in outbox. Encrypted, too. God forgive me. Uncle Tommy."

"It's not from Dad, it's from Tommy," she said, her voice choking. "What is all this about?"

Jules looked at Popeye. "So what's in the e-mail?"

"Just open Entourage. The icon's at the bottom, in the dock," Popeye said, eyeing the last slice of pizza.

Maggie touched her finger to the track pad, moving the cursor slowly along the bottom of the screen, amazed at the way the icons enlarged as the cursor passed over them. "The big E? Entourage?"

"Yep. It's sort of like Outlook. Just click once."

Maggie clicked the icon and launched the program. Within a few seconds, the Entourage mail program filled the screen. To the left were a series of folders, including one labeled "drafts."

"OK, I see the drafts folder. I'm opening it."

A list at the top right showed one message in the file. Maggie clicked on it, and an encrypted message appeared. She hit Command-F8, and the symbols transformed like magic.

"Have you read this?" she asked Popeye.

"I'm afraid I have. Real nasty stuff."

Maggie read the screen silently, shocked by the content.

"What's it say?" Jules asked, sitting forward. "Can you read it?"

"Yes." Maggie looked around the restaurant. They were the only customers, and the kitchen looked empty. "OK, this is what it says. *'Dear Maggie. As I write this, you're preparing for your father's funeral. Maybe you've already had it. I know you think he died of natural causes, but he didn't. They injected him with high doses of epinephrine. Don't expect anyone out there to figure it out. I'm sorry—so sorry for his death, Maggie. It's all because of what we know. Chuck and I just wanted to help put a stop to war. That's all. We thought we were making a defense agent that would incapacitate the enemy but not harm our soldiers. Looking back on it now, I realize that we acted like school-yard children—no, worse—we were foolish sheep with wolves for shepherds. They've twisted our research and used it to make something awful. Something that will kill everyone. Anyone they choose. Anytime. Anywhere. In minutes. Imagine bird flu combined with Ebola that works in minutes in chickens. They have intentionally unleashed it in China, hoping it will mutate and infect humans. Maybe it already has.*

"'BioStrain manufactures a microchip that monitors mRNA. Once the body's natural messenger RNA alters due to invasion by a virus, the BioStrain chip uses the information to formulate a vaccine unique to that individual. Boom. Instant diagnosis and treatment. It could save millions of lives and billions of dollars. Sounds great, doesn't it? But the puppeteers behind BioStrain plan to embed the chip with this Armageddon virus, then release it into the carrier's bloodstream upon a signal from a small command device.

"'In other words, BioStrain, which is nothing more than an arm of the shadow government, wants to program every human for

selective death! I'm so sorry for all this. I think your dad sent some of the data back to Doug for safekeeping, encrypted of course. Be sure to read through all of your father's papers. Your father tried to fight them. He was a good man, an honest man, and they killed him for it. I'm done for, too, if I don't get out of here. Don't try to find me. If I can, I'll disappear. If I can't, well, you can guess. Take care. Uncle Tommy.'"

Maggie closed the program then the lid of the computer. "Dear God," she whispered, her mind reeling from the words.

Popeye nodded as the last of his Mountain Dew twirled through the loops of his straw. "Barney's right. We're all gonna die."

"Just coffee, thanks. Black."

The perky young waitress winked at Hank Meier and sashayed toward the kitchen. Meier had spent most of his life in Eden, Indiana, and he'd come to know Sandy's Sports Bar well. Even though the new owner, Linda Kemp, had upgraded the décor, the place felt the same.

"Black coffee," a different voice said. Hank looked up and saw a tall blond woman with a knockout smile. "I don't think I've seen you here before. I'm Linda, the owner. Mind if I join you?"

Meier took the coffee and stood up. "Not at all. I wouldn't mind a little company right now."

Kemp eased her long legs underneath the booth and fixed her bright blue eyes on Meier. "I don't usually hit on customers. You just look lonely, you know?"

"You're very perceptive," he said, forcing a smile. "I don't want to sound like a bad movie, but my ex-wife can be a real stinker."

"That's too bad, um… Sorry, I don't think I caught your name."

"It's Hank. Hank Meier. I grew up over on Second Street. I live in Indianapolis now. I just came from a meeting with my daughter and her mother."

"That explains the battle scars. Are you sure you wouldn't like something stronger than coffee?" Kemp asked, turning on her charm.

"No, thanks. Look, you seem like a reasonable woman. If you had the chance to trade a rotten life for a great one, would you do it? I mean, even if it meant losing everything you thought you wanted—money, power, being an inside man, you know."

"Are you thinking of doing something like that, Hank?"

Meier stirred a packet of sugar into his coffee. "Maybe. I don't know. I think it may be too late."

Linda leaned forward and touched Meier's hand. "Hank, it's never too late. I can vouch for that. I'm betting there's a woman involved here, and she's not your ex. I know this is going to sound funny, since I sat here to hit on you," she said with a smile, "but I believe in second chances. If you've got one, grab it. Even if you have to go through hell to get there."

Meier looked up, his eyes rimmed with moisture. "Thanks, Linda. I'll do it. I'll drive up there, and I'll see if life has another chance for me."

"Good for you!"

He rose, tossed a five on the table, and touched Linda's shoulder. "And about that hell part. Keep me in your prayers. You have no idea how close to the truth you are."

The Ohio River flowed past the spot where Bill Conners had parked his Mazda, rippling gently, calling him to her banks. Leaving the car, the exhausted cameraman strolled up the brick pathway that paralleled the river until he found an empty bench. In the distance, a barge whistle called out a deep-throated warning to make way for her cargo. A flock of pigeons overshadowed the walkway for a moment, one or two of them alighting near Conners' feet.

A small boy ran past, giggling as he flew a kite along the friendly bank. Bill watched the lad jealously, wishing he could trade places, if only for a moment, so that he might return to a life free from knowledge and fear.

He had come to Madison for only one reason, he suddenly realized. To find Andy Ryder.

And kill him.

CHAPTER 21

Pippa had been listening to Daniel argue with Warren Down for almost an hour. Standing up, she stretched her long body, inherited from her tall Scandinavian father, and walked to the dirty window that faced the only real street in Los Muertos.

"I can't believe you're fighting me on this, Warren! What if those kids died of this new disease the CDC is warning us all about? All physicians in the four-state area have been ordered—that's ordered, Warren—to report any cases that look like they might be viral. Warren, think of the town, for God's sake!"

Down leaned back in his leather chair, his scuffed boots crossed on the edge of the desk. "I am thinking of the town, Tohe. I can't just let you cut open bodies without a good reason. Those kids, rest their souls, are gone, and carving them up like turkeys isn't going to bring them back. You know as well as I do that the body is sacred in our culture, that it's part of the person in the afterlife. Do you want those kids going on with scarred bodies?"

Tohe slammed the walnut desk with both hands, sending dust flying off Down's boots. "That's bull, and you know it, Warren! You don't believe in those old woman rituals and rules. Next, you'll be telling me that Meektay is right! That the gods are angry and they've put a curse on us."

"Maybe they have," the sheriff said, opening up a pack of cigarettes and lighting up. "You tell me how your way makes more sense."

"My way? Good heavens, I'm gone for a week, and it's like someone's brainwashed you. Warren, the rest of the Ibanez family has disappeared. There's no one to complain, so let me autopsy the two children. If they didn't die of a viral agent, then I'll keep quiet from now on, OK?"

Down inhaled the smoke, closing his eyes. "OK," he said, blowing a thick gray cloud toward Tohe. "I'll exhume the bodies. You have one day. After that, they go back into the ground. No extensions."

"Fair enough. Thanks, Warren."

The doctor turned to leave, but Down jumped up and put a hand on his wrist. "Watch what you do, Tohe. Meektay may be a crackpot to you, but some of us are beginning to think he may be right. Consider this a friendly warning."

Daniel pulled away, rubbing his wrist. "Thanks for letting me know where you stand, Sheriff. I'll definitely keep it in mind," he said as he and Pippa left.

Alone again, Warren Down picked up the telephone and dialed. He waited a moment, listened, and stubbed out his cigarette. "Yeah, it's Down. Let me talk to Grayson."

"So what do we do now?" Popeye asked, wiping pizza sauce from his mouth.

Maggie started to answer, but her cell phone chose that moment to jingle. "I'd better get this. It might be campus police." She flipped her phone open and put it to her right ear. "This is Maggie Taylor. Oh, uh, hi, Hank." Maggie bit her lip, unsure what she should say.

"What did she mean it might be the police?" Popeye looked at Julie, not sure whether he should stay or go.

"Dr. Taylor's office had a break-in overnight," the soprano whispered into Popeye's ear. "Come on, let's check out the jukebox and let Maggie have some privacy."

Left alone in the booth, Maggie gathered her thoughts. "So, how did it go with Karen?"

"As well as one might hope, I suppose. She hates the idea of Becka moving away, but she's beginning to realize that it has to happen sooner or later. And she agrees that Eden isn't the safest place right now."

"What place is?" Maggie asked, thinking of Foil's message. "Does Becka still want to come up on Friday?"

"She does. More than ever now. She and her mother aren't getting along all that well, so this has intensified Becka's resolve to make a break. As for me, I'm not sure I can wait until Friday, Maggie. I remember you said you might drive to Madison today. I'm not far from there now. Could we meet? I'd really like to talk."

Hank Meier lied to you. He works for the company that may have killed your own father. What does he know? Why is he trying so hard to win your friendship—your trust?

"Me, too. OK, I hope to leave Bloomington in about an hour. That will put me in Madison at, oh, three. Do you know where the Broadway Inn is?"

"Yeah, I think so. Turn right off Main?"

"That's the place. I can meet you there at three o'clock for coffee."

"Thanks, Maggie. I can't wait," Hank said, his tone genuine.

"See you then," she finished, trying her best not to reveal her rising anger. She hung up and returned the phone to the tote bag. Maggie wondered if she'd made the right choice. What had Yarber said? She'd be followed at all times. She'd be safe.

"Dr. Hunk?" Julie asked as she and Popeye returned to the booth.

"Yeah," Maggie answered absentmindedly. "Listen, you two, thanks for your help, but I gotta run. Jules, I'm driving to Madison in about an hour. Would you keep an eye on my place? Call me if anyone comes by?"

Emerson and Pop exchanged looks. "Sure," she said, shrugging. "When are you coming back?"

"By tomorrow afternoon. I think."

"Nice to know you have an ironclad itinerary," she joked, but Maggie didn't laugh. "Be careful, OK?"

"I will. Thanks again, Popeye. I'll take the laptop with me. Maybe the three of us can powwow tomorrow. Oh, how much do I owe you?"

"Nothing, Doc! Nothing at all," Bailey replied. "Consider it a contribution to the fight. If you need me, Jules knows how to find me."

"Thanks," Maggie said, gathering up her bag. "I'll pay for this, then I gotta scoot. Bye, Jules," she said, hugging her friend. She stopped by the counter, paid, and left.

Jules and Popeye exchanged puzzled glances. "She always on the go?"

"Guess so," Julie replied. "Come on. I've got a little time before rehearsal. Take me to meet this guru of yours. After what we read on that computer, I'm beginning to think you're not nuts after all."

"Thanks, I think," Popeye laughed, and they headed toward the back exit.

Doug Hilliard couldn't understand Andy Ryder's logic. "I can't believe you're leaving when Maggie's on her way here, Andy! I thought you wanted to make your move!"

Ryder wiped his mouth and crumpled up the paper that had wrapped his tuna on rye. "I do. But that phone call I just got forces me to make a slight alteration in my plans. It's only one o'clock now. I can run my little errand and be back at your place in plenty of time for the barbeque. Trust me. I do this all the time."

Hilliard wasn't convinced. "Didn't I hear you mention Bloomington in that conversation? Ironic that you're driving there, while she's driving here. Hey, maybe you could call her, Andy. Ask her to wait and ride back down here with you."

"You're a matchmaker at heart, aren't you, old bud? No, I think it's best that I drive alone. I don't want to push. Maggie's too important to me. She always has been," he said, rising and tossing the wad of paper into the trash near Doug's massive desk.

"You know, Andy, if it's something you just need to pick up, I can have one of my drivers go up there and get it," Hilliard suggested. "It only takes a phone call."

"Thanks for the offer, Doug, but this is one errand that requires a personal touch. I promise I'll be back in plenty of time. You'd be amazed just how quickly I can travel."

Doug stood and followed his lifelong friend to the door. "All right, I'll back off. It's just—well, Andy, you've had your eye on my sister since you two were kids. I could never understand how you let her slip away and marry Jackson Taylor, but what I really don't get is that you seem to be repeating past mistakes! Strike while the iron's hot, Andy!"

Ryder's eyes simmered, and a smile played at the corners of his lips. "That's an interesting expression, Douglas. I promise to keep it in mind. I'll see you tonight!" he added and left, blowing a kiss to Gina as he passed by her desk near the front of the building.

"He sure is a charmer," Gina Patterson said as she brought her boss the morning mail. "Cute, too."

"I wish my sister thought so. Oh, well! I can't force people together if it isn't meant to be! Come on in for a minute, Gina. I want you to help me pick out a present for my wife."

"Anniversary?" she asked as she followed him into his office.

"No. It's a just-cause gift. Just because I love her."

"Oh, gee, Mr. Hilliard, that's so sweet."

"Yeah, it is, isn't it?" he laughed, as he noticed Ryder getting into his car outside. "Maybe my sister will find that kind of happiness, too."

CHAPTER 22

J ulie Emerson, meet Barney Ison."

Julie craned her delicate head upward and stared, wide-eyed, at the giant before her. "You're a big one," she said, extending her tiny hand.

Ison laughed. "Yeah, I get that all the time. You're sweet and petite, just like my ex-wife. You're a fan?"

Julie blushed. "Sort of. Popeye's been telling me all about you for weeks—through e-mails. Actually, today's the first time he and I ever met in person."

"Well, then, come on into my office, little lady, and I'll tell you all about our cause. Popeye, grab some Cokes from the cooler over there. Are you hungry, Julie?"

"We just ate, thanks. Do you mind if I just had some coffee or maybe a water?"

"Got it!" Popeye said, retrieving an Evian from the cooler. "I thought you drank Coke, Jules."

"I have a rehearsal at four. Don't want to muck up my vocal cords. So, what is it you and your followers are into, Mr. Ison?"

"Barney. Just Barney. Here, sit down. Pop, bring in that kitchen chair for yourself."

Popeye followed orders and joined the other two in the small office. "You won't believe what we read on that professor's computer, Barn!"

Julie looked uneasy. "That may be private, Popeye."

Popeye shook his head, the unkempt copper hair falling into his eyes. He swept the unruly locks back without thinking. "I doubt it. Besides, this is Truth, Jules. No one owns the Truth!"

Julie sipped the water thoughtfully. "OK. I guess so."

"So, what's this about a computer?" Ison asked as he leaned back in the old wooden chair.

Popeye Bailey began to speak, and with each new phrase, Ison's eyes grew larger.

Bill Conners had been wandering the riverbank for hours. How could he possibly be considering murder? Bill had grown up in a household where you kept the Ten Commandments, you minded your Ps and Qs, and you didn't murder people. Raised a Catholic, Conners had cut his teeth on honor and duty and service to mankind; this didn't feel like service at all, at least not in the usual sense.

"It's a service in one way, isn't it?" he muttered aloud. "Ryder has to be the one who killed Jenna. The police won't believe me. Ryder's covered it up. Ryder has to pay. I can make him pay. It makes sense. Still, I can't prove Ryder did it. So what right do I have to take a man's life unless I know he's guilty? Dear God, what do I do?"

As he walked, he noticed a sign ahead for the Broadway Tavern. Food. That's what he needed. He'd eat something, then he'd decide. *Never kill a man on an empty stomach.*

Happy to have a plan, Conners picked up his pace and turned onto Broadway.

Andy Ryder slammed the door of the rented black Corolla. He checked his watch. After two. He should never have taken the back roads to get here. The detour at Seymour had thrown his whole schedule off.

Although fit, Ryder knew better than to run for his meeting. Never arrive looking like you're winded, and never break a sweat. Rules to live by—or die by if you break them. He'd learned that back in high school when he'd given himself over to The Watchers. *You're special,* they had told him. *Your unique DNA makes you specifically designed as a vessel for greatness, a clay jar fit to hold something far greater than any gold or spices. You, Andy Ryder, are privileged to host one of our own inside you.*

At first, Ryder hadn't been sure, but he soon learned that he had no choice in the matter. His mother and father had dedicated him to The Watchers even before his birth. The initial possession had hurt, terrified him, but he'd learned to cohabitate with his other self over the years. Now, Ryder liked it. Enjoyed the power it brought.

Ryder had never liked working with cattle, which is what The Watchers called those humans without a demon presence. No matter how often a handler might contact his assignment, he could never really trust the animal to do as he'd been told. Such was the situation Ryder now faced.

Walking slowly to the apartment house, he adjusted his tie, smoothed his hair, and took a deep breath. His eyes were fixed and cold as he knocked. Soon, he knew, his other self would emerge, and he had to be ready for it.

A moment passed, and the weathered door opened to the hallway. "Oh, it's you," the occupant said, his tone casual. He wore a Star Wars T-shirt and plaid pajama bottoms. His black beard had been carefully trimmed to look like a week's growth. His face showed sleep marks from his sofa. He'd been napping.

Perfect. This would be so easy.

Ryder said nothing but simply followed the man into the one-bedroom apartment. He then closed and locked the door behind him.

"So what is it you want?" Hitch asked, tossing his cat off the couch so Ryder could sit. "Here you go, Spook. Take a load off."

Ryder eyed the littered sofa. "No thanks. This won't take long."

"Suit yourself. Is this about Meier? 'Cause I took his bribe just like you wanted me to. I got a witness though. Trick saw me take it. I had to give him a hundred to shut him up. Maybe Trick should have a little accident."

"You're certainly cold-hearted," Ryder said as he eyed the apartment. "What do you do with all the money we give you anyway? This place is a dump."

"Just playin' the role, Ryder. Ison and his bunch would get snoopy if I all of a sudden bought a big place. This suits me fine. For now. I'll be wanting much more once Ison's been taken down."

"Naturally."

Hitchins sat. His soft belly hung low over thighs that had once run for touchdowns, but that had been long ago, when he'd believed in making a future. Now he knew a future had to be bought.

"This Dr. Taylor, she's Chuck Hilliard's daughter, isn't she?" he asked, popping the tab on a Mountain Dew. "She's a looker. Been hanging out with old Hank. They looked mighty chummy. She got pretty upset when I mentioned Tommy Foil's death. Maybe I could tell her more, huh?"

Ryder's eyes narrowed. "Just what would you tell her, Hitchins?"

He gulped down half the can in one swallow then wiped his bearded mouth and belched. "Oh, that her dad helped the government create a killer flu. That he and good old God-father Foil fiddled around with nature to make a virus that can knock out half the world population. That you and your buddy Grayson mean to use the virus as a way to bring on Armageddon."

"You know a lot," Ryder said softly, his face twitching. "But you don't know everything."

"Don't I?" Hitch asked, smirking.

"No. But I can fix that. Would you like to know the truth, Hitch? Everything?"

"Sure. But if you let me know more, then I should be worth more, you savvy?"

Andrew Ryder nodded. "I savvy. Here, Mr. Hitchins, let me give you a peek at the real power behind the takeover."

Ryder's face twitched again, and his eyes began to smolder. Hitchins gaped at the transformation, a look of stark horror overtaking the smirk.

"Good God!" Hitch screamed, rushing for the door, but it was locked. He fumbled for the latch, but it wouldn't budge. The black cat hissed and rushed for the open bedroom door.

"God has nothing to do with me," Ryder replied coldly as his mouth became a cavern of sharp teeth. "And soon, you'll see that He will have nothing to do with you. Greet Him for me when you stand at the judgment seat, Mr. Hitchins. Tell Him Dagon sends his regards."

After leaving Barney's, Popeye had Julie drop him off at the Morning Dove Apartment complex on the northeast side of town.

Ison had talked for nearly two hours. Julie had looked pretty numb once Barney had finished his lesson on reality. Popeye doubted she'd have much of a voice come four o'clock, but he felt sure she'd be speaking out very soon, speaking out for Truth.

Climbing up two flights of open steps, he passed by a freckle-faced boy, not more than ten years old, who reminded Popeye of himself at that age.

"Nice day, huh?" the kid said.

"Yeah. You just hangin' out?"

"Waitin' for the cops," the kid said calmly. "I figure they should be here sometime soon."

"Cops? Why?"

"'Cause of the dead guy upstairs."

Popeye stopped smiling. "What do you mean, dead guy?"

"Just a guy that's dead. Burned up. Boy that place sure stinks. Mom says it's gonna take a lot of cleaning," the boy said, reaching into his pocket for a Game Boy. "I'm on level nine. It's a tough game."

Popeye knelt beside the youth, who was apparently hardened by too much thumb action and digital death. "You don't mean he's really dead, do you, kid?"

The boy looked up, his large green eyes flat and emotionless. "My mom says so. She's the landlady here. We came to collect the rent and found the door half-open. He's dead, toasted like a marshmallow. You ever play Demon Island?"

Popeye shook his head and headed up the stairs. On the third floor, he entered the exterior door and followed a long, carpeted hallway to a knot of neighbors, carrying on a confused conversation outside an open door. As he approached, an acrid stench assaulted Bailey's nostrils, and the pizza began to churn in his stomach. The gossiping neighbors stood right outside Hitch's apartment.

"What's going on?" he asked a woman in curlers. "A kid told me someone was dead."

"Dave Hitchins. He must have been smoking and fell asleep," the woman answered, puffing on her own cigarette. "Emmy there found him when she came by to get the rent. It's awful. He's roasted. Hope you didn't know him."

Popeye fell against the fading flowered wallpaper. He could feel the blood drain from his face and the pizza rising. Bending over, he braced his hands against the wall and began to throw up.

Maggie entered the Broadway Tavern a few minutes before three. As her eyes adjusted to the darkened interior, she noticed several old friends from high school days, women near middle-age who had chosen to stay in their hometown, women who had remained close friends and had therefore never known the terror of living without an intimate support network. Women who traveled in packs. Maggie waved as one recognized her.

"Maggie? Maggie Hilliard?"

"It's Taylor now, at least for a little while longer. Hi Marcie."

Marcella Goins laughed, a nasally snort that sent Maggie back years to high school. "Oh, that's right. I think Doug told me. Maggie, you remember Emma Paige—she's Emma Righthouse now—and Patty Anderson. Still Anderson. Oh, and this is Rhonda Coleman, she's from Eden. We're all realtors. Success doesn't come easily, but when it does, it's sweet. Right, ladies?"

Maggie wanted to hurl. "That's really nice, Marcie. Miss Coleman, it's a pleasure."

"Same here with bells on!" Rhonda bubbled. "Here's my card if you're ever in need of property in Eden."

Maggie took the card and noticed the brag line—*making deals so hot, the devil takes notes.* "Interesting card," she noted. "But I don't think I would ever move to Eden."

"Keep the card, Maggie. You never know," the blond woman insisted.

"Maggie?" a man's voice spoke from a few feet away.

Taylor felt honest relief at seeing Hank Meier. No matter how she distrusted him right now, his company was far preferable to the gaggle of giggles here.

"Hank! I'm sorry, I didn't see you. Excuse me, Marcie. It was really wonderful to see you all again. And thank you again for the card, Rhonda."

Following Hank to his table in the back part of the restaurant, Maggie's shoulders began to tighten. How would she deal with this conversation? Would she just blurt out what she knew? Would that be dangerous? Was one of Yarber's men somewhere in the inn?

"I got here early," he said, his dark eyes posing questions she dared not answer. "The waitress promised to come back as soon as she saw you were here. Gee, it's good to see you, Maggie."

She sat in the chair he offered, her mind leaping to Jackson for some reason. In all honesty, their marriage still existed. Should she even be here?

"You, too, Hank. It's funny. You grew up in Eden, and I grew up here in Madison, a stone's throw away. We probably crossed paths at basketball games without noticing each other."

"I'd have noticed you. Believe me. Although, I wasn't born in Eden. My parents moved there when I was ten or so. I suppose that makes me a transplant Edenite. I remember the Angels' basketball team getting clobbered by the Cubs, but we usually trumped you in football."

"We're making small talk, aren't we? Hank, I need to talk to you about something important, but I don't know how to approach it," she began, just as the waitress arrived with a pair of water glasses and two menus.

"Hi, welcome to the Broadway Tavern. You two just visiting?"

Maggie wanted to scream. She'd almost gotten it out, almost told him about Yarber. "No, I'm from here. And my friend's from Eden, so he's practically from here. You know, I'm not really hungry, but I'll take some coffee."

The woman had to be forty at least, bleached hair, premature wrinkles, and a hard look that comes from a life without dreams. Her blue eyes lacked spark, but she made an effort to smile. *Probably divorced,* Maggie thought, noticing a white line on the ring finger of her bronzed, left hand. *And recently, too.*

"Our house blend is some really good stuff called Stromie's Blend. You've probably had it," she said to Hank. "It comes out of Eden. Best darn coffee I've ever drank."

"Sounds good," Maggie said, warming up her tone. "Your name's Edith?"

"Yeah, how'd you know? Oh, my name tag. I keep forgettin' we wear these now. Most folks call me Edie. Two Stromies then?"

Hank nodded. "Yep. And I'll have some apple pie, if you have any."

"Fresh baked. Ice cream?" she asked, scratching down the order on a light green pad.

"Why not? What's pie without ice cream? Thanks, Edie."

"You bet. Be up in a minute." The woman tucked the pencil behind a double-pierced ear and headed toward the kitchen.

"You were saying?" Hank prompted.

Maggie stared. "I'm not sure it's all that important," she lied. *Coward! You lost your nerve, that's what!*

Hank leaned in, and his face grew serious. "Then let me talk. Maggie, there are so many things in my life that have gone wrong, but I hope our relationship isn't one of them."

"Hank, I...," she began.

"Now, let me finish. I've been mustering up the courage to say this all morning. If I don't do it now, I may never do it. Maggie, I'm not the man you think me to be. In fact, I'm not sure who I am! When we met on Monday, it wasn't a coincidence—no, that's not the way I want to say it. When we met on Mon..." He didn't get a chance to finish his sentence. Before Hank could complete his thought, the front door to the tavern slammed open so hard that it shook the flowers on their table.

"Nobody move!" a tall man screamed from the doorway. "I demand to see Andrew Ryder! I know he's in here somewhere! Don't ask me how—I just do! Now, hand him over, or I'll—or I'll, I'll kill this woman!" he screamed, grabbing Marcie by the shoulders and dragging her with him toward the kitchen.

The other women at the table began to scream and cry. One ran for the front door, but the intruder ordered her to sit down. Timidly, the woman returned to her seat and began to moan softly.

To Maggie's surprise, Hank stood up and walked toward the lunatic. "Sit down, Hank!" she whispered tensely.

Hank ignored her and walked closer to the wild-looking man in the rumpled clothes. "I don't know you, buddy, but I do know Andrew Ryder, and he's not here."

The crazed man's eyes lasered in on Hank, and he pushed the woman back toward her friends. "You do, huh? Where is he? I need to talk to him!"

"What do you need? We'll help you find him," Hank said calmly, his hands open to show he had no weapon. "What's your name?"

"You'd like to know, wouldn't you? So would the cops in Washington! It doesn't matter! Once I find Ryder, I'll show them that I told the truth! Ryder can't be trusted—he, he's a liar! And more than that! I'm going to prove that he is a mur..."

Bill Conners never finished his sentence. Without warning, his body lurched backward, and a thin stream of blood bubbled from his surprised mouth. "I...I," he stuttered as his legs gave way. "God forgive me," he finished, and he crumpled to the floor in a heap, bright blood spreading across his shirt from the hole the .22 bullet had made.

Rhonda Coleman cocked her head, still holding the handgun that had ended Conners' short life.

"What on earth did you do that for?" yelled Hank, rushing to Conners and feeling for a pulse.

Coleman shrugged. "I thought he had a gun. It looked like he was about to shoot you," she explained, her lack of remorse chilling the air. "Excuse me for saving your life!"

Maggie rushed to the fallen man, checking for signs of life.

Edie appeared with the coffees, the cups clinking against each other as she trembled. "Sh-should I call the sheriff or somethin'?"

"Yeah, then call an ambulance," Maggie said. "But there's no hurry. He's dead."

CHAPTER 23

Sheesh, what a day, huh?" Doug asked as he handed his sister an iced tea. "Sorry it turned out that way, sis. This guy, Hank Meier, he still in town?"

"No, he had to leave," Maggie said simply, taking the tea and chugging it. She felt like a rag mop—limp and lifeless. She'd spent two hours answering Sheriff Driscoll's questions. Hank had received a phone call and made his excuses. Whatever confessions he'd wanted to make would have to wait, she guessed. Maybe they could still talk on Friday. She wanted desperately to believe he couldn't be mixed up with the web of evil Tom Foil had described.

"I wonder why this man wanted to talk to Andy," Angela Hilliard said. "You don't think Andy is mixed up in anything, do you?"

"What about me?" a friendly voice asked from the gate. "Hey, there, Hilliards! Hi, Maggedy Ann. Sorry I'm late. My business took a little longer than I thought."

"Hey, Andy!" Doug called from the grill. "The gate's not locked. Grab a drink from the cooler there. You missed some real excitement while you were gone. Tell him, Mags."

"I don't think Maggie wants to talk about this anymore, Doug," Angie chimed in. "Maggie, you look worn out. Maybe you should lie down for a little while."

"No, I'm all right. Hi, Andy. Hey, do you know a man named William Conners?"

Ryder thought of Jenna Dryden and how she'd looked just before he roasted her alive. Her beautiful smile, beguiling eyes, her perfect figure shown off in the tight, red dress. Conners had been the name of her cameraman. "Conners? I don't think so, why?"

"He's dead, that's why," Doug said flatly. "He burst into the Broadway Inn, screaming for you, waving a gun around, and..."

"He didn't have a gun," Maggie explained. "No gun. That woman, Rhonda Coleman, claimed she saw one, but I didn't."

"Rhonda Coleman?" Andy asked. "Who's she?"

"She shot the guy. Put a .22 slug clean through his heart. She claims it was a lucky shot. I should be so lucky," Doug exclaimed. "You want brats or burgers, Andy?"

"A burger's fine. Well done. You know I like mine charbroiled."

"Got it!"

Ryder joined Maggie and sat next to her. "So, I take it you witnessed this? Are you okay?"

She shrugged. "I guess so. The man may have been crazy, but he didn't deserve to die."

Ryder put an arm around her. The human part of him truly did want to comfort her, but the dark half of Ryder merely wanted to make sure this woman, so central to The Watchers' plans, remained unharmed, safe—for now.

"It must have been terrifying," he said, his tone soothing and slick. "Absolutely terrifying."

Popeye Bailey had never been so scared in his life. He burst into the kitchen at Barney's, his face pale, and his green eyes as large as saucers.

"Barney! I gotta see Barney now!"

Lisa Howard, who ran the coffee shop for Ison, came out of the office, a receipt in one hand and a ballpoint pen in the other. "Popeye, are you OK? You look awful!"

Bailey stumbled to her office door. A thin line of dried vomit crusted his chin. His breath smelled acidic.

"What happened?" she asked, taking him by the elbow. "Come on in here."

She closed the door and used the small bathroom sink just off the main room of the office to run cold water onto a paper towel. Coming back, Lisa wiped Bailey's chin. "You look sick. I don't think you're hot, though."

"I'm sick all right. Barney? Where's Barney?"

"Barney had to go to the radio station to record some ads or something. He shouldn't be gone too long."

Popeye closed his eyes. He felt as if his body weighed a thousand pounds. His eyelids demanded closure, and his brain was shutting down. "I'll wait. Could I have some water?"

Lisa filled a clear glass with cold water from the sink. "Here. Maybe I should call the Health Center and make you an appointment."

"No! Don't tell anyone I'm here except Barney. Let me know when he gets back. I—I just wanna sleep. To forget about it for now. Just sleep."

"You look like you could sleep for days," Angie said as she and Maggie washed up the barbeque platters and utensils.

"Why don't you go relax with Andy? I can get this. Most of it's paper, anyhow."

"You work too hard," Maggie replied, drying one of the large platters. "You need to rest more, Angie. You know, this baby you're carrying is a little miracle, and you need to nurture it."

"Him," she whispered proudly. "And maybe a her, too. Twins."

"Oh, Angie! How wonderful! You did talk to Dr. Pryor about the amnio, right?"

"We did. And it's scheduled for next Monday. The ultrasound showed two tiny babies, though. One is clearly a boy, but the other was kind of shy. The tech couldn't tell the gender."

"I'll bet Doug's in seventh heaven. He always wanted a boy."

A sad smile crossed Angie's face. "Yeah, we tried for so long, but it just wasn't happening. Doug pretended it didn't matter, but I know it did. He's really a wonderful man, Maggie, but then I don't have to tell you that. You grew up with him! Maybe it's part of some bigger plan for us to have children late in life."

Maggie thought about Charlotte. Her precious girl. Snatched away from her. Cold and dead. "I'm not so sure about plans, but if there are some cosmic blueprints, I'd like to have a chat with the architect."

"Girl talk? Or can we mere men join in?" Doug asked from the doorway to the den.

"I told Maggie about the twins," Angie beamed, finishing the last of the plates. "Maggie, you go on in and visit with Andy. I know he's the main reason you came down here."

Doug laughed and hugged his pregnant wife's expanding tummy. "Hey there, my lads. Did you hear that? Your Aunt Maggie has a boyfriend."

"Doug, you're the limit!" Angie laughed, and Maggie left them to enjoy a few minutes alone.

"So, Major Ryder," she said, entering the den. "What can you tell me about BioStrain?"

Ryder's head jerked up from the newspaper he'd been reading. "BioStrain? Why would you ask me about that?"

"Turns out it's the company Dad worked for. And it has a hefty government contract to produce a vaccine for this avian flu, should it become infective to humans. I'm betting it's all in those papers, which is why you wanted them. So where are my copies?"

Ryder blinked. "Waiting to be made, I guess. Sorry. I've been swamped this week. I can bring them on Friday. Remember, I said I'd be in town."

She'd forgotten all about Andy's promise to call her at the end of the week. Hank and Becka would be coming to Bloomington on Friday as well. When it rains, it pours.

"That sounds good. What's in the paper that has you so intrigued?"

"Nothing much," he said. "More about the flu. It's hit Iowa pretty hard. Looks like you were right about the pigs. Two hundred feeder pigs were slaughtered in a little town called Mayfield. This is going to play havoc with the agricultural economy."

Maggie reached for the paper. "All from one little virus. I'm surprised it's mutated so quickly. They must be pulling out their hair at the CDC."

"You'd know more about that science stuff than I would," he said, keeping a straight face. "So you're going to New Mexico on Saturday?"

"Yeah. Did I tell you that? In all that's happened this week, I can't remember."

"I was having lunch with Doug when you told him. Why's your week been so hectic? Finals?"

She nearly mentioned the computer, but something in her cried caution. "Finals, yeah. Well, that and having my office broken into."

"You're kidding? Who did that?" he asked, showing surprise.

"I don't know yet, but I will," she promised with a smile. "Soon, I'll figure out everything."

"Barney, thank heaven you're here," Lisa said, pointing to Popeye's sleeping form. "He came in about an hour ago, talking crazy. He said he could only talk to you."

"Thanks, Leese," Ison said, walking into his office and gazing fondly at Bailey. "Hey, Pop, wake up, man. You gonna sleep here all night?"

Bailey jerked awake, staring wide-eyed at the man who'd become more of a father than his own dad had ever been. "Barney! Oh, gee, man! Thank God! I gotta talk to you—now!"

"Calm down, kid. We can talk. Let me check the day's numbers first..."

"No time!" Popeye poked his head around the corner, looking at the evening crowd, wondering if Hitch's killer waited among them. He felt trapped. Turning back to Ison, he grabbed the big man's arms. "Man, you have to listen to me, but—look, Barney, we can't talk in this public place. Will you just take a short walk with me? Outside in the fresh air?"

Ison nodded. "OK, Pop. Anything to make you happy. Lisa! I'm gonna head to the bank to get some change. Pop's goin' with me. Back in five."

Lisa waved, and Barney led Bailey to the alley behind the store. Once outside, Popeye began to talk nonstop.

CHAPTER 24

Friday

Maggie left Madison by noon on Thursday, kissing Angie and wishing her and Doug all the best with the babies. She promised to visit again as soon as she returned from New Mexico.

Thursday had passed without event, except that Hank Meier had called three times, leaving messages on Maggie's machine as she screened her calls. Detective Hendricks had called and left a message once, promising to come by the office on Friday morning. Julie had stopped in after her last final, and the two friends had huddled over a pot of decaf coffee while Julie shared all that Barney Ison had told her. Finally, past midnight, exhaustion had forced the two women to retire for the night.

Maggie yawned, still tired after a night filled with bad dreams, and sipped at her morning coffee. She had been sitting for nearly an hour, staring at the computer that Tom Foil had risked his life to send her. Risked? Lost his life. He'd paid for his defiance, for his patriotism, with his life. Dead scientists, that's what Popeye said. She wondered if he and Barney Ison were right. But scientists aren't stupid! How can any company, even a diabolical one such as BioStrain, manage to keep the true nature of their research from its own researchers? It didn't make any sense.

The phone rang, pulling her back to reality. "Hello?"

"Hey, Maggedy Ann. It's me. Andy Pandy."

Maggie jumped at the name. What about Maggedy Ann gave her the creeps lately?

"Andy. I hadn't expected your call. What's up?"

Ryder feigned hurt. "Gee thanks. I thought we had a date. I'm in town like I promised. Am I too late for breakfast?"

"I can't do breakfast. I have an early meeting at my office, so I already had a cereal bar and washed that down with a slice of cake," she answered, still processing Ryder's motives. "I don't know, Andy. I have a lot to do before tomorrow."

"We could make it dinner instead, if that works better for you."

Maggie began to recall her nightmare's terrifying imagery and the name Maggedy Ann. She thought about Ryder and his possible involvement with BioStrain. And those dreams! It was Ryder who had sent Meier to follow her. Ryder, who had stolen her father's papers.

"I can't do dinner either, but I will meet you for a quick dessert at Barney's Café—do you know it?"

"Oh, yes. I love that place. An interesting bunch of people hang out there. Sure. Barney's sounds fine."

"Great. How about seven? But I can't stay long."

"I'll cherish every minute you can spare, Maggedy Ann. See you at seven. Oh, I have copies of your dad's papers with me."

"You do? Great! I'll see you at seven. Bye."

Maggie hung up and stared at the telephone. *What an amazing world! Pick up a phone and talk to anyone, anywhere.*

Share a joy, a laugh, order an execution. Had Andy ordered such an execution for Tom Foil or the other scientists? And what about Hank's involvement?

Doug had said Andy wanted something in their father's papers. Maybe he thought she had information as well. Did Andy know about the Armageddon virus? What about DARPA? Andy had said he no longer worked for Justice, so who signed his paychecks now?

Could she trust anyone?

Andy Ryder stood in front of a mirror in a nearby Bloomington hotel room, combing through his hair. *Funny,* he thought. *It's so easy to fool the humans. So easy to make them dance to our tune.*

In the mirror, his normally light blue eyes had changed color, and they smoldered back at his other self. As the demon took control, Ryder's body reshaped into a hideous beast, his demon's natural form. Dagon's multi-colored scales glistened in the incandescent lighting of the bathroom, and his claws clicked as they touched his ancient face. Sharp teeth caged a leathery tongue, which protruded from mammoth jaws as he spoke aloud.

"Stupid cattle. Proper handling, that's all it takes. A whisper in the ear, a dream in the night. A promise of power, and they fall all over themselves to do our work for us. A few weeks more, and everything will be in place. And then the true invasion can begin."

Dagon began to laugh, a hideous, earth-shaking laugh that rattled the mirror as he changed back into the small, human shape of Andy Ryder. Satisfied with his appearance, the thing shaped like a man clicked off the light switch and headed for his meeting with Maggie Taylor.

"Mornin', Maggie May. I figured you'd ducked on out to New Mexico when you didn't show up yesterday."

"Sam Fountain, have I ever told you how handsome you are?" Maggie asked and kissed the bashful professor's cheek. "Thanks for noticing my absence."

Sam rubbed the spot and followed Maggie into her office. "Ah, gee, how could I not? You didn't miss much though. The Optometry School dean came by asking if you'd thought about their offer for the fall. Oh yeah, and that Detective Hendricks, he came by to see you. You okay, Maggie?"

Maggie sat down and began cleaning up the mess her midnight visitor had left in her office, made worse by Hendricks' investigation. "Does he have a suspect yet?" she asked, settling Jackson's photo in its place on the desk.

"He says he might. They got some prints they can't account for. He figures that's a good start."

Trueblood appeared in the doorway. "Dr. Taylor, you have visitors."

Maggie looked up, expecting to see one of Yarber's shadowy men in the hall. Instead, Hendricks and a campus officer waved from the open doorway.

"Not again," Maggie moaned. "Come on in, Detective."

Hendricks stepped carefully, making sure not to disturb any of the paperwork that still littered the carpeted floor. "Just now cleaning up, I see. I heard you were out of town, Dr. Taylor. I thought we had a deal that you'd call me when you left. I had to hear it from Dr. Fountain here."

Sam shrugged. "Sorry, Maggie. I didn't mean to rat you out. I'll be across the hall if you need me."

"I understand you have some prints that might lead to an arrest," she said, retrieving the morning *Herald* from outside her doorway. "Do you mind, Officer?" she said as she inched past the tall policeman.

"Sorry, ma'am."

Hendricks whispered something to the young policeman, who left and walked back to Trueblood's office. "He's new. Don't mind him. Dr. Taylor, did you know someone called David Hitchins?"

Hitchins? "I don't think so," she said honestly, although the name did sound familiar. "Why? Do you think he might have broken in?"

"We don't know yet. It's a possibility, since our computers show a partial match to his right index to a print taken off your office door. But the match is only on four points, so it's not enough to pin it on Hitchins, not that it matters."

"What do you mean? Aren't you going to talk to him?"

Hendricks unwrapped a piece of gum and popped the stick into his mouth. "I would if I could."

The phone rang.

"Excuse me, Detective, I'm expecting a call. Hold that thought," Maggie said.

"Maggie Taylor," she answered.

"Hank Meier," a pleasant voice replied. "It's Friday. I just wanted to make sure we're still invited."

Had she been that indifferent on Wednesday? "Of course. Is Becka on her way?"

"Actually, she has a friend from high school who lives in one of the campus sororities, so she stayed there last night. I'm coming down from Indy now. Does ten o'clock still work for you?"

"That'll be fine."

"You okay? You sound sort of, I don't know, odd."

"I have company, so I can't talk much."

"We can make it later, if you like. Ten's only an hour away."

"No, that's fine. I'll be done by then. Be careful."

Hank laughed softly. "After Wednesday, I was about to say that to you. Becka and I will meet you at ten."

"I can't wait to meet her," she answered.

"Bye, Maggie."

She hung up, hoping the flush she felt in her cheeks wasn't visible.

"A friend?" Hendricks asked.

Rats. He sees it. "Sort of. You were telling me about someone named David Hitchins. Why haven't you at least brought him in for questioning?"

Hendricks blew a small bubble. It popped, and he scowled as he wiped the strands of gum from his lips. "I would ask him, if he weren't dead," he said flatly, wrapping the useless gum in a tissue.

"Dead? How?" she asked, dumbfounded.

"You know, we're still trying to figure that one out. Are you sure you never heard of Hitchins? He had your name written on a note we found on his fridge."

"My name? That's crazy! Wait—unless he really is the guy who broke in here. But why would someone I don't even know want to break in here? I don't keep drugs. I don't keep..." She stopped suddenly, her eyes wide. *The computer. What if Hitchins worked for BioStrain? And why did the name sound so familiar?*

"You think of something else, Doc?" prompted the detective.

"Is it possible this guy went by the nickname Hitch?" she asked tentatively.

"Could be," Hendricks said as he considered opening a second stick of gum. "You know a guy named Hitch, Doc?"

Maggie shut her eyes. *This just gets worse and worse.* "Not really, but I had an encounter with a guy called Hitch at Barney's Café. That was, let's see, on Monday evening, I think. He came up to my friend and called him some names. I guess I didn't take it too well."

Hendricks pocketed the stick of gum and waved to the officer down the hall. "OK, well, I think that's all I need for now. We'll try again to get a match on the prints. I can't guarantee anything though, there isn't much left of him."

"What do you mean?" Maggie asked, not sure she really wanted the answer. "How did he die?"

"Toasted, Doc. Like this morning's bagel, only a lot darker. The smell ain't comin' out of that place anytime soon, I can tell you that. Call me before you leave on Saturday. Maybe I'll have more."

CHAPTER 25

Nate Beacham's toast popped up, brown and golden, just the way he liked it. "Amy! Breakfast's ready. I have to eat quick! Frank wants me to run over to Los Muertos to check on some deaths there!"

Beacham buttered the whole wheat slices and set them on a blue and white china plate. "You want some toast?" he called then jumped when his wife of thirty years came up behind him.

"Sure," she said and kissed him. "Frank's got you running off to where?"

"Los Muertos. Remember the piece Lyle wrote on that religious leader up there? The one who claims to be descended from the Aztec Lord of the Dead?"

"Mickey? Meety? Something like that?" she asked, opening the refrigerator to get the milk.

"Meektay. Lunatic, if you ask me, but then who's asking? Anyway, I'm doing a follow-up since Lyle's in the hospital with that broken ankle. Four deaths in the last two weeks or so. It might be this flu. Frank thinks it's a big story."

"I hope so," she said sweetly. "I have a hair appointment, then I'm having lunch with Kimberly. I guess we'll meet up again later."

"Just like always," he said. "I'd better run, hon. I'll call you when I get back in town."

Nate grabbed the toast and dashed out the front door and into the morning heat. Ninety already. The sunspots were killing their flowers. So much for ever putting in a real lawn. He kicked at the multihued rocks that served as turf and beeped his car door open.

Sliding in, Nate adjusted the mirror and mentally reviewed his plans. He wished he could have told Amy the real reason he wanted to drive to Los Muertos, but the truth about BioStrain and the flu vaccine would frighten her, and Nate Beacham loved her too much to let her spend even one moment in fear. Amy had waited for him during his time in Vietnam, and she'd stuck with him through the drug rehab he'd required after he came back. Amy deserved nothing but the best, and Beacham spent every day trying to find new ways to give it to her.

As he backed the car toward the street, he waved to his neighbor, Sid Friedman, wondering how he and Marta would take it if they knew a secret lab almost directly beneath their feet worked on the very virus everyone feared.

Nate knew how he felt.

Terrified.

"This must be Becka!" Maggie gushed as Hank arrived with a lovely young woman.

Hank beamed and put an arm around his daughter. "My pride and joy. Becka, this is Dr. Taylor."

"Hi, Dr. Taylor. You're really nice to make time for me and my dad today."

"It's no problem, Becka. I'm still cleaning up my office from the break-in, so do you mind if we meet downstairs?

There's a serviceable canteen down in the basement where we can talk in private. Oh, Hank, I hope you have some ones. I don't seem to have any change."

"I've got it covered," he answered as all three followed the stairway to the lowest floor of the building. Ahead sat three soda machines, two snack machines, a water fountain, a change machine, and five tables, each surrounded by four chairs.

"It's not much, I know. We're planning a really nice student lounge for the end of the summer. It's being built on the other end of the basement, but for now this will have to do. The pop machines take dollars. Hank, if you'd spring, I'd love a Pepsi."

"Becka?"

"Just some bottled water if they have it, Dad. Thanks."

"Come on, Becka. Let's sit down."

Maggie led the girl to the cleanest table, and the two of them sat. "You're premed?" Maggie asked.

"For now. Dad thinks I should look into pathology. Do I need to do an M.D. to go into forensics?"

Maggie smiled. "Actually, most forensic pathologists do an M.D. first. You can do a Ph.D. at the same time. I did. Pathology's my thing." Hank turned around and offered a grin, glad to see the two women hitting it off.

"I thought you were a molecular biologist."

"That's right. I have two Ph.D.s, one in physiology and one in molecular bio. So, my specialty is finding out the cellular reason for death. Or rather, it would be if I worked in the private sector. You want to go into police work?"

Hank joined them, setting down their drinks. "She's looking at the FBI. No Evian, hon. This'll have to do."

She picked up the mineral water and nodded. "That's OK. Thanks, Dad. The truth is, Dr. Taylor, my mom's not really happy that I'm looking at IU. I can go either way, but Dad doesn't want me in Eden any longer."

Hank shrugged. "So sue me for wanting to make sure you're safe. I thought your mother had softened a bit when I left. Don't tell me she's ranting again."

"Dad, she's just having a hard time letting go. Just like someone else I know," she continued, looking directly at Hank with a big smile. "She's still not crazy about me moving, but I reminded her that you're paying for school, so she's okay with it."

"Looks like it's up to you," Maggie answered, popping the tab on her Pepsi. "Why not talk to some of the students here and take a little time to think about it?"

"I'd like that," Becka answered. She looked past Maggie and her dad at the machines. She twirled a piece of highlighted brown hair around her finger. Maggie studied her. *A slight overbite, but the girl has charisma.* Maggie could see something wrong behind the brown eyes, though. Becka clearly wanted to please her father, even if it meant changing schools.

Watching the girl, Maggie went back in time in her mind, seeing herself trying desperately to please her own father. Charles Douglas Hilliard had demanded perfection of his bright daughter, leaving Doug to follow whatever path he chose. Maggie had always believed her father's love fell best on the male twin, so she'd spent most of her childhood vying for any scraps of attention he might offer her. Charles Douglas Hilliard hadn't loved Charlotte much better. Or so Maggie had thought. She'd always believed her father had wanted a grandson, but made do with a granddaughter. She'd realized how wrong she'd been at Charlie's funeral. Her father had cried like a baby.

"Becka," Maggie said, leaning in to whisper. "Becka, you have to do what makes you happy. Believe me, your dad wants that, too. Right, Hank?"

Hank looked puzzled but agreed. "Sure. It's just that…"

"It's just you don't know how to say it, right?" Maggie finished with a wink at Meier. "Becka, you can be anything you choose, but don't go for pathology unless you're willing to put aside a lot of personal time. It's an all-consuming path."

"I know," she said thoughtfully. "Mind if I just walk around campus for a while?"

Hank started to object, but Maggie stopped him again. "Go on, Becka. Where are you staying?"

"Delta Gamma House. I might take the bus back over there and see if Helen is back from registration. Is that okay, Dad?"

Hank looked at Maggie, who nodded. "Sure. Uh, you want to stay here again tonight?"

Becka nodded. "If that's okay. Mom's gone all weekend, so I don't have to worry about being home."

"What about Buster?" Hank asked.

"He's at the vet's. Mom's having him fixed, 'cause he's been getting into the neighbor's yards. You know, he actually climbs that high fence you put up. It's kinda weird. A lot of the dogs in Eden have been acting sort of funny lately. Anyway, the vet said Buster should be fixed before he's a year old, so Mom left him there for the weekend. I'm supposed to pick him up on Monday."

Hank shrugged. "Sounds like you have it all lined up. OK. Have fun, sweetheart. Do you need any money?"

Becka laughed. "He's always asking me that, Dr. Taylor. Thanks, Dad. I have plenty. I work, remember?" She kissed him lightly on the forehead. "See you tomorrow, Dad. You and Dr. Taylor have a good time," she added with a wink.

Leaving the water on the table, Becka waved goodbye as she headed up the stairs to the north exit.

"She's got a mind of her own," Hank said after Becka was out of sight. "I hope I didn't waste your time, Maggie."

"Not at all. Look, I'm probably barging in where I don't belong, but you need to give Becka some space. She wants to please you, Hank, but she needs to find her own way. She may not want to work for the FBI. Who knows? She may even find a great guy and settle down."

Hank laughed. "I guess she could. Funny, I just assumed that she wanted to follow my plan for her."

Maggie stood up and tossed her empty can into a recycle bin. "I need to make some phone calls in my office. I can call you later."

Hank rose as well and followed Maggie to the staircase. "Maybe we could meet for lunch," he suggested. "I never got to finish my speech the other day."

Maggie shivered, remembering Bill Conners' pale face as he crumpled into a heap of death. Rhonda Coleman had been proclaimed a hero, which made Maggie want to scream. The world was going mad.

"Lunch? Maggie? Am I being thrown to the lions, here?"

Maggie blinked and shook her head. "No, no, I'm sorry. Lions? Oh, say, that's a good idea. The Irish Lion. Do you know it? Say eleven-thirty-ish—it's on Kirkwood."

"I know it well. Great food. Okay. I'll get there early and save a booth. That all right?"

"Yeah, that will help. I may be a few minutes late."

"Eleven-thirty, then," he said, hope filling his voice.

"Right. Eleven-thirty-ish."

Hank kissed her on the cheek and headed up the stairs to the exit. After he'd gone, Maggie returned to her seat at the table, staring at the empty can he'd left. Suddenly, she had an odd thought. Picking up a napkin from a condiment table, she grasped the can by the top and left the canteen, headed for Trueblood's office, where she hoped she still might find Detective Hendricks lurking about.

CHAPTER 26

M aggie parked the Santa Fe in the small A lot off Kirkwood. Her faculty permit gave her access to prime parking spots on campus, and the summer drop in attendance
meant she had her pick of spaces. She shut off the engine and
stared at the entrance to the Irish Lion. She had a few minutes
before meeting Hank. Their meeting on Monday seemed so
long ago. Meier's charm drew her like a magnet, but she had
to wonder who this man was. Was it wise to let him pursue a
relationship with her? Over the past five years, Maggie permitted alcohol to dull her senses, but now she was sober, and she
wanted clear eyes and a clear head.

She thought about the prints she'd left with Hendricks. The
detective had taken the soda pop can, zipped it into a plastic
bag, and promised to get back to her later today, providing the
prints could be found in the local database. If not, he'd have to
send them to the Indiana Bureau office for processing. *What
would the prints reveal about Meier?* she wondered.

This was turning out to be one busy day. Just after Hank
and Becka left, Yarber had called to arrange a meeting. Maggie
had asked him about Meier, but the tight-lipped military man
had simply said she should watch herself. *Thanks, Major.* One
more phone call to make before going into the Lion. Maggie

pulled out her cell phone and dialed the familiar numbers, her hands shaking. *Nervous about talking to your own husband? Silly!*

"Hi, is Dr. Taylor available?" she asked, hoping the receptionist would say no.

"Sure. Is this Dr. Maggie?" the girl asked. "He said to put you right through. Give me a minute."

Maggie watched a lanky student on a skateboard weave in and out of parked cars. *The guy must think he'll live forever,* she thought. *Kids his age have no sense of mortality. Just like Charlie.*

"Hi, Mags."

"Jackson. I only have a minute, but I wanted to let you know I've given it a lot of thought. If you still want to go, I'm game."

"I'd been praying you'd say that, Maggie. Believe me, this will be good for us. What time do we leave?"

What have I done? Too late. Can't take back the invitation now.

"I'll pick you up in the morning at six sharp."

"I'll be ready. Thanks, Mags. See you tomorrow morning."

She ended the connection and closed the phone. Her hands shook, and she longed for a drink. She'd have to see the house again, the house she had shared with Jackson and their daughter. The house with all the bad memories.

Shaking her head to clear her thoughts, Maggie locked up the Santa Fe and headed across the street. As she entered the dimly lit interior, she couldn't stop wondering if she'd stepped through the looking glass as well. Ever since her father's funeral, she'd felt unsettled. She sensed a change in the world around her, a sense of doom. Just like Alice in a nonsensical world, she could easily lose her head.

Maggie had spent a lifetime surviving by her wits, but could she still trust them? More to the point, could she trust Hank Meier? And since it was Andy who'd sent Meier her way originally, could she trust him?

As she walked past the bar, she could see Hank sitting in the second booth. Waving, she passed by a redheaded waiter and joined Meier.

"Eleven-thirty-ish on the nose," she said as the waiter followed her to the booth.

"What's the special?" she asked while Hank perused the menu.

"The roast leg of lamb is very good today. We also have a super bacon potato soup. Order any rollog and you can add seasoned or cheese fries for only an additional dollar today. I'd also recommend the corned beef sandwich, finishing off with whiskey pie or our Bailey's cake."

"It all sounds good," Hank told the young man. "OK, I'll have the soup and the corned beef sandwich for now."

"No cheese fries?" Maggie asked.

"We could share them," Hank answered.

"Done. OK, then, I'll have the Celtic salad with soda bread, please."

"What to drink?" the waiter asked, winking to a passing female student.

"I'll have a Murphy's Stout. Maggie?"

She looked at the long list of Irish beers, and she could almost taste them on her tongue. Closing her eyes, she passed the menu to Hank and swallowed. Opening her eyes, she looked at the waiter. "Iced tea."

"Long Island?"

"Just good old iced tea with lemon. Thanks."

"You don't mind me drinking, do you?"

Maggie shook her head.

"I'm very proud of you," Hank told her after the waiter had left.

Maggie held her breath. For a moment, Hank's voice sounded just like Jackson's. Jackson, her tall, lean husband with killer gray eyes and Sherlock Holmes brain. Jackson, who could make her laugh with a word or weep with a touch. Jackson, who would be sitting beside her on a 747 jetliner to Las Cruces in less than twenty-four hours.

"You're becoming a special friend, Hank," she said as their drinks arrived. "I don't want you to get the wrong idea, though."

Hank tried to smile, but he couldn't hide his disappointment. "You're still in love with your husband."

"Am I? Really, Hank, I don't know. Maybe that's one of the reasons I said yes to him when he asked to go with me to see Pippa. If we spend a little time together, and the old magic is there, then maybe it's worth a shot, don't you think? If it's not, then, well, I don't know. Am I crazy?"

Meier sipped the ale thoughtfully. "Maybe. I'm not exactly objective, you know. Look, Maggie, I'm going to lay my cards on the table. When I met you on Monday, I wasn't looking for a relationship; in fact, I figured on spending the rest of my life alone. Now, all of that is changed, and I keep seeing you and me in a little house with a dog, a cat, and the whole shebang."

"A cat? Ooh, I don't like cats," she answered lightly.

"Two dogs then."

Both laughed, and Hank took her hand. "What I'm saying is, when you get back from New Mexico, if you want me, I'm here. OK?"

"Fair enough, but please don't count on me. I'm not very reliable. Jackson can tell you that."

"If you ask me, Jackson's a fool for ever letting you go."

Maggie raised her iced tea glass and clinked it against Hank's beer mug. "I'll drink to that!" she said with a grin.

"Now, before we get lost in those fries, I have to tell you something, Maggie. It's what I started to tell you in Madison, but... Well, here it is. I've told you that I work for a company called BioStrain, and that's true, but I don't really work in..." Hank made a face then reached into his pocket. "Sorry. My cell phone's vibrating."

"Vibrating?" she cocked one eyebrow. "Go on. Answer it."

"Thanks." Hank opened the phone and checked the caller ID. Grayson. He had suspected as much. "I have to take this. I promise it won't take long," he said. "Mind if I go outside?"

"Oh, the other woman, eh?" she joked. "No, go on out. I'm going to eat all the cheese fries while you're gone."

Hank offered a weak smile and left the restaurant. Once outside, he sat on a park bench. Kirkwood Street teemed with color and life, but Hank could see nothing beyond the silver cell phone in his hand.

"This is Hank."

"Still seeing our little doctor, Dr. Meier? That's good. But your services will no longer be required. Once she's here in New Mexico, you can go back to your previous assignment, that gaggle of Internet spies there in Bloomington."

"Mr. Grayson, I'd rather remain on the Taylor assignment, if that's all right. I've gotten very close to her, and she trusts me."

"Does she? Are you aware that she recovered your fingerprints from the aluminum can you left with her this morning? That doesn't count as trust, Dr. Meier."

Hank nearly dropped the phone. Had Maggie actually taken his prints off the can? Grayson had to be bluffing.

"She's bringing her husband to New Mexico, Mr. Grayson. If you let me continue with her, I can break that up."

"No need, Dr. Meier. If Jackson Taylor becomes a nuisance, we can deal with him. The desert sun is very hot, and people have been known to lose their way. Now, if you want us to keep paying your daughter's tuition, just do as you're told. She is so very bright. Perhaps one day she'll come to work for BioStrain."

Grayson hung up, and Hank closed the phone. A knot of fear gnawed at his stomach. Grayson knew. He felt sure of it. Grayson knew he'd lied about Pippa Anderson. He might even know Hank intended to defect. He had a week, maybe less, to get his ducks in order and find a way to keep Rebecca safe.

Returning to the booth, he offered a thin smile. "Sorry about that, Maggie. Hey, you ate all the cheese fries."

"I told you I would. Was that your boss?" she asked innocently.

Meier flinched. "Why would you ask that?"

She took a sip of tea then wiped her mouth with a white linen napkin. "Sorry, I didn't mean to step on toes. If you have another woman on the hook, that's fine."

"Another woman?" he asked. He gulped the last of his ale. "Forgive me. You're right. It was my boss, and he isn't very happy with me. In fact, I need to make a few calls to keep him off my back. Mind if we call it a day?"

Maggie smiled, a dazzling effect when she wanted to impress a man. "Not at all. In fact, I have a hot date with a guy from DARPA."

"DARPA? The government agency?"

"The same. I have my little secrets, too, you know. Hank, it's been a fun week, getting to know you and now Becka. Maybe you should take her out tonight, just the two of you. Talk about her future. I'll need an early night if I want to be up with the chickens. I'll call you when I get back from New Mexico. I still have that card you gave me with your number."

She was brushing him off, sending him packing. "I'd like that, if you really mean it," he said, helping her out of the booth. He walked her to her car, lingering as she unlocked the door. "You will call me, right?"

"I promise."

She kissed him on the cheek, but he pulled her close, holding on to her as if this would be their final embrace. "Good-bye, Maggie," he whispered. Then he kissed her, fully on the mouth, an intense, desperate kiss as if saying good-bye forever.

Hank walked away, not turning back once, leaving Maggie alone in the parking lot, wondering if she'd just made a big mistake.

Nate Beacham savored the last of his lunch and waved to Susie Thayer. "Miss Thayer! I think I'd better be about my business."

Susie emerged from the steaming kitchen, a towel over one shoulder and a spoon in her right hand. "You done already? How'd you like that chili? Good, huh?"

Nate rubbed his flat tummy, still fit from years of sit-ups. "Twelve alarm, if anything, but the best I've ever had. And I know chili!"

"Thanks," she said proudly. "That'll be six dollars even."

Nate removed a ten from his wallet and handed it to his hostess. "Is that all? Boy, I wish you'd open a branch in Las Cruces! Here you go. Keep the change."

"Thanks! You still want to know about Meektay?"

"Yup. Can you tell me where he'd be this time of day?"

Susie frowned. "Unfortunately, I can. My brother's mixed up with that crazy man. Meektay's got a place about three miles outside of town, but he usually hangs out on top of Ford's Mesa. I have no idea why, since I thought the high places were just for ceremonies. Meektay says you have to get high to reach the gods."

"High? Which kind?" Nate asked, knowing all too well what drugs can do to a man.

"Both kinds," Susie said simply. "Here, I'll draw you a map of the area."

Within minutes, Beacham's car again pointed toward a story, this time heading south to a place called Ford's Mesa, where his life would change forever.

"Is a booth OK?" a tall waiter asked at Mother Bear's.

"Sure," Maggie replied, noting the restaurant appeared rather crowded for midafternoon. "I'm meeting someone. He should be here in a few minutes."

"Here you go," the young man said, laying out silverware wrapped in red napkins and handing Maggie two menus. "I'll bring you some water, if you like, Dr. Taylor."

"You know me?" she asked. He didn't look familiar. Not one of her students.

"Sort of. My girlfriend's in medical school right now. Emily Scott. She just finished a gross anatomy class with you. She said the final was a killer."

"Sure, I know Emily. She's a good student, and she'll make a fine doctor one day. Tell her I said hi."

"I will. She says you're the best teacher she's ever had. Well, I'll go get your water."

Unexpected. I'm a fine teacher? Then why do I feel like such a bum?

199

She glanced at her watch. Three-twenty-five. She still had five minutes before Yarber arrived, so she took out her cell phone and pushed the number for Campus Police.

"Hi. May I speak to Detective Hendricks?"

"Just a moment," the woman answered.

"Thanks, Miss," Maggie said, taking a short sip of water.

"You're welcome," Hendricks' brusque voice answered on the other end of the phone.

"Sorry, Detective. I didn't expect such a quick connection. This is Maggie Taylor. Do you have any results yet?"

"Those prints you gave me? Let me see," he told her. "I'm looking at the report now. Sorry, Doc. Looks like your man isn't in our database. We'll send it on up to Indianapolis for them to have a look-see. Now, you're flying to New Mexico tomorrow, right?"

"First thing in the morning. The plane leaves at eight."

"Can I reach you on your cell?"

"Sure. I'll take it with me. I'll give you the number."

"Got it already, if that's what you're using now. Our incoming calls are all screened. Dr. Taylor, one more thing."

"Yes, Detective."

"Be careful. I know you think the office break-in was an isolated incident, but in my opinion it's a lot more than that. This Hitchins guy—he had quite a record, but nothing in burglary. I'm betting someone hired him to pop your office door. Watch your back."

"Thanks, Detective. I'll do that."

Maggie hung up just as the waiter returned with two glasses of ice water.

"Awful, isn't it?" he said, setting the glasses on the table.

"What's awful?" Maggie asked, returning the phone to her bag.

The youth, a lanky artsy type, pointed to the small television set mounted over the cash register. "Looks like that flu's spreading to humans. The president's supposed to speak tonight. I hear he's going to announce vaccinations for everybody. Me, I'll be the first in line. This flu is a nasty way to die. So, you want to order now or wait for your friend?"

Maggie gulped. Flu vaccine. BioStrain must have finished the project. Armageddon stood waiting at their very door.

CHAPTER 27

In the underground lab, Arnie Smith couldn't believe what he was reading. "Are you sure about this?" he asked Eve. "These numbers have to be wrong."

Eve Martin shook her head. "These are right. Sam and Rick went over them as well. Besides, the data has already been crunched by the team in China. It's right. I just don't get it."

Smith scanned the pages again, turning them in his hands. "Come with me," he said to Eve, and he led her out of his office, past the break room, and into a small storage closet in a hall past the restrooms.

Once inside, Smith checked the ceilings and shelves. "OK, I think we can talk here."

"You sound paranoid, Arnie. What gives?"

"You said you don't get these results? Well, I get them, but I don't want the all-seeing eye of BioStrain to know I do. This is the only place without video or audio equipment installed."

"You mean we're being watched?"

"I was told it was for our own security, but I've been thinking a lot about Tom Foil. He came to me the morning he died and told me that he thought BioStrain had sold us out. He went on and on about some big conspiracy involving our research, how BioStrain is really building the ultimate, selective weapon that could wipe out anyone—whole groups, even—with the touch of a button and make it look like something viral."

Eve leaned against a stack of towels. "He'd been under a lot of strain, Arnie."

"Yeah," Smith laughed scornfully, thinking of his beautiful wife and fighting rising panic. "Too much BioStrain. Six weeks ago, we field-tested a solution that was supposed to be a weakened version of H5N1. You saw the workup."

"Yeah, you'd altered the hemagglutinin gene to make the virus less harmful. The point being to produce an aerosolized vaccine that would protect our troops and maybe even civilians from bioterrorism."

"Sounds really good, doesn't it? It did to me when I signed up. So many people don't want to take flu vaccines, don't like the pain. But if you could aerosolize it, make it user-friendly, everyone would sign up, and you'd eventually eradicate the virus in humans. That's not what happened. Someone took our research and used it to strengthen the virus, then they combined it with Ebola to create something that makes the Spanish Flu look like the sniffles."

"Oh my God! They combined Hong Kong flu with Ebola? Then—then, what happened to Tom wasn't an accident?"

"You're catching on. Who knows what else they've put in that biochip they've sold the president on. I'll bet he doesn't know, either. And I'm beginning to wonder now if Chuck Hilliard's death was accidental. He and Tom worked together at our test site, a little farm ten miles or so from Los Muertos. They found this chicken with a brood. It wasn't supposed to be there! Now, I think it was put there on purpose. What if it's loose? God help us, Eve! What if this thing is loose?"

Martin closed her eyes, her head swimming. "The China team—do you think they know?"

"They must if someone there faxed this to you. Grayson had our team working on the H5N1, so Mel Winston's team must have been working on the Ebola side of the equation. Do you know who faxed this to you?"

"I think Mel did."

"Listen, Eve, don't tell anyone else. Go to our fax machine and see if you can remove the incoming entry in the database. If you can't do it, get Rick—he knows how. He's done it before. I'm going to take Martha and drive to the house for the weekend. I suggest each one of you does the same. I have a cell phone there that's an old one, analog, so it doesn't have GPS. Can't be tracked. Are you starting to understand me?"

Eve nodded. "Maybe we shouldn't say much more. I'll get Rick and Sam Dotson. Pete's taking a nap right now, but I'll nudge him and get him going. Where should we meet?"

Smith thought for a minute. "Los Muertos. It's that little town about thirty minutes north of here. Drive in circles, so Grayson can't guess where we're going, then meet me at Dr. Tohe's office."

"Tohe? You know the doctor? Can we trust him?"

"Tom Foil was close to Tohe's girlfriend, a gal named Pippa Anderson. Meet me at Tohe's clinic," he said, checking his watch, "in twenty-four hours. That'll be just enough time for us to leisurely go to our homes for the weekend, pack, and then drive in different directions, finally meeting up there. Got it?"

Eve nodded, her lower lip quivering. "I've got it. We'd better go back to your office. They'll think we're up to something."

Smith nodded. "You're right. Mess up your hair!"

"Huh?"

"Mess it up, like you've been in a heavy make-out session."

"Make-out session? What the—wait a minute, I know where you're going. OK." She unbuttoned the top button of her light blue blouse, scratched her skin to make it turn red, used her hands to tousle her thick blond hair, then kissed Smith fully on the mouth. "That puts lipstick on your lips. It's more convincing."

Smith blinked and blushed to his ears.

"That color looks good on you, Arnie. Now let's go."

"Good afternoon, Dr. Taylor."

"Have a seat, Major Yarber. Hungry? This place has great food."

Yarber wore a light beige shirt over khakis. He appeared surprisingly casual for a military spy. "Maybe a slice of pie, if they have any. You look surprised, Doctor. Even government men can have a sweet tooth."

Had he smiled just then? Maggie nodded, letting Yarber hail the waiter. "Sorry. The key lime pie is fabulous."

The tall waiter returned. "Ready?"

Yarber looked to Maggie. "Oh, OK," she said, looking at the menu. "I guess I'll have some ice cream and a cup of coffee. Sugar and creamer."

"What kind of ice cream, Dr. Taylor? We have cinnamon, chocolate, peppermint, black walnut, and spumoni."

"Let's see. How about the spumoni? That sounds good."

"Sir?"

Yarber looked up, offering the boy a real smile. "I hear you have key lime pie. I'll try that with coffee. Sugar and cream for me as well."

"Sounds good," the waiter replied, taking the menus. "Back in a few minutes."

Maggie stared. "Gee, Major, was that a smile? I didn't know you DARPA guys had it in you."

"Oh, I'm full of surprises, Dr. Taylor, as are you. I understand you submitted Dr. Meier's prints to the local police for identification. It's nice to see your wits are sharpening."

"My wits have totally abandoned me, Major Yarber. What do you know about Hank Meier? You can save me a lot of digging by telling me. Can I trust him?"

Yarber's blue eyes narrowed. "Don't trust anyone, Dr. Taylor. That's rule number one."

"And rule number two?"

"Refer to rule number one."

"Fine," she said, leaning forward. "So why should I trust you?"

"Because I can keep you alive. And because I represent a large consortium of patriots who want to put a stop to the shadow government. For years, non-elected men and women have been putting on a puppet show we call democracy. Some of us are sick of it. We're tired of taking orders we know hurt America. I can't go into the identity of the puppeteers, but I can assure you that they are very dangerous individuals, and they will stop at nothing to attain their evil ends. Most people assume the President and Congress run the country, but it's not true. These shadow people run it, have for a long time. The President's a good man, but he doesn't see the Truth. His eyes aren't open."

"But yours are?" she asked, feeling like a player in a movie.

"At the cost of a dear friend's life, yeah, they were. I've been afraid to blink ever since. These shadow people are ruthless. The deaths of your father and Dr. Foil are evidence of that."

"So they did kill my father," she whispered tightly. "What can I do to help?"

"Are you still flying to New Mexico tomorrow?"

"You tell me. Am I?" she countered.

"If you're brave enough, we want you to go. I noticed you added a ticket for your husband, Jackson. Good. You'll feel safer with him along, I think. Tell him what I've told you only if necessary. We'll have someone watching you at every moment."

Both stopped talking as the waiter returned and served their desserts and coffee. "You know that presidential speech tonight, Dr. Taylor?"

"Yeah?" Maggie asked.

"They're saying now that it's going to be the most life-changing broadcast in history. Imagine the ratings, huh?" He laughed and returned to the kitchen, leaving Maggie staring at Yarber.

"Government issued vaccinations in the form of the Bio-Strain chip. Is this a shadow government operation, Major?"

Yarber poured two packets of sugar into his coffee along with a slight pour of creamer and began to stir. "Welcome to the other side of the mirror, Alice."

The shaman known as Meektay watched the Cutlass circle the mesa. "Third time around," he said to Ray Bindell. "You know this man?"

Bindell popped another slice of peyote and shook his head. "Man, I don't know anybody who'd drive that piece of junk. Forget about it. It's some lost tourist."

The mystic's eyes followed the car as it slowed to a stop. "A man's getting out. This is a bad sign. I saw a dead owl this morning. Bad sign. Where's Matt Thayer?"

"Chickened out. He's decided to turn back to that Jesus stuff we learned in Sunday school. He's a turncoat, man. You oughta let me slice him open. We could use him for tomorrow night's sacrifice instead of a pig."

Meektay pulled back from the mesa's edge, took up his warm pipe, and began to smoke again. "I think the gods will provide a sacrifice, Ray. We bring the pig by faith, but you never know what prank the gods might play. Bring Matt tomorrow night. Force him to come by threatening his sister. He'll forget all about the Hebrew gods. Of that you can be dead certain."

Maggie arrived at Barney's Café just before seven. Before leaving her apartment, she'd hidden the laptop in a box marked "Christmas Ornaments" inside the storage closet. Satisfied the laptop would be safe for a while, she'd grabbed her tote bag and headed out. Now, as she entered the popular coffee spot, she wondered if meeting Ryder might not be foolishness. *Don't trust anyone. That's rule number one.*

Walking to the counter, she leaned over and called. "Anyone here?"

It took a minute, but a small woman finally appeared, wearing a ballpoint pen behind one ear. "Sorry!" she gasped as if she'd been running. "I didn't hear you."

"That's OK. A large hazelnut with two sugars and a little whipped cream."

"Ordering for me?"

Maggie whirled around, surprised to find Ryder. "Andy! You scared me!"

"I did?" he asked with a big grin. "Sorry. I would never dream of scaring you—not on purpose."

Lisa leaned toward them both, her pen poised on an order form. "Is this together?"

"Yes," Ryder answered, withdrawing a crocodile skin wallet from inside his jacket pocket. "I'll have a large house blend, black."

"OK. Your order will be ready in a minute."

"Come on, let's sit." Ryder motioned to a table. "I'll get the coffees when they're done. You look flushed, Maggedy Ann."

She flinched. She was starting to hate that nickname. "I've had a long day, Andy. The President's speaking tonight, did you hear? Do you mind if we cut this short? I want to be back before eight."

"I won't pretend I'm not disappointed, but I understand. We could watch it together if you like—in my hotel room."

Maggie nearly jumped out of her chair. "I'd better make it a solo event, Andy, sorry. I still have to pack."

"Looks like our coffee's ready," she said, seeing Lisa appear at the counter.

Andy got up to fetch the coffees. "Where's Barney, Lisa? I thought he was usually here in the evening."

The manager shrugged. "Can't say," she said honestly. She knew that Barney and Popeye had left town, but Ison had told her nothing more—for her own protection as well as his. "He might be in later."

"Tell him Ryder stopped by." Andy returned to the table, set the cups down, and sat across from Maggie. "So, is Jackson back in your life?"

She tilted her head and raised an eyebrow. "Now why would you ask me that?"

"I hear Jackson is going to New Mexico with you."

"Who told you that? Doug?"

"No. Hank Meier told me. Remember? The man I sent your way about transferring his daughter Rebecca to IU. He said you and he hit it off. I'm jealous, Maggie. I thought I was the secret love of your life."

"I don't know if I even have a life right now, Andy. Yeah, Meier came by my office to talk about his daughter, and we've spent a little time together. His daughter's a gem, although he wants to recut her facets and make her into his image. She loves him, and she'll probably end up in a career she hates."

"Are you sure you're not talking about yourself?"

She sipped the coffee. "Have you hung out a shingle that I don't know about, Ryder? Besides, you start that analysis bit on me, and I'll give it back in spades. I know you better than anyone. Or do I?"

Ryder smiled. "You know me as well as any human could."

"And don't you forget it," she countered, taking care not to reveal her suspicions. "Anyway, Jackson is flying with me to New Mexico to see—Carol." She'd nearly said Pip. For some reason, she didn't want Ryder to know about Pip. *Rule number two—refer to rule number one.* "I'll be back in a few days. Will you still be around?"

"You'll see me again. I promise."

"Good," she answered, wondering what he really meant. "We have a lot to talk about."

"More than you can ever imagine, Maggedy Ann."

Hank Meier had been sitting by Griffey Lake for over two hours. The small, out-of-the-way spot provided a nice place to think, and he'd been doing plenty of that. He looked at Rebecca's photo, always first in his wallet, and wished he'd made better choices for her and Karen. He should have taken that job in Seattle back before Becka was born. If he had, he felt sure he and Karen would still be married, and Becka would be safe.

Now, he had to choose between doing the safe thing and doing the riskier, more noble thing. Grayson hadn't given him any other alternatives. He could either blow the whistle on BioStrain and take his chances with the Justice Department, or he could play it safe and follow Grayson's orders.

As Grayson's head muscleman, Ryder had given Hank the simple assignment of watching Maggie Taylor for a couple of weeks. Simple. He'd blown it by letting his heart do the watching instead of his brain. Hank knew Grayson intended to force Maggie to work in the New Mexico lab, and he knew the kinds of methods Grayson could employ to do so—fat wads of cash for some, fistfuls of threats for others.

Maggie wouldn't be swayed by offers of riches, so Hank knew Grayson would threaten to harm or kill anyone Maggie loved. That meant Jackson. Hank's dilemma was that part of him would love to see Jackson out of the way, but only part. Thank God, his years of being a yes-man operative for BioStrain and its international band of Illuminati thugs hadn't crushed his soul completely. Just most of it.

As he watched a phalanx of Sandhill cranes flying low over the lake, he realized there might be one more alternative. Opening the glove compartment, he withdrew an MK 23, Special Ops handgun. In his twenty-six years with Grayson and his kind, he'd used the weapon only six times in the field. Twice in self-defense, once to signal a fellow agent, and three times to kill. As he felt the gun's weight in his hand, he considered the ten-round clip and the last alternative. Maybe it was time to kick that kill number up to four.

CHAPTER 28

Barney and Popeye had been on the road since Wednesday night. They'd spent the first night at a truck stop, sleeping in shifts. Then Ison had circled down to North Vernon, turned east, and driven into Ohio, where the pair met a man named Spencer, who gave them camping equipment and a small food supply. Thursday night brought them to a campground, where Popeye learned the fine art of sleeping on the ground.

Come dawn, Barney had prodded his protégé awake with campfire pancakes and strong coffee before packing up and pointing the sedan toward Indianapolis. That was hours ago.

"Hungry?" the tall man asked Bailey.

"A little, I guess. I keep thinking about Hitch. Shouldn't we have called Trick and told him where we're going?"

Ison punched the cigarette lighter. "Not if we want to protect him. What he doesn't know, he can't tell. We can send him an e-mail from the next Starbuck's we pass. I think there's one in Indy. Speedway, maybe. But we're going to have to watch any electronic trail. No paper trail either. It's cash in hand from now on, Pop. We'll take money out in small amounts at different ATMs. Once we're in Michigan, I got a friend who can put us up. I've got money in banks all over the country, in different names with different social security numbers. We'll have enough to live on."

"Maybe," Popeye said. "But after what the shadow government did to Hitch—oh, man, the smell!—you know they're after you. Your face must be plastered all over, Barn. Won't all the police state officers recognize you? Walking into a bank will be like walking into the freakin' FBI!"

The lighter popped out, and Ison picked it up, setting the glowing end to the tip of a cigarette hanging from his lips. "I've got that covered. I'm part of a big network, see? It's the local folks who opened the account. I've just been sending money to them, and they keep part as a thank-you and deposit the remainder. I know it sounds like I'm putting a lot of trust into these men, but they're like brothers. We can depend on them. The war's begun, Pop. And we're on the front lines."

Ison returned the lighter to its position in the dash, just below the CB radio, and pointed the car toward Marion County.

"How long of a drive is it going to be, Arnie?" Martha asked as she handed him the last of her bags. "Do we have time to stop and get something to eat?"

Arnie handed his wife a Snicker's bar. "I bought a box of these when I stopped to fill up the tank. I don't want to take too much from the house, 'cause it will tip them off. We're supposed to be heading to the mountains for a little R & R. Grayson's bonus money was in cash. That will keep us from having to make a large withdrawal. Fifteen thousand in small bills should keep us going for a while."

Martha snapped the seat belt into place and removed her shoes. "Yes, I think it should, but what about the house? What about Florence?"

"Florence will be fine. She thinks we're heading to the mountains, too. If we told her the truth, we might be placing her life in danger."

"Couldn't we have taken the nice car?" she asked, unwrapping the candy bar.

"Not after what happened to Tom Foil. Besides, it'll be kind of nice to drive this old jalopy for a change. I've been working on this baby for ten years, and it runs fine. It just needs a little more spit and polish."

He choked the large steering wheel to the 1950 Ford, a dinosaur of a car with a huge interior and a new engine. "I've kept this under wraps for a long time, and I checked it over before packing. If they planted something in Tom's car to control it, then we can't take a chance by driving the Lexus. Sorry, Martha."

"That's all right, Arnie. I kind of like this car. Remember our first date in it?"

Smith grinned from ear to ear. "Very well," he said, putting an arm around his bride of twenty-four years. "Like it was yesterday."

She leaned over against his shoulder and offered him a bite of the Snicker's. He bit down, tasting paper, and they both laughed.

"We'll be okay," he promised. "I won't let anything happen to you, Martha. Not a thing."

She closed her eyes and gave him the last of the bar. If Arnie said it, then it must be true. Within minutes, she had fallen asleep.

"Good evening, fellow Americans."

"Hurry up! The speech is starting!" Julie called out. Maggie emerged from the tiny kitchenette, holding two large glasses of iced tea.

"Thanks," Julie said as she took the drink. "This is the speech that's gonna change everything, huh?"

Maggie sat down, tucking one foot beneath her body. "Shh."

On the small color television, the President smiled into the cameras. "America is a strong nation, a mighty nation, a nation blessed by God. But we are also a careful, stalwart nation, long accustomed to the diligence required as we tread lightly upon the razor's edge called freedom. Many of you have lost sons or daughters, husbands or wives, fathers or mothers to the battles we now fight to maintain that freedom. Some have been lost in Iraq. Some in Syria. Some in the new front in Iran. But a few have been lost to an enemy we cannot see with naked eyes, an enemy that would steal our breath, our blood, our bounty in a moment, in the blink of an eye. An enemy that science calls influenza.

"As I speak to you tonight, over one hundred thousand animals have already marched to slaughter, all because of this invisible enemy. But now that enemy strikes at our very doors. Our very homes. And it stalks our children. I've been told that the avian influenza strain that reached our shores earlier this year has now mutated, regrouped, as it were, for a new battlefront, and it has gained the capability to infect human beings. China has already suffered the loss of over three hundred men, women, and children—all since April. Even conservative estimates indicate the current rate of infection in that country will result in nearly a million deaths by the year's end."

"America cannot permit this to happen. Not to our neighbors, not to our friends, and certainly not to our loved ones. And so it is that I am announcing the first major event in medicine since Salk's vaccine in the early 1900s. Beginning on Tuesday of next week, the biowar on the influenza virus will launch a major attack—through the tiny point of a needle so small you won't even feel it. I know this for certain, because I received the first inoculation this morning.

"This life-saving vaccine, a monumental achievement in science, will be carried within a microscopic monitoring device called the BioStrain chip. While it sounds like science fiction, I can assure you, it is science fact. This amazing little device will not only protect the recipient from this devastating strain of influenza, it will also automatically update itself and encode a new vaccine each year. But it doesn't stop there. The name BioStrain refers to the straining ability of the chip. Each time your body or my body is infected by a virus, the chip will know it, because it will strain blood proteins in a way that allows them to boost our immune systems, fine-tune them, and enhance them so that no one need ever become sick again. Yes, you heard me correctly. No more flu. No more colds. No viral infections at all. None. The savings in healthcare dollars alone will be enough to feed an African nation for a hundred years. The number of lives that will be saved is inestimable.

"But the amazing BioStrain chip does not stop there. Within its tiny circuits, not much larger than a blood cell, is a transponder that will automatically send a message every five minutes. No longer will a missing child go unfound. Within minutes of a kidnapping, police can locate the child and even identify the kidnapper. My friends, we are entering a new world of safety and peace and health, the likes of which the world has never before known. Initial inoculations will take place in at-risk groups and newborns. Due to limited numbers, the chip will be available only to U.S. citizens. If you are not a citizen, you have one month to identify yourself and undergo procedures for naturalization. I know that this amnesty period for illegals will not make me popular with some, but I believe it is the only humane way to approach this life-changing event. Following the month of amnesty, anyone without the chip must prove citizenship to receive it. I urge you, if you are not a citizen, please take advantage of this one-month door of opportunity, because after that, the door will close for good.

"My fellow Americans, this is the dawn of a new age. Criminal offenders will no longer be able to hide in the shadows. Terrorists will no longer blend in. America, the strong nation with the big heart, opens her arms to embrace those who obey the law, but those same arms will discipline those who break it.

"Tuesday, local FEMA personnel will begin identifying at-risk individuals. When you receive a letter of notification, please respond at once. I did. My family did. I pray you will, too. Let us become all the stronger as we defeat this ravenous predator upon our sacred shores. Thank you, and may God bless America."

Julie Emerson hadn't touched her iced tea. She stared, open-mouthed at Maggie. "What the heck did we just hear? Barney Ison's right, Maggie. It's nothing more than a countdown to Armageddon."

Maggie wanted to answer, but she found her voice gone. Tom Foil had died trying to reach someone with the Truth, her father had died as a spy for the Truth, now she had to fly into the very heart of the Shadow of Lies. She prayed her courage would prove equal to that of her father and Foil.

CHAPTER 29

Saturday

A re you sure Las Cruces has an airport?" Jackson asked as the airliner began its final approach.

"If not, we'll land in a bean field or something," Maggie said, not even looking up. She kept her eyes on the book she'd been reading, *America's Phoenix* by K. C. Adamson. Popeye Bailey had recommended the book as a good place to learn the basics about what Barney called the Shadow Government. Only days before, she would have laughed at such a phrase, but after talking with Yarber and witnessing what she'd seen and heard, Maggie had no doubt an unseen cabal had its collective claw around America's throat.

Jackson kept jabbering. "A bean field? In this place? More like a cactus patch. Is Pip meeting us?"

"Nope. We're renting a car. I want my own wheels. More control."

"Now why doesn't that surprise me?" he asked, looking out the window at the line-etched desert. "It looks almost like those Nazca lines. Maybe that place actually was an airport for aliens!"

"Sit back, goofball." Maggie closed the book and dropped it into her tote bag, on top of the TiBook. "I called Enterprise and set us up with something good on gas. I'm told filling stations can be few and far between around Los Muertos."

"What kind of town is named 'the dead'?" he asked. "No really. Pip must have found something else to keep her there. Maybe this guy Toehead."

"His name's Tohe. T-o-h-e. It's Navajo, I think. Do you plan on acting your age anytime soon?"

"Sorry, Mags. I'm just trying to keep it light. Really, I'm looking forward to seeing Pip. And spending time with you."

That smile of his. It broke through her gloomy mood like a lighthouse beacon in the night. "You make me crazy, you know that?"

"Yeah. And it's nice to hear it again. Oh, looks like we're landing."

Half an hour later, Jackson sat behind the wheel of a champagne-colored 2002 Elantra with Maggie in the passenger seat and a map of the area between them. "Could you grab that map and see how many miles it is to Los Muertos?"

Maggie pulled her hair into a ponytail and checked her lipstick. "Yeah, OK." She took the map and intentionally held it upside down.

Jackson drove a minute. "Well?" he asked, not turning.

"I can't seem to find it," she said in her best ditzy voice.

"What?" Jackson asked, turning at last to see. "You're holding it upside down! No wonder!" he said, half irritated. When she began to laugh, he pulled over to the side of the two-lane road. "Now who's the goofball?" he asked, breaking into a delicious grin.

The two continued to laugh for several minutes, alone in the desert, just the two of them, closer than they'd been for years. "It feels good," she said, wiping a joyful tear. "I've missed this, Jack."

"Me, too. So, what now? Do we have a map that's right-side-up?"

"I'll see," she giggled and turned the map around. "It looks like we have about an hour to drive. Fifty miles or so."

"That works. We have a full tank of gas, we're an hour out of Los Muertos, and we're wearing sunglasses."

"Hit it," she said, her laughter filling the car.

Putting down his right foot, Jackson did just that.

They arrived in Los Muertos by noon, parking off the main street, behind the cantina. As they got out, billows of sandy dust greeted them, blowing into their eyes, noses, and hair.

"Nice place," Jack said as he locked the car. "Where did you say Pip would be?"

"She said to meet her at Tohe's office. Excuse me!" she called to a passing woman.

"Si?" the woman asked.

"Habla Inglés?" she asked.

"Yes, I speak English," the woman said a bit irritated. "This is America. You must be tourists, no?"

"Visitors," Jackson answered. "We're looking for Dr. Tohe's clinic. Could you tell us where it is?"

The woman smiled. *She responds better to a man, of course,* thought Maggie. "Dr. Tohe's office and clinic are two doors down from the cantina. If you walk past the cantina, you'll see the sign on the door. I think the clinic is closed, though."

"Closed? I hope not. We're supposed to meet Dr. Tohe and another friend."

"I don't know. I just know the sign said closed today. You can go knock if you like." She winked at Jackson then walked away.

"Come on, Cassanova," Maggie told him, pulling on his arm. "This way."

They walked past a place called Susie's Cantina, and the smells that came through the screen doors were heavenly. A Pepsi sign had been hand-painted on one of the doors, and Wonder Bread on the other. Half a dozen patrons sat scattered around the tables or at the bar, and Maggie heard what sounded like Louis Armstrong's version of *Mack the Knife.*

"Not the music I'd expect from a southwest cantina," she said to Jackson.

"Maybe not, but I like her taste. We'll have to get to know Susie. Hey, there it is."

They stopped in front of a clapboard house with a bleached-out green door. A small sign read, "Clínica Médic de Los Muertos—Los Muertos Medical Clinic." Beneath this permanent sign a cardboard sign had been hung from a nail. This temporary sign read, "Cerrado Hoy—Closed Today."

"The woman was right."

Maggie ignored Jackson and knocked. "They said we should meet them here."

A moment passed with no answer. Maggie knocked once more and noticed a curtain move slightly in one of the two windows. Seconds later, the door opened, and she saw Pippa Anderson's tall figure, strawberry blond hair in pigtails, and a broad smile on her handsome face.

"My darling friends!" Pippa exclaimed, hugging them both and bringing them inside. "Come in! I'm so sorry if you thought we weren't here. We had to close to conduct two autopsies. Daniel's in the back now. We didn't want any of the townsfolk to come in while we were doing them. They're very superstitious about cutting into bodies. Come on back with me. You're not squeamish, are you, Jackson?"

"Who me? Nah. Watch Mags, though. She's likely to start grading Daniel on his performance."

"Very funny," Maggie scolded. "Is it all right with Daniel if we observe?"

"Sure," Pippa said, leading them through a door marked "Private" and into a cramped operating room.

"Hey there!" Daniel said over top a tiny body. "I'm just starting. I'd welcome your opinion, Maggie. Jackson, I hear you're more an internist, but feel free to help. It's a little cramped. The low budget life of a desert doctor."

Jackson took a cursory look at the patient, a slight girl of about three years. Her brown skin had paled in death, and she had a chalky appearance, but her hands and face were marred with large gashes and purple mottling.

"Cyanosis? Heart attack or poison maybe?" Jackson asked.

"She did have a history of congenital heart problems, but it could also be poison," Tohe answered, reaching for a scalpel. "Apparently, her baby brother died a few days before. The mother fell ill, too, from what we know, but the family has disappeared, which doesn't make any sense to me. Rosita, that's the mother, used to help in the clinic, and she'd talked about attending school to become a medical assistant. Very bright but dirt poor. Her husband is an illegal, so it's likely he feared an investigation. After that speech the President made last night, he's probably halfway into Mexico by now. The kids here were buried in the yard near the family's trailer. Good thing we got to them when we did. From the wounds, it looks like the vultures found them before we did."

Though a hardened medical man when it came to diagnosis and treatment, Jackson had never really cared for pathology, so he begged off. Pippa left, too, suggesting she take Jack to Tohe's adobe home about a mile outside of town.

"Guess Jack's not into puzzles, huh?" Tohe said with a grin. "Here, Maggie, you better put on this mask and gloves. I don't want to take any chances."

Maggie donned a surgical mask and snapped on latex gloves while Daniel began the initial Y incision. "Most docs don't really like autopsies. I didn't at first, but you get used to it. To me, it's the least you can do for the dead. You know, figure out what or who killed them."

"That's why I always wanted to go into forensics," Maggie explained as she watched Tohe's work. "Nicely done," she said, clearly admiring his technique. "So, what do you suspect?"

"Truthfully, I don't want to see what I expect, but I'm afraid I will. I met with the head of the CDC recently about a new virus that we're supposed to watch out for. It has a virulence rate of fifty percent."

"Did you say fifty? Daniel, you didn't mean fifty."

"That's what he said. But flu's spread by sneezing, so we should be safe."

Maggie's face grew pale. "Daniel, close up. Close her up now!"

"What do you mean?" Tohe asked.

"Close her up! Close her up now! Wrap the body in plastic and ice to preserve the tissue then call the CDC. The same with the other one. Come on!"

Tohe considered arguing, but she had the mad look of extreme determination in her eyes, so he closed up the incision and wrapped the body as Maggie had told him to do.

After they finished storing the bodies on ice, Tohe dialed the number he'd been given at the conference for the CDC.

"Special Operations," a man answered.

"I may have reached the wrong number. This is Dr. Daniel Tohe calling from Los Muertos, New Mexico. I was given this number at a CDC conference."

A pause. Then Daniel could hear whispers.

"Of course," the voice said at last. "Sorry for any misunderstanding. I'm new, and I wasn't aware that our line would be used as a hotline. Do you have an outbreak to report?"

Tohe sighed. "I'm not sure," he said, looking at Maggie. "We have as many as four dead from something that works very fast. I have a colleague here who was helping me with an autopsy when she realized we might be dealing with a totally new virus."

"One that spreads through any fluid, alive or dead," Maggie whispered as she scrubbed up with alcohol.

"You're kidding!" he gasped. "Blood-borne?"

"Dr. Tohe?" the man's voice called from the phone.

"Sorry, uh, we may have a new virus—a very bad one."

"Have you already begun the autopsy, Dr. Tohe?"

"Just the initial Y incision. We've covered the bodies and put them in a separate room—on ice, of course, but they can't last long."

"That's fine. You and the other doctor need to shower and burn the clothes you are wearing. No one is to leave or enter Los Muertos until we approve. Do you understand? By the way, is the doctor you mentioned Dr. Maggie Taylor?"

Tohe stared at the phone. "Yes, how did you know?"

"We were informed that she would be flying to New Mexico. She is an expert cellular pathologist. Please, ask her to remain there. We will send a team out there at once. We'll call you as soon as we have an ETA. Where can we reach you in about an hour?"

Daniel gave the man his home telephone number. "Call me anytime. And thank you."

"Thank you for calling. You did the right thing. Goodbye, Dr. Tohe."

The connection closed, and Daniel hung up the receiver. "They'll call me at home once they know exactly when the team will arrive. Right now, you and I have to shower and burn our clothes."

Maggie didn't seem the least bit surprised. She reached into her handbag and found her cell. In minutes, she'd dialed Jack to ask him to bring her suitcase.

"Why?" Jackson asked. "Are we leaving already?"

"No," Maggie answered tensely. "Just get here. I need a change of clothes. Ask Pip to bring a change for Daniel. He and I may have been exposed to a virus, so we'll need to wash down with disinfectant and burn our clothes."

"Maggie, what is going on?" Tohe asked once she'd hung up. "What do you know that I don't?"

Maggie's face grew dark. She would have to tell Jack everything, which would put him in danger, too. Tensely, she whispered, "Something that will scare you to death, if this exposure doesn't do the trick first."

An hour later, Maggie, Daniel, Pippa, and Jackson had all scrubbed and burned the clothes they'd been wearing in the clinic. The foursome now waited for the CDC's call in the cool interior of Daniel's two-hundred-year old adobe home. Walls a foot thick surrounded the structure, and the sloping shapes of the rooms kept the ambient temperature near seventy degrees year round. At one corner of the living room, an arched brick fireplace stood proudly as the center of attention. Navajo and Hopi art decorated the walls, and an old Bible rested on a large teak pedestal, the pages open to Psalm 22.

"That was my mother's favorite psalm," Daniel explained as he finished the tour. "She loved to read about Christ's suffering because she said we all must remember every day how much He sacrificed for mankind. She must have read that to me a thousand times. God rest her sweet soul."

Jackson put a hand on Tohe's shoulder. "I had a mom like that. One in a million. It's nice to know she had a sister out here."

Maggie and Pippa came out of the kitchen, one with a tray of iced tea in tall glasses, the other with a platter filled with Swedish spritz cookies.

"I know these aren't Mexican or Indian," Pippa said as she set them on the coffee table, "but I like making them. Norwegians always get to choose dessert."

Daniel rubbed his hands and eagerly helped himself. "Pippa makes the best cookies, but wait until you taste her apple cake. She's going to make one tomorrow night, I think."

"I'm not sure Maggie wants to talk about dessert right now, Daniel. You said on the phone this morning that we needed to talk about more than just Tommy's death," Pippa said. "Did you mean your dad's death as well?"

"That's part of it," Maggie said, leaning back against the plump couch cushions. Jackson sat next to her and sipped his tea.

"This has something to do with this new virus the CDC is investigating. And I'll bet it's connected to the chip the President mentioned in the speech, right?" asked Daniel. He wiped cookie crumbs from his hands and took a sip of tea. "You knew about it before I even mentioned it. That's why you panicked about the bodies."

Maggie nodded, ignoring Jackson's odd expression. "I knew a virus had been manufactured. I didn't know the CDC was aware of its real nature."

"Hold on!" Jackson said at last. "Start from the beginning, please! Some of us aren't up to speed!"

Maggie nodded. "Fair enough. To my knowledge, it all started when Dad and Uncle Tommy joined up with an insidious little company called BioStrain."

Arnie Smith had been driving in circles for nearly seven hours, and he needed rest. "Mind if I pull into this motel and sleep for an hour or two, Martha?"

His wife had spent most of the trip dozing, and she looked up sleepily. "Huh? What time is it?"

"Nearly noon. We're not supposed to meet up in Los Muertos until four this afternoon."

"I could drive, Arnie. It's a flat road, and I don't mind driving in the daytime."

Smith touched her auburn hair, delighting in the silky texture as it slipped through his fingers. "I know you could, Mart, but you still look tired."

Her eyes had a dark look, especially beneath the lids. "Yeah, pretty tired. I don't know why."

"Well, I suppose we could arrive early and wait for the others at Dr. Tohe's place. No reason why we all have to pull into town at the same time."

Martha shifted in the wide leather seat. "These springs could use an update. It seems to me that it's better everyone doesn't get there at the same time. Don't you think so, Arnie?"

"I do. Los Muertos is less than an hour from where we are now. We'll head right for it. Go back to sleep, Sweetheart. I'll wake you when we get there."

As she put her head down, her left hand slipped next to his, and he reached down for it, bringing the slender fingers to his lips for a soft kiss. As he did so, he noticed something odd about Martha's nails. The nail beds had the slightest tinge of blue. Quickly, Arnie glanced at the other hand and found the same light blue hue showing beneath the clear polish. He leaned over to check her face, and her lips still showed pink, but Arnie knew he had but a short time to get her to Tohe's. Despite his precautions, the company must have discovered his treason and found a way to punish him—through his beloved wife.

Scientist Eve Martin lit a cigarette and smiled. "Two more hours," she said, running her fingers through Grayson's thick, platinum hair. "Although I'd bet at least one of them shows up early. Possibly Arnie."

Grayson stretched out on a long, velvet chaise and stared at the ceiling tiles of the bunker suite he used for his trysts with Eve. "You're sure he doesn't know you work for me?"

"Not the slightest hint. He's a typical scientist. He sees the data, but he can't add it up without a push."

"Good," he said, reaching for her shoulders and pulling her down for a kiss. "You've done well, my dear. And you'll be suitably rewarded."

Eve pushed away from Grayson and sat on the edge of the chaise. "I suppose I'd better be going soon, if I'm to make it to Los Muertos in time to meet the others. I need to ride out this charade to the last."

Grayson sat up beside her, swinging his long, muscular legs onto a silk Persian carpet that covered the concrete floor. "You deserve so much more than this hole in the ground."

She smiled and took a bobby pin to fix her mussed hair. "Oh, I plan on having much more. Diamonds would be nice for a start."

"A petty imagination," he whispered, kissing her ear. "Think much bigger than diamonds."

She turned to face him, her eyes bright. "How much bigger?"

"As big as the world, my dear. For that is what I shall control once the BioStrain chip has been implanted in every being on this planet. Then all shall bow to me, or they will die. Nice, huh?"

"Very nice," she cooed, tickling his ear with her long nails. "And where do I fit in?"

"I'll show you," he whispered. "Watch and learn."

Grayson left the chaise and walked to a large, glass-topped desk on the other side of the room, opposite the door. He opened the middle drawer and reached inside. "This will amaze you," he told her, lifting a small metallic box from the open drawer. "See this? It's my magic wand. It makes me a king! A great wizard! Master of the Fates! *And the Angel of Death!*"

Eve jumped up, adjusted an earring, and laughed. "Oh, my! And what does this wondrous box do, my deadly angel?"

Grayson's cold eyes fixed upon her, and he grinned, showing gleaming white teeth. "It destroys," he said simply and pressed the button.

Eve cocked her head, puzzled by his cryptic response. "Destroys? Destroys what?"

"Not what, my dear. Whom."

"Whom?" she asked, still failing to grasp her fate. "I don't know what you mean. I—uh—what's happening—to—me?"

Eve's eyes blurred as the blood vessel walls in her body began to disintegrate. The microscopic chip that Grayson had implanted during Eve's initial health check and vaccinations for working with BioStrain hummed as it released an encoded, recombinant viral blend into her bloodstream. In just minutes, her lungs filled with blood, which then congealed due to an added ingredient even the China team knew nothing about.

"Grayson!" she choked as blood began to ooze between her white teeth. "Not me! Not—no, not...!"

"Yes, you, my dear. I had to test it, you know, to verify that it works. Your microchip contained the fast-acting version of the virus. I'm pleased to see it surpasses even my expectations. Now, Arnold Smith's dear wife? Well, we implanted the slower acting viral mix in her chip. Just in the interest of research. I activated that chip about an hour ago, which, oh let's see, should give her another twenty minutes at the latest."

"Ant...ti...dote?"

"Antidote?" he repeated, laughing. "Don't be silly! Of course I wouldn't make an antidote! However, there is a vaccine. But then you would have needed to take that at least a month before I pressed my little button. Sorry."

He leaned over and gave her a light kiss. Horrified, Eve reached up to attack his face with her nails, but she lost her balance and fell at his feet. Grayson watched stoicly as spasms shook her body like a leaf in a great wind, and purple blood foamed from her silent mouth.

"I am sorry, you know," he said, knowing she was dead. "Oh dear. I shall need to replace this carpet. Ciao, darling. I've much more to do in the next week or so. For starters, I'm meeting with the President next week to receive a commendation for my brilliant research. On Tuesday, the first production lines will form, injecting my little creation into human after stupid human. Of course, the unsuspecting cattle that call themselves citizens will never realize they're being injected with their own personal time bombs. Fitting, don't you think?"

Blood covered her blond hair and blouse, and her hands and lips had turned a hideous purple.

"Dear me, Eve. You've certainly looked better. Purple is just not your color. Tsk. Tsk."

Delighted with his sick joke, Grayson left the suite and headed toward his office on Level Seven, where a large control center gave him access to anyone in the world via GPS tracking. He whistled a nonsensical tune as he entered the hidden car that would take him to his private level. Time to give the scientists in China their bonuses.

CHAPTER 30

Maggie took a breath. She'd been talking nonstop for nearly an hour, trying to remember every detail of the past week and how those events added up to a shocking plan to control every person in the country, if not in the entire world.

"Where's the laptop?" Pippa asked as Maggie finished. "You did bring it with you, right?"

"It's in my carry-on bag. I'll get it." It took a minute, but Maggie soon returned with the black tote bag. Reaching inside, she retrieved the silver TiBook and opened it on the coffee table.

"This yellow note is the one I told you about, the one Tommy put on here to direct me to the Entourage program." She clicked the Entourage icon, and in a moment, everyone could see the unencrypted message regarding BioStrain's plans.

Pippa took Tohe's hand to calm her shaking. "This is terrible! Good heavens, the President has that chip! Can this Illuminati group really do this to us? Where are the laws?"

"Laws have been changing for years now," Jackson said, standing and walking to the fireplace. "I haven't said much to Maggie before about this. Truthfully, Mags, I was afraid to tell you what I believed. You've been pretty fragile since…since Charlie's…accident."

Maggie looked him squarely in the face. "You can say it, Jackson. Charlie's death. She's dead. Just like Dad and Tommy. It's taken me five years to face that reality. But I realized that if I don't face her death, I won't be able to live," she said. "So what have you believed that you didn't tell me about?"

Pippa refilled Jack's glass while he told of an old conversation he'd had one Christmas with Charles Hilliard.

Don Yarber had been watching Meier since Friday. Although he'd only been with the DSO for a year, he'd honed his skills in Iraq as a member of the elite counterterrorist group, SEAL Team 6. Yarber's unique abilities hadn't gone unnoticed, and he'd received a commendation and a job offer two days after his tour of duty had ended.

As he sat now in the last seat of a Southwest airline first class section, his eyes never left Meier, who sat two seats ahead. Considering what Yarber had learned about Meier's close connections with BioStrain and his sudden, rather intense relationship with Maggie Taylor, the major figured Hank had been assigned to co-opt Maggie to join BioStrain or to kill her if she learned too much.

What Yarber hadn't yet figured out was the relationship between Meier and Andy Ryder. Ryder, a former Justice Department operative, had suddenly and without explanation switched to the CIA the year Charles Hilliard had joined BioStrain. Ryder's friendship with Hilliard reached back to Maggie's childhood, and it was a bond that could either be treated with caution or used to their advantage.

Yarber's predecessor had chosen to exploit the relationship by keeping Ryder on a short leash. Ryder followed Hilliard, and the DSO followed Ryder. As time passed, and more and more of his colleagues died or disappeared, Hilliard came to realize how dangerous Ryder had become, that little Andy Pandy Ryder, his daughter's childhood friend, had changed from a loveable panda into a ravenous wolf and couldn't be trusted.

That's when the DSO had stepped in and asked Hilliard to spy on Maggie's old beau, a decision that had most likely gotten the aging scientist killed.

"Nice work on that crossword," the attendant remarked as she passed by Yarber. "I never can do that one. Too tough. Can I get you anything?"

Yarber tucked the number two pencil behind his ear and shook his head. "No thanks, ma'am. I'm just fine."

"OK, but if you need anything, Major, I'm only a call away. And I just want to tell you how much your sacrifice means to all of us. Captain Green and Cocaptain Roberts both served in Vietnam, and I worked as a nurse in the first Iraq War. We saw you come on board, and we just wanted you to know that you're appreciated."

Yarber blushed, an affectation but effective nonetheless. He'd learned to fake humility and put on southern charm whenever necessary. Most people, even seasoned operatives like Meier, found it easier to trust a man with a thick drawl. Once they landed in New Mexico, Yarber planned to put it on good and thick.

Barney and Popeye had stayed overnight in Speedway before leaving just after dawn for Michigan. They arrived at a small farmhouse north of Lansing on Saturday morning, too late for breakfast and too early for lunch. Both men needed a break from sitting and were thrilled to see a friendly face at the farmhouse door.

"Is that you?" called a petite woman from the doorway. "Barney Ison? Shucks, it is you! We got Keller's message that you'd left Speedway this mornin'. Come on in! This must be the fella that Keller mentioned."

Pop lagged several steps behind his friend and mentor, struggling to keep up with Ison's long legs.

"How ya' doin', Edna!" Ison said, picking up the small woman and giving her a bear hug. "I don't suppose you have any pancakes?"

"I will in ten minutes! You two come in and take a load off. Tank'll be here in less than the time it'll take you to eat. He's at the bank in town. Oh, and we got a car for you to drive. Leave that one here, and we'll send it to a guy we know to give it a new look. There's two empty rooms upstairs if you need to rest. Come on in, Bluto!"

"It's Popeye, ma'am," Bailey said, nearly falling through the doorway.

"Sorry. Ain't good with names. Popeye. I'll try an' remember it. That your real name, son?"

"It's good enough."

Barney slapped Bailey on the back and laughed. "His real name's Theodore, but he loved spinach so much as a kid, everybody started calling him Popeye."

"Is that so? Well, it's a good story, but I think I'd like Ted better. Sit on down, boys. I'll get you some coffee."

"Do you have any Mountain Dew?" Bailey asked as they slouched into a pair of kitchen chairs.

"Why would I have that?" she asked soberly. Seeing Popeye's face, she broke into a smile. "Just kidding! Keller sent us a list of your favorite foods and the like by e-mail. We got a couple of cases out in the milk fridge. I'll get a cold one for ya', son. Here are some cookies to tide you over 'til I flap those jacks."

Following a farmhouse breakfast, Barney huddled with Tank Jones, Edna's husband, about the next stop on the Freedom Route, as he and the other members of the Alliance called it. Tank, a Vietnam veteran with a hook on his left arm, scribbled with his right as he explained the plan to Barney and Popeye.

"Pop, I understand you're kind of new to the Alliance, so I'm going to explain some things that Barney here already knows. First of all, we believe the government has all but locked the door on our cells. We believe you can't retain a freedom you no longer have, so we fight to regain the freedoms we've already lost. We work in small groups. Each one of us puts his life in the hands of the rest. Me and Edna and one other guy I won't name are all members of one local group. Each group consists of three people. We know about Keller in Indy, and we know about Larson, the guy I'm sending you to in Wisconsin. He knows about me and the next one, and so on. Get it?"

Popeye nodded.

"Barney, I reckon you ought to see what's been posted to the website from New Mexico."

"What's that?" the radioman asked, patting a stomach filled with twelve pancakes.

"Another dead scientist. Eve Martin, a statistician and biologist. Can you guess who she worked for?"

Barney nodded. "BioStrain."

"Bingo. You heard the President's speech, I suppose?"

"On the radio, yeah. It's no surprise to us, is it, Tank? It goes without saying that no one in the Alliance will take this chip—this Mark."

"You got that right, brother," Tank said, lifting a small gold cross from the inside of his shirt. "If it means we die, then we die. To live is Christ, to die is gain."

236

"Amen, brother. Tank, we can't stay too long. The last days are in the wings, and me and Pop have to find a temporary bunker I can broadcast from."

Tank thought for a moment. "I may have just the thing you need, Barn. If I told you I knew of an old motor home that's been refitted to serve as a mobile radio station, would you be interested?"

Ison looked at Pop, eyes wide. "I'd be more than interested, Tank. I'd say where and how much?"

Tank Jones glanced at Edna and nodded. "It's in a Quonset hut on my granddad's old farm, 'bout fifty miles from here. Granddad's hobby was shortwave, so he rigged up his Winnebago so he could stay in touch on the road. I can give you the keys and a map. Won't cost you a dime."

CHAPTER 31

Maggie," Jackson began, "your dad loved you more than you will ever know, but he couldn't always show it the way you wanted him to. You and I had been married for three years, and we visited your mom for Christmas and to celebrate our anniversary. The day after Christmas, we visited your dad over at Doug's place. Chuck was in town for just a few days, but he'd come all the way out to see you and Doug."

"I remember," Maggie said, her face sad with memories.

"This would have been '84. That was the year everyone expected the government to take over, like in Orwell's book, *1984,* but none of it happened."

"Yeah!" Pippa said, sitting next to Daniel. "The biggest thing to happen that year was the new Mac computer. Brilliant commercial."

"I didn't think you watched television," Daniel complained, pinching her lightly.

Pippa giggled and tapped him on the head. "I did back then, silly. Everybody did. But now television is nothing more than a steady stream of sex, violence, and bad jokes."

"And that's just the news," Maggie chimed in gloomily, catching Jackson's winking eye and finally smiling.

"Not much of a year, or so we thought. What I didn't tell anyone is that Maggie's dad told me some stuff that turned my blood cold. Chuck worked with the Defense Department then, stationed in White Sands. We figured he must have something to do with defensive biological warfare. That night, Chuck told me about something he referred to as Project Armageddon."

"Ooh! Biblical!" Maggie said. "Are four horsemen coming next?"

"Don't laugh, Maggie," Tohe said soberly. "The prophecies in the Bible are true. There is a day coming, and soon, when those horsemen will ride and bring war, famine, pestilence, and death."

Jackson nodded. "And then the tribulation will come to shake the world, and the men of the earth will wage war against Jesus Christ, but they'll be doomed to lose before they even suit up. Jesus will speak and all the armies will fall dead."

Pippa looked, and her eyes shone with joy. "You're a believer! Jackson, that's wonderful!"

"Good to know you're a brother, man," Daniel said, standing up momentarily to shake Taylor's hand.

Maggie said nothing, just sank more deeply into the couch, making herself smaller, hoping they wouldn't put her on the spot.

Jackson continued. "It is good to find a brother and a sister. The truth is, I only became a Christian last year. It took that long for all that Chuck had said to mix with what I'd begun to read in the Bible and finally start to make sense. I've spent most of my life warming a church pew in one place or another, but it only made sense to me recently. I guess I was slow on the uptake."

"Better slow than never," Daniel said.

"Yeah. Well, like I said, Maggie's dad told me about this Project Armageddon, which centered around a hypothetical nanochip, so small that it could be implanted through a hypodermic needle. This theoretical biochip would carry the person's financial, medical, and civic information. Plus— and this would be the real reason people would accept the chip—the tiny processor would be able to verify and catalog all the naturally occurring messenger RNA in the body and report on any new strands discovered. A new strand would indicate a viral contaminant, which would send a signal to a central location that the carrier needed to be isolated until his or her health could be assessed. I know that's not exactly what BioStrain's created, but it's close. In fact, I'd say the chip Grayson has foisted upon America is far worse than Chuck had ever imagined.

"Anyway, back then, the Macintosh was all the rage, and the processor size was huge and slow as a turtle compared to today's machines. I couldn't dream then that anyone could ever shrink a chip down to less than twenty microns, but nanotech-nology has already achieved that. We read about it all the time in medical journals. Nanomedicine is the wave of the future now, but back then it sounded like science fiction.

"Even though I didn't completely believe Chuck, the thought of health-tracking sounded like a great idea at the time, and I told him as much. Chuck shook his head and said he'd begun to doubt the wisdom of such technology. He'd con-sidered the possible misuses of such knowledge. He told me how knowledge had been the very first temptation in Eden, and that it remains the greatest temptation today. That's why we became scientists, especially you, Mags. We're curious. We want to know more. Satan promised secret knowledge, and Eve fell for it. And she died for it—first spiritually, then physi-cally, and Adam did, too, because he also fell into the devil's temptation."

The phone rang, and Daniel left to answer it. Pippa moved closer to Maggie and took her friend's hand. "You okay?"

"Yeah, why wouldn't I be? My dad worked for some secret government types who want to bring us closer to Armageddon, and my husband has gone off the deep end. I'm just great."

"Sorry you think I'm nuts, Mags, but it is nice to hear you call me your husband again."

She looked up, her eyes softer but still full of questions. "Maybe it's nice to say it, too."

"That was the CDC calling back," Daniel said as he returned to the living room. "They want both bodies, and they want the Ibanez family, if we can find them. I called Sheriff Down right after I hung up with the CDC. He's not the most cooperative official I've ever met, but he's promised to check out their relatives in Mexico. It's a start, I guess."

"Mexico? Is the CDC going to contact the World Health Organization and the Mexican government? They should know they may have a possible epidemic on their hands."

"Dr. Grover—he's the team leader—assured me that all the formalities would be taken care of on their end. He said he and the team will arrive here around midnight."

"Midnight?" Pippa said, her eyes wide. "Is it so contagious that they'd come in the middle of the night?"

"Apparently so. And from what I read in Tommy's note, this is a viral cocktail that could decimate the world population if left unchecked." Daniel sat next to Pippa, and then remembered one other detail. "I forgot to tell you this, Maggie, but the man I originally spoke with seemed to know you were here."

"That's odd," Pippa said. "How would the CDC know your travel plans?"

Maggie thought about Yarber, and how he'd told her she'd be followed at all times. "My government shadow must have alerted them."

"Shadow?" Jackson asked. "What are you talking about?"

"Major DARPA. One of the last things he told me was I'd be followed—protected, he said. So watch your steps, everyone. We're being tailed." She laughed, but stopped abruptly when no one cracked a smile.

Jackson shook his head. "No, it's more than that. Something about this is way off. Don't you feel it? Why would the CDC rush out here to see two bodies that might have died from an unknown and virulent strain of influenza, as they're calling it? Why wouldn't they ask you to send samples or, for goodness' sake, autopsy the bodies under controlled conditions yourself, say transport them to Las Cruces by ambulance?"

"Good questions, Cowboy," Maggie said, standing and stretching. "But I'm going to need more than a few cookies and iced tea to find an answer. I'm starved! Pip, why don't we bag the kitchen and head to that cantina in town?"

"That's a good idea. After that, I need to go back to my trailer and pick up some more clothes," Pippa said. "If we're going to start burning everything, then I'll need a bigger wardrobe."

Within fifteen minutes, the four friends had claimed a corner booth at Susie's, menus in hand.

"What's good?" Maggie asked, her stomach screaming for food.

"Everything," Pippa said. "Try the steak sandwich. It comes on a big tortilla, and she puts homemade chipotle sauce on it with onions, peppers, and mayonnaise."

"What?"

"Yeah, she loves mayo, puts it in almost everything. She adds peanut butter a lot, too. Susie's father is from Minnesota. Susie was born there, in fact, so her dishes are sort of mixed up. She makes a dynamite cold fruit soup. I gave her the recipe. You should try it! Nothing beats it on a hot day."

"When isn't it a hot day here?" Maggie asked, fanning herself with a menu. "Hey, what's going on out there?"

Pippa and Daniel turned around so they could see the street. Outside, a car had barreled into town, struck a light post, and was lurching forward, wheels spinning.

"What does that driver think he's doing?" Jackson asked.

Daniel put on his hat and headed for the door. "Some drunk kid, I'd say. Susie! I'm going to get Warren!"

The others followed Tohe out the screen doors, where the day's heat blasted their faces. The car, an old black Ford, had finally stopped in the middle of the street.

"Stupid kids!" Daniel was saying under his breath as he approached the car, but he stopped as soon as he could see inside.

"Oh my God! It's a man and a woman, and they look injured! Jackson, get the driver!"

Tohe pulled open the passenger door and began examining the woman while Jackson ran to the other side to help the unconscious driver.

"He's in bad shape, but alive!" Jackson called, checking for bleeding.

Tohe rose up and removed his hat. "I wish I could say the same for his wife, my friend. She's dead."

Don Yarber knew how to blend in when he needed to. Once he'd landed in Las Cruces, the former SEAL rented a hotel room under a false ID, Major Harold Langley, paying for a week in advance in cash. Inside the hotel room, he shaved his moustache, gelled his hair, and put in brown contact lenses. He then exchanged his military uniform for faded jeans, a Hawaiian shirt, and a baseball cap. He slung a Nikon camera around his neck, tucked a local newspaper underneath one arm, and left.

In this tourist garb, Yarber rented a small sedan from a local dealer, again using a fake ID, this time in the name of Jeff Michaels. As Michaels, he checked into a different hotel, this one much more upscale. He used a credit card with the alias and told the assistant that he'd be staying for a week, sightseeing.

By Saturday afternoon, the new, altered Yarber roamed the streets of Las Cruces as Jeff Michaels, but his casual demeanor belied his real activity: following Hank Meier. As he sat in the rented car, the major watched a tiny screen on what appeared to be a cell phone. A curious passerby would think him a harmless yuppie tourist playing a game on a PDA phone when, in actuality, his artificially colored brown eyes were watching the blip, blip of Meier as he drove through Las Cruces and into the desert.

Satisfied that he knew Meier's destination, Yarber set the tracking device monitor on the passenger side and started up the engine. Pulling into traffic, he aimed the car for the source of the blip—a low mesa just south of Los Muertos.

"Martha? What about—uh—Martha?" the man asked. His eyes watered endlessly, but his mouth cracked from dryness. "Martha?" he croaked.

"He's losing fluids fast," Tohe said as he and Jackson helped the man onto an examination table in the clinic. "This can't be simple dehydration. Look at his eyes. See the cloudy corneas. And there's massive contusion in the conjunctiva. He's bleeding internally."

"Mar-tha."

Maggie ran up, a dark blue handbag in her hands. She held up a driver's license. "The woman's name is Martha Smith. The next of kin on her insurance card is Arnold Smith. My dad used to work with a Dr. Arnold Smith, Daniel! Ask him—sir, sir!" she screamed, rushing to the man's side. "Are you Dr. Smith? Are you from BioStrain?"

Smith's eyes grew round, and he began to shake all over. "B-Bio-St-Strain. Y-yes. Smith. Y-yes. V-virus. Tri-triggered. Ch-chip."

"Chip? Did you say chip? A microchip? In your blood?"

He nodded furiously. His eyes rolled into his head, and he passed out.

"He's barely holding on," Jackson announced. He'd been listening to Smith's heart, which alternately hammered and slugged. "He doesn't have much time. His lungs are already taking on fluid. If this is the viral cocktail Foil wrote about, then this man's vascular integrity is breaking down. He's going to bleed to death, and we can't stop it!"

"Why isn't it working as quickly on him as it did on his wife? Could their chips have been triggered at different times?"

"Maybe, but I don't think her death was this violent. She didn't bleed out. This is madness. What did these men do?"

"He's awake again!" Pippa called. "Dr. Smith?"

Smith tried to sit, but spasms racked his lungs.

"Don't try to talk," she said.

Maggie pushed in. "No, Pip, we need him to talk! Dr. Smith! Were you trying to get out? Is that why they triggered your chip?"

He nodded, a weak but clear shake of his head.

"Dr. Smith, we want to expose this. I'm Maggie Taylor. I'm Charles Hilliard's daughter. Tommy Foil was my godfather."

Smith's hand came up to Maggie's face. His nails had turned a dark purple. He gasped for air. "Da-ta. My c-case. All there. Pass-password is Ar-ma-geddon."

"Dr. Smith?" Maggie asked, taking his hand. "Doctor?"

The hand relaxed, and a foamy blood oozed from Smith's lifeless mouth.

"Everybody in the shower!" Tohe ordered. "Wrap these bodies! Put them on ice and shower! Burn your clothes! Pippa, call Warren Down! Tell him to keep everyone away from that car!"

CHAPTER 32

Hank Meier checked his map. He'd only been to the desert lab once, but he felt sure he could remember it when he saw it. He'd stopped his rental car in the middle of the highway, about forty-five miles outside of Las Cruces. It looked familiar, but he couldn't be sure which mesa disguised the entrance. He held up the hand-drawn map, comparing the features to the landscape.

Three mesas stood ahead, majestic guardians of a living desert, dotted with desert primrose, Mexican poppies, chicory, and desert lily. Meier's dark eyes skipped over the watercolor beauty of the wildflowers—he had no time to appreciate such glories now. He had to reach BioStrain before Maggie found it. He had to kill Rex Grayson.

"Hey, Meektay! What you think, huh?"

The tall, muscular shaman sized up the old, black Ford that sat, doors open, in the middle of Main Street. "Looks like trouble," he said at last. "Blood. Don't touch it. It's not clean."

"Good idea, Meektay," Sheriff Down said as he swaggered to the accident scene. "No one's to touch the car. The two who came in it are now dead. Unless you and these boys are anxious to join them, you'd better go on home."

"This is a sign," Meektay announced. "We have angered the gods of our ancestors. Blood requires blood."

"And just what does that mean?" asked Down's deputy, a toady fellow named Mitch Kean.

"It means more will die," the religious leader said simply and then faced the setting sun and spread his arms to the heavens. "Tonight, I will ask the gods to cleanse those who believe. At midnight. On the mesa."

"Not without a permit, you're not!" Kean said, stepping toward Meektay.

Down grabbed the zealous deputy by the arm. "Back off, Kean. If someone's foolish enough to go up there and dance around some chicken blood, let him. It's not our job to police religion. Come on, we gotta button up this area."

Reluctantly, the deputy helped Down throw a tarp over the car and tape off the area around it. As they finished, a dark blue sedan pulled into town and slowed, finally parking just behind the covered auto.

"You can't park there!" Kean called, waving his arms in the air. "It's a restricted area!"

Both doors opened on the car, and two men exited, one large, one thin. "Dang," Kean said to Down. "Looks like we got Laurel and Hardy here."

"We get that a lot," Rick Albertson said good-naturedly, extending his hand to Down. "Contrary to popular opinion, though, I'm not Oliver Hardy, but Rick Albertson. Laurel over here is actually Pete Wilder. We're supposed to meet a colleague here. What's going on?"

"I'm Sheriff Warren Down, and this here's my deputy, Mitch Kean. Sorry about the Laurel and Hardy remark. I hope your colleague wasn't in this car. Both of them are dead."

Wilder shot Albertson a dark look. "A man and a woman?"

"Sure enough. The bodies are inside the clinic there."

"Thanks, Sheriff. Is it okay if we go in and see?" Wilder asked.

"Sure. Dr. Tohe can help you. Just move your car, if you don't mind. We need to keep this area secure," Down finished, tipping his hat.

Albertson and Wilder walked toward the clinic, their stomachs in knots. "Rick, do you think it's Arnie and Martha?"

Rick Albertson knocked on the locked door. "If it is, then we're both dead men."

Wearing her third outfit for the day, Maggie followed Jackson, Daniel, and Pippa into Susie's Cantina. She now carried Arnold Smith's laptop in her totebag.

"Susie! We're going to set up shop here for a while. Is that okay?"

The owner appeared, wearing a bright red apron over a tank top and blue jeans. "Sure. No one's coming in here tonight anyway. All the boys followed Meektay to the mesa. Even Matt, though he promised he wouldn't go. And Warren's gone to Las Cruces."

"Why would he go to Las Cruces now?" Daniel asked, looking at Jackson. "That doesn't make any sense."

Maggie opened up the PowerBook and pushed the on button. "There's a lot that doesn't make sense lately, but maybe Arnie can help us. I'd like to think he didn't die in vain."

Susie came over and took drink orders. "I got some enchiladas and rice pudding if you're hungry."

"Enchiladas and rice pudding? Another Minnesota-Mex meal?" asked Jackson.

Susie grinned. "Don't knock it 'til you've tried it. How about a lutefisk pie?"

Maggie grimaced. "Susie, you're a lovely lady, but those dishes make me want to hurl. I don't suppose you have a pizza tucked in that kitchen anywhere?"

Susie laughed. "Dr. Taylor, you're in luck. I just happen to have a recipe for pizza that will knock your socks off. Even the Bindell boys love it. Want to give it a try?"

"It doesn't have rice or fish on it, does it?"

"Not a bit. Shredded chicken all right?"

Jackson thought about the abandoned chicken farm BioStrain had used as a test site. "No, thanks. How about plain old disease-free cheese?"

"You got it, Doc. I'll be out in a few minutes with your drinks."

Maggie looked at her husband over the laptop. "Cute, Jackson. Real cute."

Jackson winked, happy to be in her good graces again. "So, Sherlock, what does Dr. Smith have to tell us?"

"I'm not sure yet. I wish Julie's friend, Popeye, were here right now. The files are all encrypted."

Susie returned with four Cokes and a basket of tortilla chips. "The salsa's good and hot," she warned. "My dad may have been a Swede, but my Mexican mom taught me to make salsa that will strip paint. Enjoy!"

She started back for the kitchen but stopped as the screen doors swung open. "Welcome to my cantina!" she said to the newcomers. "You look hungry. Sit down!"

The taller of the two men pointed to Daniel and the others. "Is that Dr. Tohe?"

"Oh yes. You sick?"

"Not yet," Albertson replied. "Come on, Pete."

The two men approached Daniel and the other three. "Excuse us. You're Dr. Tohe?"

"Yes. Can I help you?"

Wilder drew up a chair and looked to Albertson. "I gotta sit down, Rick. I'm getting the shakes."

"Sure, Pete. You need some juice, or something?"

"Nah. I got some candy. That'll do."

Daniel looked at the shorter, thinner man. "Diabetes?"

Wilder nodded. "Yeah. Stress is driving my sugar levels crazy."

"Stress?" Maggie asked, looking up from her task.

"Let me explain," Albertson began. "I'm Dr. Richard Albertson, and this is Dr. Peter Wilder. We're with BioStrain. Does that mean anything to you?"

Daniel rose and pulled up another chair. "Sit down, Dr. Albertson. We've been waiting for you."

CHAPTER 33

Darkness had fallen by the time Hank Meier found his way into the secret entrance of Ford's Mesa. Beneath what looked like a manhole near the mesa's craggy base, on the northwest side, his sunburned hands located a steel lever that opened a sliding door disguised to look like stone. Once inside, the door automatically resealed, returning the entrance to its ancient appearance.

Checking his watch, Meier figured it would take him nearly an hour to thread his way down through the maze of tunnels that led to the main interior of the installation. He checked his pistol and extra ammunition clips. He knew most of the guards had been given the weekend off, so he should be able to proceed without much opposition. However, should he require it, the MK 23 stood ready to assist.

Warren Down had been watching Meektay and his followers for over an hour. As per Grayson's orders, the sheriff had left his overzealous deputy in charge of Los Muertos for the evening so Down could shadow the religious group. Grayson had expressed concern that Meektay's choice of Ford's Mesa as a ceremonial site could prove dangerous to the project. Down found it difficult to believe the pseudo-religious leader and his well-meaning cult could in any way affect the project's perfectly timed progress, but he followed orders nonetheless.

Down took a sip from his canteen, filled with homemade tequila, then lifted his compact high-power binoculars to his eyes. As he watched the procession of some fifty or so citizens, mostly young boys, Down chuckled. He kept thinking of the $250,000 that Grayson had deposited into a Las Cruces account in Down's name. A nice retirement. For starters. Warren Down had news for Rex Grayson. A quarter of a million wouldn't cover a lifetime's silence. Down had plans to soak BioStrain dry.

"Arnie's dead? Dear God! We're all dead then."

Albertson and Wilder stared at Daniel and the others. "Arnie knew too much. And so do we," Rick said gloomily. "I'm no prophet, but I'm thinking you guys know too much, too. In fact, it's my bet that this whole town will be erased from the map. If I'm going to die, then I want to find a way to stop BioStrain. You with me, Pete?"

Wilder nodded wearily. His blood glucose had slowly leveled out, but he looked pale. "What do Arnie's files say, Dr. Taylor?"

Maggie had been fiddling with the encrypted files for almost half an hour. "Wait a minute!" she cried at last. "I got it! Take that, Popeye!"

"You're in?" Jackson asked, leaning over the table to peek at the screen.

"I sure am," she said. "I had to change the user preferences. Arnie was right. His password had been Armageddon, but not in the files. The password was in the account settings. I now have access as the root user! Woo hoo!"

"I married a computer genius," Jackson bragged. "What now?"

Albertson scooted his chair closer. "Go into the Word documents. Just open Word and check out recent files."

Maggie clicked the W icon in the dock, waited a few seconds for the program to open, then clicked on recent documents. To her surprise, she found an entry named *For Martha*. "I think this is it," she said and opened the file.

Meier inched his way along the dark tunnel, descending further into the desert's bedrock with each step. So far, he'd encountered no one along the winding maze. Up ahead, a dim light shone from around a corner. Meier could hear voices and weeping. He stopped to listen.

"I'm hungry," he heard a voice whisper.

"I know, but we don't have any food right now. Go to sleep and dream of your favorite foods."

"When will the bad man bring Maria back?" the boy asked.

"I don't know," the man's voice replied. "Sleep now."

"Shut up!" a harsh voice ordered. "You, kid! Get away from the door. Get back, both of you! And no talking!"

Meier pressed against the cool rock wall, listening to the heart-wrenching exchange. He could imagine the man, possibly the child's father, locked in a cage, terrified and helpless. Meier knew that feeling, but he had to rise beyond it. Closing his eyes, Meier began to pray.

"God," he said, moving his lips but making no sound. "Please forgive me for all I've done, for my defiance and rebellion. Forgive me for doubting You. Please send someone to help Becka and Karen. I should never have left my family,

God. But I can help this small family, maybe. I want to believe in You. Help me, God. Please, help me."

Meier finished the prayer and took a deep breath. Gripping the MK 23, he rushed around the corner and began to scream.

CHAPTER 34

Maggie and the others read through Arnold Smith's confessions, tears streaming down their cheeks. It soon became clear that Smith had been brought into BioStrain with a full understanding of the company's sinister goals. Smith had only wanted to provide a comfortable life for his wife, whom he loved passionately. A man named Rex Grayson had recruited Smith, promising millions of dollars in exchange for Arnold Smith's complete loyalty. Despite his personal convictions, the compassionate scientist had ignored his own feelings and his faith for profit and power. He'd sold out his friends and colleagues while ignoring his own soul.

"'I can't take it anymore, Martha,'" Maggie read aloud. "'I was a fool to ever put our comfort above the safety of the world. I've abandoned all I ever cared about, the very reason I got into science, to help people. Now, I'm murdering them. One by one. Group by group. Nation by nation. Please forgive me, Martha. I've found a vaccine, but it has to be administered at least a month in advance, but even then there's a chance it won't help. This chip monitors the messenger RNA and uses that information to alter the native form of the embedded virus. This demon chip actually constructs an individualized virus that infects and kills only that chip's carrier. This means BioStrain and the dark power that drives it can selectively kill *anyone at anytime—without having to worry about that body infect-ing others. It gives absolute power to whoever wields the control box. I helped create this monster, Martha. And I'm terrified that I'll burn in hell for it. May God forgive me.'"*

Yarber parked his rental car behind an outcrop of rock and decided to walk to Ford's Mesa. He'd watched as Meier found the entrance, and planned on following immediately, but the sudden appearance of another car had stopped him. The former SEAL kept a careful eye on the newcomer. The man had binoculars, but instead of training them on the lab entrance, he watched a group of young men who were climb-ing up the mesa, some barehanded, some on what looked like a rope ladder. It took the group nearly an hour to make it all the way up, but once there, they began lighting a bon-fire.

Yarber had read a report about a local religious cult that believed in animal sacrifice to Aztec gods. This had to be it. *Why would this man be interested?* Yarber wondered. As he left the compact car behind, the DARPA operative decided to find out for himself.

Hank Meier flew toward the surprised guard like a madman. Arms askew, gun at the ready, the outraged Meier flew in headfirst and sacked the burly BioStrain jailer, taking him down in one movement.

"What the...!" the guard shouted as the lunatic knocked the wind out of his lungs. "Umph!"

Hank loomed over his victim, gun drawn. "Keys!" he shouted, his dark eyes blazing with rage and terror.

"I ain't got no keys!" the big man blubbered, struggling to free himself from the crazed intruder.

"Keys now, or I ventilate that thick head of yours!"

In the cage, the small boy trembled next to a middle-aged man with broken glasses and what looked like a dislocated shoulder. Both looked dirty and ill-treated. The boy grew brave and ran to the bars. "God sent you!" he shouted, pointing at the guard's belt. "The keys are there! On the belt!"

"Oh, those k-keys," the fallen man stuttered. "Mr. G-Grayson ain't gonna let you leave h-here alive!"

"We'll see about that," Meier answered, removing the man's belt. "Here, kid!" he called to the boy and tossed the keys through the bars. The boy ran to the man, who used the keys to open the cell.

"I don't know who you are, but thanks is not enough!" the man shouted. "What can I do to help?"

"That arm looks bad," Meier noted. "You ever use a gun?"

"Three years in Nam says yes," Nate Beacham answered. "Never mind my arm. I'll hold the gun if you want to use my belt to tie this guy up inside the cell. We can use the key to lock him in."

"You read my mind, soldier," Meier said, handing the weapon to Beacham. "Name's Hank Meier."

"Nate Beacham," the man answered. "Pleased to meet you. Very pleased! This is Miguel Ibanez. He and his sister were captured a few days ago and brought here. Both their parents died here. Maria, that's the girl, is here somewhere. A group from BioStrain has been performing tests on the kids. For some reason, they leave me alone. They say my blood is all wrong."

Hank pulled the belt tight. He took the guard's own handkerchief, crushed it into a tight ball, and stuffed it into the man's jaws. "I don't want to hurt you, man. It's Grayson I want.

If you had any idea what your boss means to do to the world, you'd be helping me. Sorry I have to leave you here, but I'm on a tight schedule."

Meier locked the guard inside the cell then pocketed the keys, hoping they might help in the tunnels ahead. "What was that about wrong blood?" he asked Beacham.

"Something about immunity. They've been taking tubes and tubes of the children's blood. They still have Maria. They took her away this morning."

"They were exposed to the virus," Meier concluded. "You're lucky they didn't expose you, Beacham. They must have a reason for keeping you alive."

"We gotta find Maria!" the boy cried, pulling at Beacham's good arm.

Meier put a hand on the boy's dark head. "I'll find her, if she's here, Miguel. You help Mr. Beacham to go find help."

"Now, wait a minute!" Nate objected. "I'm not leaving you!"

"Take the boy and get out of here! If you follow the tunnels, they'll take you to a secret entrance at the foot of Ford's Mesa. If God lets me make it all the way to the labs, I intend to blow this place sky high."

Nate considered his options. "Miguel can find that alone. You can't do this by yourself, Hank."

"Don't argue with me! What was your rank in Nam?"

Beacham blinked, puzzled. "Final rank was Second Lieutenant."

"I finished up Captain. Now, this is an order, Lt. Beacham! Take this boy to safety!"

Beacham bit his lip, not wanting to leave, but Miguel's fearful eyes settled the issue. "OK. God be with you, Captain!"

"And the same to you, Lieutenant. Now go!"

Beacham and the boy headed back up the tunnels toward the entrance and freedom. As he watched the pair turn the corner, Meier took one last look at the guard, said a silent prayer, then headed deeper into the installation to find Rex Grayson.

CHAPTER 35

So what do we do now?" Albertson asked. "We can't just sit here and wait. BioStrain knows about Arnie, so they know he headed to Los Muertos. It's a good bet they're on their way here now."

Wilder nodded. "Probably. But Grayson can take you and me out in a heartbeat. You can be sure we both carry that chip, Rick. Just like Martha and Arnie."

"Maybe there's a way to deactivate it," Jackson suggested. "You can't just give up."

"There's no way to deactivate it," Wilder said. "It's fool-proof. God knows how many people are carrying the chip already! Grayson led us to believe we had years to go before human testing would begin. He lied about that. Maybe the chip's already been put into circulation."

"Circulation! Ha, funny," Albertson said, gloomily. "Look, if I'm goin' down, I'm taking Grayson with me. What do you say we go back to the lab, buddy? I doubt Grayson would ever expect that."

"I'll go with you," Jackson said, standing.

"No you won't!" Maggie blurted out, pulling his arm. "That's suicide!"

Daniel Tohe looked around the table. "My friends, there are unsuspecting people the world over who will die if someone doesn't stop BioStrain from distributing this chip on Tuesday. We can't think of ourselves, otherwise the madness we've witnessed here will be multiplied by millions. I agree with Jackson. We'll go with you two, if you want to return to fight. Pip and Maggie will stay here and wait for the CDC. They can tell Dr. Grover all that we've discussed, and Maggie will have the files on the computers for proof. Grover can see that the government puts a stop to BioStrain. For our part, we men will take down Grayson."

"You men?" Maggie repeated. "This is nuts! You're all nuts! But if you're mad enough to risk it, then we're not letting you go without us!"

"You're staying here!" Jackson said sharply, rising to his feet. "Margaret Ann, I've let you down again and again since Charlie's death. I allowed you to drift into a self-imposed isolation, I allowed you to blame yourself, and God help me, I blamed you, too. If you can forgive me, then I'll promise to do everything I can to make up for it once this is all over. But right now, I'm not going to let you risk your life, when I have the power to stop you. Understand?"

Maggie stared, her mouth agape. "Jackson Taylor, I've waited years to hear you admit to me that you blamed me for Charlie. Why on earth did you have to pick now to make me fall in love with you again?"

Jackson pulled Maggie to her feet and took her into his long arms. "I've been a fool, Maggie. I love you."

"I love you, too, you idiot," she answered, kissing him with years of unspoken passion.

"What about me?" Daniel half-joked, looking at Pippa.

Pippa touched the Indian's cheek. "Promise me you'll come back in one piece, and I promise I'll marry you," she whispered.

Tohe's blue eyes twinkled, and a tear slid down his cheek. "I'll hold you to that. I have witnesses."

"Come on!" Albertson said. "Before we all lose our nerve! We'll need a car that doesn't have any tracking devices."

Daniel held up his keys. "We'll take my jeep."

The skies over Los Muertos had turned into a sea of ink dotted with brilliant stars. Maggie and Pippa sat on the porch of Susie's cantina, waiting for Grover and the CDC team to arrive. The men had left nearly an hour before in Daniel's jeep.

In the distance, a line of headlights brightened the road and kicked up a plume of dust and sand. "That must be Grover," Maggie said. "Susie! I think they're here!" she called into the closed screen doors of the cantina. Across the street, she could see a light blink to life in the sheriff's office. "I thought Down had disappeared," she said to Pippa.

"That's probably Kean, the deputy. He's a smarmy little rodent. Down probably told him to greet the feds. Makes Kean feel important. Which makes me wonder all the more where Down went."

As she finished talking, the head car to the caravan pulled into town. The entourage consisted of the lead car, a black sedan with tinted windows, two ambulances, a white box truck, and a second smaller car. The sedan parked in front of the cantina and a tall, angular man emerged.

"Are you Dr. Grover?" Pippa asked.

"I'm Winston Grover," he answered, showing an ID badge. "Where is Dr. Tohe?"

Maggie stood and extended her right hand. "I'm Dr. Maggie Taylor, and this is Pippa Anderson. Daniel Tohe sends his regrets. He's on a call right now."

Pippa looked to Maggie, her face showing surprise, but she said nothing. Maggie must have her reasons for not telling where Tohe had really gone.

Grover shook Maggie's hand and then reached for Pippa's. "I'm sorry we're meeting under these circumstances. Can you show me where the bodies are?"

"Sure. Follow me," Maggie said, leading him to the clinic. "They're inside. We wrapped them up tight. Your men have Hazmats?"

Grover smiled. "We'll take all necessary precautions. It's fortuitous that you were here, Dr. Taylor. Your reputation is well known and well respected. May I ask where your husband is?"

Maggie started to answer then stopped. Now why would this man care about Jackson's whereabouts—and how did he even know Jackson had come along? Had Yarber's spy told him?

"How did you know about Jackson?" she asked, point-blank.

"Well, I think Dr. Tohe told me."

Maggie unlocked the door to the clinic and walked inside. "I see. So, what is the procedure in outbreaks such as this?"

Grover glanced around the meager facility. "First we need to know the extent of the infection. You and Dr. Tohe were exposed, but you appear to be well enough. Still, we'll need to quarantine you until we have all the answers."

"Quarantine? I don't think so," Maggie said simply.

"I'm afraid you have no choice in the matter," the smarmy deputy said as he led the rest of the team into the clinic. "Dr. Grover has full jurisdiction here, Dr. Taylor. He can do whatever he pleases. And I'm here to make sure no one resists."

"Thank you, Deputy Kean," Grover said. "Could you help my men with the bodies, please?"

"Sure," Kean said, leading the team toward the back of the clinic.

Pippa entered, her face full of confusion. "Maggie, they're rounding up everyone in town. Kean said they're going to have to hold all of us. Is that right?"

Grover emerged from the back room, wiping his hands with alcohol pads. "Too bad about Dr. Smith," he said, nodding to the team. "The usual procedure, Mr. Canton. A full cleansing."

"Cleansing? What do you mean by that?" Maggie asked as several team members shoved her out of the clinic and back out into the street.

"We're very sorry, Dr. Taylor, but your services are required by Mr. Grayson. Gentlemen, secure the deputy and anyone else left in town then burn it. Burn it to the ground."

Don Yarber had been watching Warren Down for some time, and he'd begun to wonder just whose side the rotund sheriff was on, but he had no more time to pursue it. The agent clicked his watch once, and the device chirped to life.

"That you, Major?" a distant voice asked.

"You weren't asleep, were you, Price? You're still watching Dr. Taylor, right?"

The man's voice snapped to attention. "No, sir! I mean, yes, sir! I mean I wasn't sleeping, sir! I have Dr. Taylor in my sights right now. She's been sitting on the porch of a cantina for a while. The CDC just arrived."

"CDC? Take another look, Price. I spoke with Mitchell of the CDC just an hour ago. They won't be here until noon tomorrow."

A pause.

265

"Sorry to take so long, but I had to get closer. Looks to me like the group is removing the bodies to a couple of ambulances. Dr. Smith and his wife are among them."

"How about Albertson and Wilder? Did they show up?" Yarber asked.

"Yep. You figured that one right down to the ground, Major. But they took off in Dr. Tohe's jeep about an hour ago. Hold on."

Yarber trained his field glasses on Down once again then up at Meektay. Yarber figured the religious ceremonies were part of a ruse to keep anyone from discovering the lab's secret entrance. Nothing like drawing attention to a place to keep people from really looking at it. Yarber had used that trick many times.

Up on the top of the mesa, the bonfire rose high into the stars. The followers had begun to whoop and sing while dancing like a bunch of whirling dervishes. The whole thing gave Yarber the creeps.

"I'm back," Price said. "Dr. Taylor disappeared, and I had to see where she'd gone. Major, I think this Grover guy put her and Miss Anderson into a white box truck. Should I try to rescue?"

"Negative. Not on your own. Follow them and keep me posted. I'm putting in a call to Washington."

Yarber closed the communication by clicking the watch a second time. Above the mesa, Meektay and his foolish band of worshipers had begun a blood sacrifice meant to appease ancient gods. They needn't have bothered.

Blood would be spilled beneath the mesa tonight.

CHAPTER 36

Maggie kicked at the two men holding her. "Let me go, you big oafs!"

Pippa, who had already been tied and gagged, watched her friend with a mix of admiration and fear.

"Get in there!" one man yelled as he pushed Maggie into Pippa. The taller of the two knelt down and slapped Maggie, knocking her backward. "Not so tough now, huh? Tie her hands and feet and gag that mouth of hers! We have to finish the cleanup before dawn."

Following his boss's orders, the short man bound Maggie securely then slammed the truck's overhead door shut. Sitting in the darkness, Margaret thought of Jackson, Daniel, and the others, and her heart tightened.

She looked toward Pippa, even though she couldn't see her in the pitch-blackness of the truck's interior. *Please, God, if you're there, if You really exist,* she said in her mind, *protect Jackson. Please! Don't take him from me, too!*

To his astonishment, Hank Meier had made it all the way into the main body of the installation without meeting up with any more guards. From what he could recall of the layout, he felt sure the first elevator must be straight ahead and on the right. Taking a deep breath, he tiptoed ahead.

Daniel shut off the jeep. "Look up there," he said to the other men. "That's Meektay. He's summoning the gods with fire and blood."

"Local color?" Jackson quipped. "So are we going in there with just our brains or does anyone have a weapon?"

Albertson, who led the way toward the mesa entrance, stopped. "If we can make it to the armory, we might be able to break in."

"Keep thinking good thoughts," Daniel told him. "Didn't you say most of the guards had been given the weekend off? I wonder why."

Rick Albertson shook his head. "Probably to allow Grayson to implement the plan without too many witnesses. Most of the guards are just local people who took a good job with good pay and benefits. Poor schleps. They've probably been chipped as well."

"Shh!" Daniel called ahead. "Less talk, more stealth. The desert has great acoustics."

On they walked, Albertson and Taylor, followed by Wilder and Tohe. Overhead, they could hear the mad cries of Meektay's worshipers as they prepared to slit the throat of a pig and cover themselves with blood. Below, the men's eyes fixed on two shadows emerging from the base of the mesa. One tall, one very short.

"What the...?" Albertson whispered.

The tall figure saw them and began to run toward them, waving his arms wildly.

"Friend or foe?" Jackson asked Albertson.

The scientist shook his head. "Danged if I know. But it looks for all the world like a man and a little kid!"

Warren Down put away his binoculars and smoked a cigarette. Time to go back to town. He'd left Kean alone long enough for Grover and his men to clean up the town. Once back, Down could honestly say he had no idea what had happened to Taylor or the others. He'd left his deputy in charge, so if the authorities blamed anyone, it would be Kean.

Maybe Grover and his henchmen took care of Kean, too, Down thought with a chuckle. Down had never liked the upstart deputy. He knew Kean planned to run for office in the fall, and Down had no intention of giving up his lucrative position to anyone, let alone a little rat such as Kean.

Just as the sheriff turned his car toward Los Muertos, he saw a long line of vehicles heading toward the mesa. *Must be the cleanup crew,* Down thought. Driving on, he soon met the caravan and stopped his car for a moment. As he'd expected, Grover and another man exited the lead car to greet him.

Down laughed again. Stupid gringos. He'd make sure to memorize their ugly faces so he could use it as leverage for more kickback pay from Grayson. The more he knew, the more he earned.

"Good evening, señors," he said as Grover approached the patrol car. "You are out on a lovely evening."

"You must be Sheriff Down," Grover said matter-of-factly.

"I am the very same. Did my deputy make you welcome in Los Muertos?"

"He did."

"That is good. Well, I'll see you around sometime. Be sure to stop in when you are in the neighborhood!"

"We'll make sure we do that, Sheriff. Mr. Canton, take care of this," Grover said as he returned to the sedan.

Down stared for a moment, then smiled at Canton.

"So, you goin' to take care of me, huh? I like that. I think we can settle on a small price as a down payment," Down said, smiling up at the man.

"We'd rather settle in full right now," Canton said, showing a mouth full of gleaming teeth. Then he fired a .22 caliber slug into Down's soft brain.

"Don't shoot!" the man cried as he ran toward Albertson. "We need your help!"

Taylor ran ahead. He reached the pair in moments, followed soon by the others. "What are you doing out here?" he asked the man.

"Are you OK?" Tohe exclaimed once he saw the man's face. "What happened to you?"

"It's a long story," the reporter panted. "There's another man inside who rescued us. We were being held prisoner. Miguel's sister is still in there! I wanted to stay and help, but he insisted I escape with Miguel."

"Your arm's dislocated, I think. Here, Jackson, can you see it?" Tohe said. "What man is inside?" he asked as the two doctors examined Nate Beacham's shoulder.

"His name's Meier, I think. Sorry, they knocked me out a couple of times, and my brain's not working its best. Usually, I can remember everything I read or hear. He—ouch!—he's got a handgun, but that won't be enough. These people are armed to the teeth. Ow! Oh, that—that really hurts..."

"Jack, he's going to faint!" Tohe cried. Albertson carried Miguel while Jackson and Daniel helped Beacham to the jeep. It took several minutes before they had settled the pair into the vehicle. The reporter insisted he should go with them, but Daniel convinced him to regain his composure then drive back into town for help. He also gave Beacham his cell phone, which the reporter used to call Frank Levatino and his wife.

"We'll find Maria and this guy Meier. She is in God's good hands. You take Miguel and find Sheriff Down and Deputy Kean."

"I'll do my best," Beacham promised. "God be with you!"

He reached for the keys to start the engine, but a sudden explosion startled all of them, and every eye turned in the direction of Los Muertos.

"Good Lord!" Nate cried, hugging the boy close.

Daniel and the others stared, dumbfounded at the distant blaze, already reaching to the sky, rivaling the pyre set by Meektay.

Albertson shivered. "Grayson's covering his tracks, destroying all the evidence. We're next, Pete."

Wilder set his jaw and slapped his friend on the shoulder. "If we're goin' down anyway, let's take a few bad guys with us. What do you say, men?"

Jackson and Daniel couldn't help thinking about Maggie and Pippa. "Do you think they got out?" the medicine man asked Taylor.

"I'm betting on my wife," Jackson replied. "And on God."

"Amen," Daniel said, fighting tears. "Come on, brother. Let's go."

CHAPTER 37

The box truck skirted away from Ford's Mesa for several miles then turned onto a dirt road that led to an abandoned filling station.

"Everybody out!" shouted Canton. "Shall we bring the women inside, sir?" he asked as Grover left the car.

"Take them down to Level Six, Mr. Canton."

"Yes, sir."

Canton led the other men into the leaning structure and opened the door to what had once been a restroom. The shark-toothed gunman pulled on a blackened towel rack, and a trap door opened a few feet away.

"Take them on down," he told the men who were leading Maggie and Pippa. "Take them to Grayson. You know how he loves the ladies."

Yarber had seen Canton execute Down but knew it was pointless to interfere. Truth was, he was glad there was nothing he could've done. Down had gotten what he'd deserved. Now, as he gazed at the red horizon where Los Muertos burned, Yarber knew he had no choice but to go in after Meier. He clicked his watch to signal Price.

No answer.

Not good, Yarber thought. He didn't like losing a man, but he liked leaving him even less. He'd have to deal with that later. For now, his path lay down and into the belly of BioStrain.

"Well, Maria, are you comfortable?"

The ten-year-old winced and wriggled against the nylon straps that bound her to the gurney. "You are a bad man!"

Grayson shrugged. "So it would seem. But you, my dear child, are very important. Apparently, you are immune to my little virus, and that intrigues me. While I've been able to save some of your blood for study, I'm beginning to think keeping your whole body would be safer. Do you like the cold, Maria?"

"No. Why did you kill my mother and my father? What did you do to Miguel? Why do you do these bad things?"

Grayson gazed upon Maria's unlined, brown face and stroked her dark hair thoughtfully. "Because I'm a bad man, Maria. That's all. Now, you rest awhile. When Dr. Grover arrives, he'll turn you into a freezer pop."

Maria screamed and fought against her bonds, but Grayson merely laughed.

"No one is around to hear that lovely voice of yours, my dear. And now, I must leave you. The next time I see you, I'll be king of the world, and you'll be dead."

He kissed her forehead and left the room, whistling as he entered the elevator for Level Seven.

Maggie and Pippa followed their captors along the winding corridors of BioStrain Labs, pushed and shoved each time they lagged behind. Deputy Kean complained nonstop, mouthing off to the one called Canton.

"You're gonna be sorry! I ain't supposed to be part of this. You ask Sheriff Down! He'll tell ya'! You better let me talk to Grayson, or else you're gonna be real sorry!"

"Shut up!" one of the men yelled, slapping Kean across the mouth. "You've got a big mouth, you know that?"

Canton said nothing. Soon the last elevator took them into the open lab area, where Maggie's father had once worked. Seeing the many stations, benches, PCR machines, bioseparation units, analyzers, and other sequencing equipment, she knew at once where they were.

Canton stopped and indicated a small room adjoining the main lab. "Put them in there. Tie everyone down, except Dr. Taylor. Grayson wants her alive."

Kean squirmed like a chicken at the block and began to scream. Pip stared at Maggie, her lips moving in silent prayer.

"You can't just kill us!" Maggie screamed.

"Of course we can," Canton replied. He pressed a button on his cell phone. "We're here, sir. We have the Taylor woman and the others. What are your orders?"

"I'll be there in a moment," Grayson's clipped accent replied. "Make the good doctor comfortable."

"So this is where you cooked up Armageddon?" Maggie asked one of the guards. "How many scientists are dead because of what they knew?"

"Not enough," Canton answered, motioning to the guard. "There's another guest in the room next door. See to her."

The tall guard nodded and entered a darkened room adjacent to their own, leaving just two guards and Canton to watch the prisoners. Kean kicked the gurney with his heels, making a thudding sound. "Let me go!" he demanded. "You can't do this to me!"

"What is it Grayson wants?" Maggie asked Canton.

The expressionless assassin shrugged. "Power. Isn't that what all men want?"

"You'd be surprised," she said, looking at Pippa and Susie, who remained unconscious. "But how will this chip give him power if he kills everyone off?"

"I can answer that, Dr. Taylor," came a soft British voice from the elevator. "What a pleasure it is to meet you at last. I knew your father well. An extraordinary mind. I presume you've inherited that same beautiful brain. To answer your question, the nanochip is a control device. That is the secret of power, you know. Control. It's remarkable what one man can force another man to do when one holds the keys to life and death. I hold those keys, Dr. Taylor."

"Really?" she asked, summoning up all her courage. "Then why do you need me? Your stooge said you want me alive. That means I have value. What possible use can I be to someone with the keys to life and death?"

Grayson examined each of the prisoners as he spoke, pinching Kean then caressing Pippa and Susie, clearly in his element. His movements were controlled, unhurried, almost graceful. "Good question, Doctor. You see, a small obstacle has appeared on my horizon. I've discovered someone who is resistant to the virus. While that doesn't present a huge problem—I have backup measures, of course—it is a puzzle. I want to know why she's immune. That's where you come in."

"Me? Why would I work for you?"

Grayson stopped in front of the door used moments before by the absent guard. "Because, if you don't, then little Maria will die."

He pressed a button to open the steel door, revealing a clinically white room where the oversized guard loomed over a small form strapped to a gurney.

"That is Maria Ibanez. I've read your dossier, Dr. Taylor. I know how much you have grieved over the loss of your daughter five years ago. How you must have blamed yourself for letting her stray so close to the dangerous mud hole where you would one day build a luxurious swimming pool. I know that you never once swam in that pool. I know that you gave away your cat—Mariah, was it?—how you blamed the poor kitty for making your precious daughter slip and fall to her death. Such a pitiful tale! Now, you hold the life of another young girl in your hands. Would you fail her as well?"

Maggie stepped forward and stared at Maria. The girl slept peacefully, drugged from her last injection, unaware of her plight.

"Well, Doctor? What is it to be?"

CHAPTER 38

Yarber had memorized the interior plan of BioStrain's lab, thanks to the map Charles Hilliard had sent to DARPA. As the well-trained former SEAL slipped along the cool tunnels, he made no sound. He carried a Khukuri knife and a Glock 26 sidearm with plenty of rounds. He'd seen only one guard, who'd already been incapacitated, but he had no intention of taking anything for granted.

He'd almost made it to the elevator bank, when he heard footsteps coming up behind him. Taking care to remain unseen, Yarber stole into the next tunnel and waited.

Maggie had little choice. Grayson had locked her in with Maria and the guard then left to return to what he called his throne room. Clearly, Grayson was a madman. Maggie wondered how her father and Tom Foil had managed to work for such a monster for so many years. Then she remembered Major Yarber's words of her father's courage. Charles Hilliard had ended his life as a spy in the belly of BioStrain, and Maggie hadn't even been able to thank him for it.

"Who is it?" a small voice called.

The sleeping drug had worn off, and Maria Ibanez's large brown eyes flickered open. "Mama?"

Maggie leaned down and touched the girl's cool brow. "Your mother isn't here right now, Maria. I'm Maggie. I'm going to take care of you."

The guard said nothing, but his expression made it clear he would not permit Maggie to do anything rash.

"Who is he? Is he with the bad man?" Maria asked, pointing to the guard's blank face.

"He—he's watching us, that's all. Can't I untie her?" she asked the guard. The brute shook his head.

"Sorry, Maria. Try to relax."

"The bad man wants to kill me," Maria whispered, her eyes filling with tears. "Are you an angel sent to help?"

Maggie fought tears and gave the child a kiss. "I'm not an angel, sweetheart. But God knows you're here, and He'll send help. I promise."

Rex Grayson surveyed the glittering panel in front of him. He touched each dial, savoring the warm glow of each diode, reveling in the knowledge that this small electronic panel gave him control of every man and woman wearing a chip. Starting Tuesday, one injection at a time, every person in America would eagerly receive the life-saving chip, completely unaware that death swam in their veins. Within a year, the entire world would host a nanochip, each one unique to that individual. And every chip would transmit its precious signal to this lovely panel.

"It's all going so well," he said aloud in the darkened room.

"Not well enough," a voice called from behind him.

Grayson spun around, startled for a moment, then he began to laugh.

"Why! If it isn't dear little Henry Meier, the lovesick operative from Indiana! Did you travel all this way to thank me for setting you up with Dr. Taylor, Hank? Completely unnecessary, I assure you!"

"You're a sick snake, Grayson! You'd use your own mother if it suited your goals."

"Oh, yes. I would. And I have, but let us not malign the dead. Please, come in. You're just in time to watch me as I activate a few chips."

"I don't think so," Meier continued, raising his weapon high. "You forget my original training, Grayson. Remember? Being a salesman was just my cover. I've been taught to kill, and nothing will please me more than to prove it to you."

Grayson shook his head. "Not this time, Dr. Meier. Mr. Canton?"

Meier turned sharply, just in time to see Canton's fist before it smashed squarely into his jaw. Meier crashed to the floor with a thud, his weapon sliding into Canton's big feet.

"Now that's better," Grayson cooed. "Help Dr. Meier to a chair, won't you, Mr. Canton?"

Canton yanked Meier by the arm and dragged him to a chair.

"Very good. Oh, Mr. Canton, can I assume that our good doctor has settled in with her new charge?"

"Yes, sir. And Dr. Grover is with them."

"Wonderful! Dr. Meier, you can watch as your precious Dr. Taylor becomes personally acquainted with our little chip. Won't that be fun?"

"You evil…!"

Canton slammed Meier's head with the butt of his gun, nearly knocking him unconscious.

"Careful, Mr. Canton. We wouldn't want Dr. Meier to miss anything."

Canton stepped to one side, ready to apply further discipline as needed.

"There we are," Grayson said happily. "Now, I just press this button and we get to see the lab on Level Six. Oh, look there! A full house!"

A giant plasma television screen lit up. One side of the screen showed a private lab, where a line of gurneys held Pippa, an unconscious Susie Thayer, and a fidgety Deputy Kean. The other side of the screen revealed a smaller room where Maggie watched over a small child. In the background, a guard towered over them both, making sure Maggie obeyed Grayson's commands.

They've got Maggie! Meier thought, terrified. *And that must be Maria!*

"Who should we inoculate first, hmm? Let's choose. Eeny, meeny, miney, mo. Here's the one whose life will go!"

Grayson's bobbing hand fell upon Kean. "Dr. Grover, our first contestant this evening will be the intrepid and most unfortunate, Deputy Kean."

Meier lunged forward, but a hard swing of Canton's hand slapped him back into the chair. "This is murder!" he cried, but Grayson merely laughed. "You're mad, Grayson!"

"Perhaps," he replied. "Proceed, Dr. Grover."

On the screen, the man who'd claimed to be from the CDC filled a syringe with a clear fluid and injected the contents into Kean's immobilized arm. Kean wriggled against the needle, but the thick straps used to bind him to the gurney held fast. "What are you doing?" Kean screamed.

Meier's eyes fell upon the other prisoners, including Pippa Anderson, whose gag kept her silent. Meier could see her pale eyes, though, wide with terror.

"This little cocktail of mine is very potent, Dr. Meier. I've added a bit of spice that even Smith and his cohorts had no knowledge of. Would you like to see? Oh, what am I thinking? Of course you would! Mr. Lyle, will you please open the window so Dr. Taylor can watch as well?" The beefy guard pressed a button and one steel wall slid aside, revealing a large window that permitted a clear view of the other room. "Grover, I suggest you stand back. I'm about to demonstrate the BioStrain chip's best-kept secret."

Smiling with devilish delight, Grayson pressed a red button on the control panel, located the unique signature for Kean's chip, and punched a black button. Instantly, Kean's body jerked into rigidity, as if electricity ran through his veins. His mouth twisted, and his hair stood on end, while a sickening sizzle filled the air with smoke and steam.

Inside the small lab room, Maggie stared in horror, her hands on the glass. Meier could see the terror etched on her face and in her wide eyes.

"Fascinating, is it not, Dr. Meier? You see, my little chip has the power to turn the body's own electrical field against itself. I thought of it while watching a documentary on spontaneous human combustion. I reasoned that this rare event must be the result of the body's shorting out, so to speak. It's an amazing phenomenon. Smelly perhaps, but amazing, nonetheless."

"You're sick, Grayson!" Meier snapped as Kean caught fire. The blaze grew white hot within minutes, consuming flesh, fat, and bone. By the end of ten minutes, little remained of the unlucky deputy but a sickening smell.

"So who's next?" Grayson asked, his eyes alight with madness. "How about your pretty little doctor, Margaret Taylor? Or better yet, that charming girl who has so captured Dr. Taylor's grieving heart. Shall I choose?" He pressed a white button and a speaker came to life in Maggie's room. "Dr. Taylor, which one of you will be next to volunteer? You or the child?"

Maggie looked around, searching for the source of Grayson's grating voice. "I thought you needed me and the girl," she bluffed.

"Possibly. I'm not really sure any longer. It occurs to me that it might be much more fun to watch you sizzle like our deputy here. So, which is it? You or the girl?"

"Do not answer!" the girl screamed. "He is a devil! A bad man! God, help us! Help us!" she cried, but the guard slapped her hard, leaving a welt on the smooth cheek.

"Take me!" Maggie cried. "I'll do it! Just promise you won't hurt the girl!"

Grayson smiled and nodded to Meier. "Very well. Dr. Grover, please prepare a solution for our dear Dr. Taylor, and make it a strong one. I'm sure she wants to go out in a blaze of glory!"

CHAPTER 39

Jackson Taylor followed Albertson's footsteps carefully, making as little sound as possible. Incredibly, they'd encountered only one guard, bound and gagged in a small cell halfway inside the installation.

"How much further?" Tohe whispered to Wilder.

"Just a few minutes to the elevators, then it's down two hundred feet to Level Six."

"And the armory?" Jackson asked.

"It's on Level Five, if we make it that far."

"Let's keep positive," Tohe said, as the four turned a corner and ran headlong into a human wall.

Outside, high atop Ford's Mesa, Matt Thayer pretended to dance like the others. Ray Bindell's threats against Susie terrified the youth, but his belief in God filled him with guilt for participating in the grotesque ritual. Ray appeared to be lost in the dance. Matt prayed that Ray and the other followers would soon become so drugged that no one would notice if he stole back down the mesa and back to town.

The piglet that Meektay and the others had hauled up the side of the mesa squirmed and squealed against the ropes that bound it to the rock that Meektay called the sacred stone.

Thayer backed away, trying to disappear amidst the pagan throng of dancers. Another youth beat a drum while the dancers sang and cut themselves.

Meektay held a stone knife in his right hand and steadied the piglet with his left. The man who claimed to be a reborn Aztec then held his right hand up to the stars and swung down with ferocity, slicing through the piglet's throat, exposing its vertebrae, and forcing a river of bright red blood to squirt in all directions.

Matt Thayer reached for the cross his mother had given him. The horrifying picture of devil worship drove home the true source of Meektay's hellish powers. Matt doubled over and began to vomit.

Maggie now lay strapped to a large gurney, a tight gag covering her mouth. Inside the smaller lab, she could see Maria. The guard had untied her so the child could witness the horrible death of the woman who had promised to protect her.

"Dr. Grover, are you ready for our next lucky guest on *You Bet Your Life?*" Grayson's laughter filled the speaker.

Grover waved and began filling the syringe. Meier's heart banged against his chest, and his ears filled with a roaring sound. He no longer cared if he lived or died; he only knew that he had to stop Grayson.

Summoning all his courage, Meier jumped from the chair, swung at Canton, knocking the man to the floor, and threw his full body weight against Grayson.

Grover held the syringe aloft, making sure no air remained. He stroked Maggie's dark hair off her forehead. "I promise this won't hurt," he told her. "Consider yourself a pioneer for science, Dr. Taylor. Just the first of millions to join the New World Order."

Maggie struggled against the tight straps, praying that God would provide a miracle, that He would at the very least keep Maria and Jackson safe, and that she would be allowed to be with her dad and Charlie once the pain had passed.

"This might sting just a little," Grover said as he positioned the syringe over Maggie's forearm.

Maggie closed her eyes, preparing herself for the bite of the needle and the moment of her death.

But she felt nothing.

She opened her eyes. Dr. Grover hovered over her gurney, syringe still poised near her arm, but his eyes had fixed in place, frozen, as if he'd gone to sleep with them open.

A second passed, and Maggie heard footsteps coming from somewhere outside the room. It was then that she noticed a tiny trickle of blood at the corner of Grover's frozen mouth. A second later, he collapsed to the floor. Dead.

"Maggie!" she heard a voice call. "Maggie, honey!"

Jackson!

As if in answer to her prayer, Jackson Taylor rushed up to his wife and kissed her beautiful face. "Let's get out of here," he said, kissing her again. Maggie began to weep, as her husband untied her arms and legs and removed the painful gag from her mouth.

"I love you," she cried, falling into his arms.

"No time for that!" a man called from the opposite side of the room. "We have to find Grayson!"

Maggie sat up and blinked. "Major Yarber!" she cried, her heart singing.

Jackson helped her off the table. "We ran into the good major in the tunnels. He's the one who took out Grover, and just in time apparently," he added, looking at the pile of ash that had once been Deputy Kean.

"Maria Ibanez is in the other room!" Maggie shouted to Yarber, but the keen-eyed agent had already discovered the entrance and short-circuited the door, forcing it to open. A short struggle followed, but soon the guard lay in a heap near the open door.

Maria rushed past Yarber and into Maggie's open arms, smothering her with kisses. "See? God did send you as an angel!" the girl cried as she wrapped her arms around Maggie's neck.

Albertson and Wilder stood near the elevator. "Come on, men! Grayson's on Level Seven!"

Hank Meier had gone mad. Every limb swung at Grayson, scratching, kicking, and punching, all in a desperate bid to save Maggie from suffering the same fate as Kean.

"Canton!" Grayson screamed, trying to fend off Meier's advance. "Canton, get over here!"

Canton, who had been knocked out briefly when his head hit the floor, pulled himself to his feet and started for Grayson.

"Shoot him!" Grayson shouted. "Don't just stand there, you idiot! Shoot him!"

Canton steadied himself, blinking to clear his blurry vision. He lifted his weapon, held Meier's head in his sights, and pulled the trigger.

Meektay laughed like a hyena. Blood poured from the piglet and covered the shaman's hands in crimson. "Smear your bodies with the cleansing blood!" he proclaimed, and the intoxicated dancers followed his orders, striping their arms and faces with blood and shouting to the skies.

"Death is our life! Death is our life! Blood, blood and fire! Fire and blood!"

Meektay stopped and looked at the crazed followers who had once called themselves human. Laughter filled his mouth as his face began to twitch. "Behold!" he cried. "I am your god!"

The dancers stopped and stared toward their new god. Meektay's body and face began to change shape, widening, hardening, shifting into a new form, one moment an ox, another moment a lion, another an eagle, another a man. Finally, the shape stretched toward the stars and grew an enormous tail with scales that shimmered in the fire's light.

"A dragon! The feathered serpent! Quetzalcoatl!" the dancers shouted, uncertain if they should bow down to worship or run.

Matt Thayer knew which to do. "This is no god!" he screamed and ran toward the flying serpent. "Only God in heaven reigns! In the name of Jesus Christ, I command you to fly!"

The glittering dragon stopped, foul breath streaming from his nostrils. Thayer lifted the gold cross up high and held it up to the monster's face. "You have no power over me or my sister!" he proclaimed.

"Then go!" the monster spoke, hot spittle spewing onto Matt's face. "Go back to God! And tell Him how I do hate Him for loving you so much!"

Thayer backed up, cross held high, until he reached the rope ladder that led to the bottom of the mesa.

The dragon now turned to the others in the group, sharp teeth dripping fire. "If you love me, you will honor me with a proper sacrifice!" he bellowed. "Ray Bindell! Tonight, you will become a part of eternity!"

Bindell began to shake visibly. "No! N-no!" he screamed, suddenly sober. "In J-Jesus' name! Leave me alone!"

"Foolish boy," the dragon replied, breathing fire as it spoke. "You must truly believe to invoke that name," and a roar of flame shot from its nostrils, consuming everyone, including Ray Bindell.

Satisfied to have led so many away from the truth of Christ, the dragon flew high into the night air, its scales gleaming in multi-hued beauty, then it turned and flew down, right through the rock, and into the heart of the mesa.

CHAPTER 40

Hank Meier should have been dead, but Canton's aim had been slightly off, due to his poor vision, and the bullet had only grazed Hank's ear. Blood gushed down the left side of his face, but Hank held on to Grayson, knocking him to the ground.

Canton had no intention of missing a second time. He held his weapon high and aimed once more. "This time you die," he promised Hank.

"I don't think so," a voice said.

Canton whirled around, but a roar of flame caught him off guard, incinerating him on the spot.

Meier looked up, certain he'd either died or gone mad. A giant dragon loomed over both him and Grayson, nostrils filled with smoke and eyes ablaze.

"I'm here for Grayson, Dr. Meier," the great serpent spoke, its tail swirling above its huge head. "You, I shall save for another day. Now go."

Hank pushed himself up, steadied his shaking legs, and tiptoed around the dragon. "I'm dreaming, right?"

"If you choose to think so. Now go."

Meier crept past the dragon and out the door. Once Meier had left, the creature's shape began to shimmer as it once again transformed itself. Grayson lay on the floor, hands over his face, blubbering and begging for his life.

289

"Let me go," he pleaded as the creature's shape shifted to that of a man.

"And why should I do that?" the man-creature asked. "You've failed us, Grayson. We offered you power and pleasure, all if you would simply worship us, but you chose to worship only your own petty desires. A mistake, my dear Grayson. A fatal mistake."

Grayson looked up, shock covering his face like a mask. "Ryder!"

"It's so nice to be recognized," Ryder replied. "But it's not enough to save you, Grayson. Not after what you've tried to do to Maggie. God denied us Maggie's firstborn child, Charlotte, but we will not be denied access to the mother nor to the child she will have one year from now. Margaret Ann Taylor must survive for our plans to survive. Generations of engineering and careful planning culminate in Margaret Ann Taylor, and no one, not even God, will take her—not from us—not from me. We have a very special place reserved for you, once God has thrown you out of His sight. You could have had the world, Grayson. We—I and the other Watchers—we gave you our knowledge, set you up to become king of this world, but your own human greed has proven more powerful than your loyalty to our cause. Now we shall choose another to carry on our work. You, on the other hand, have other fish to fry, so to speak. Well, at least the frying part is true."

Grayson opened his mouth to plead for mercy, but his words never escaped. A flash seared through his body, and within seconds he had turned to cinders.

The demon called Ryder took a scoop of ash between his hands and let it run through his fingers. "Ashes to ashes. Dust to dust. What is it God sees in you humans, anyway?"

With that, he disappeared.

EPILOGUE

I s that from Pip and Daniel?" Jackson asked his wife, as he packed the last of her clothes into the Santa Fe.

Maggie held several letters, the last ones she'd collect at this address. "Yes. They're having a marvelous time on their honeymoon, and Pip says Susie Thayer has moved back to Minnesota. She's opening a Mexican diner there. Guess that figures, huh? Oh, and she included a picture of Maria. She also says that Yarber's government contacts show that both Maria and Miguel were born in the U.S., so she and Daniel can proceed with the adoption. They'll both be attending school in Las Cruces this fall while Nate Beacham and his Vietnam buddies rebuild the town of Los Muertos, which they say will be renamed Salvation Springs."

Jackson closed the gate on the overstuffed Santa Fe. "A happy ending all around. This is everything, right?"

Maggie kissed his cheek. "For now. Julie promised to bring any other mail to our new house along with anything I may have forgotten when she comes to visit this weekend with Sam Fountain."

"You can't have forgotten anything, Mags. Unless you want to take the sink with you."

"When we have such a beautiful sink at the new place? Have I told you how much I love that house, Jackson?"

Taylor leaned against the car and shook his head. "A few dozen times, but it never hurts to hear it again. Oh, did I tell you I got a call from Yarber yesterday?"

"Really? He's not going to recruit you or anything, is he?"

"Hardly. He just wanted to let us know that the renegade chips have all been destroyed, and the New Mexico site was cleaned out and sealed up. He claims we can expect a commendation from the President for our part in stopping Grayson's bid for world domination. Good thing our President is an honest man, huh?"

Maggie leaned against the car, lost in thought. "Maybe. But what about the so-called regulation chips the program implanted? Sure, the President may have backed off the mandate that everybody is required to have them, but that's subject to change. I don't know, Jackson. I'm beginning to wonder if Yarber's rule number one isn't right."

"Don't trust anyone?" he asked. "Mags, you have to trust someone. Me, for instance."

She leaned over and kissed his cheek. "Excellent point, husband."

"So why is it you still have that faraway look, wife?" he persisted.

"Who me? OK, you got me. I was just wondering about Hank Meier."

Jackson grinned and patted her hand. "Thought so. Didn't he go back to his wife and daughter?"

"He did. That's another happy ending for you. I guess we'll be seeing him soon enough."

"How's that?" Jackson asked, opening the driver door.

Maggie hopped into the passenger side and buckled up. "He lives in Eden now, remember? We'll be neighbors."

Jackson started up the engine and looked at his wife. "Are you sure you want to leave IU and start teaching at Eden College? It's a much smaller fish tank."

"Maybe," she mused, "but I like small tanks. They're much safer. Besides, Eden's close to Madison, which means close to family, and I intend to be a very involved aunt once Angie has the babies."

"Twins!" Jackson exclaimed, checking the rear view mirror before shifting out of park. "That's going to be one noisy household."

"But a nice kind of noise," Maggie said as Jackson pulled into traffic. "Bye, bye, Bloomington! Eden, Indiana, here we come!"

As the Santa Fe turned onto Third Street, a tall man watched from a nearby corner. His eyes followed the SUV until it had disappeared over a hill.

"See you soon, Maggedy Ann," the man said, as he climbed into his own parked car. He glanced in the rear view mirror, momentarily catching sight of his smoldering scarlet eyes and began to laugh.

THE END

For now…

MYTHARC
"THE GREAT MYTHARC OF MANKIND"

Warning: Once you've connected the dots, your concept of our world will change forever. Are you sure you want to continue? Or would you rather remain asleep?

The real war began long ago—long before mankind began to fashion killing machines, long before human generals plotted campaigns over the bodies of bloodied men, long before the lust for power became the greatest of all human sins. Before the births of Socrates, Solomon, or Shakespeare, Evil struck the first blow in the war for control of men's souls.

Throughout the millennia since, the Shadow has altered his form again and again to fool mankind into trusting his insidious lies. A snake, a dragon, a mythological god, a politician, a bashful poet. Or more cunningly, he infiltrates God's camp in the guise of a priest or preacher, spewing forth doctrinal lies. This consummate conniver has but one plan: to defeat God at every turn. But God strikes back, sometimes with His eternal hand, sometimes through His mighty angels, and sometimes through the creation made slightly lesser than the angels, Man himself.

It is these lost tales of God's human warriors that we hope to present. Tales such as that of a beggar named Simeon, befriended by an antediluvian preacher named Enoch who walked with God and was no more. Or that of Denko, a sixth century shipwrecked sailor who stumbled across a tribe of giants in the days just before a megalithic asteroid crashed into Earth and plunged mankind into an age of darkness. Then there's the story of Elizabeth Branham, a wealthy English heiress who uncovered a nineteenth century plot to unseat God and crown Satan as Prince of the World. And the battle fought by a gentle doctor who strove to convince a small Kentucky town that the 1918 flu epidemic killing their loved ones is not the secret rapture, even though a man who claims to be a preacher twists God's own word and proclaims it to be the season of sheep and goats.

Follow the path forged by John Thundercloud, a Winnebago Indian in the 1950s, who can see into the realm of the Shadow. He must prevent the Enemy's followers from opening the Seven Gates of Hell that will unleash those kept in chains, even if it means the loss of his own life. Experience the battle through the lives of Light Warriors, Katherine Adamson, Joe Unes, Matt McGlone, Maggie Taylor, and Daniel Tohe, who know all too well of the terrifyingly thin line that separates night from day, slavery from freedom, and Shadow from Light.

Husband and wife authors, Sharon K. Gilbert and Derek P. Gilbert weave a complex pattern of literary threads that rip through that thin line to reveal the spiritual warfare that surrounds us. Sharing characters, timelines, and events, the Gilberts will take you on a thrill ride unlike any you've ever experienced—because what you read is real. The battle is real. The Enemy is real.

And he has set his sights on you.

Are you ready for the Truth? Do you have the courage to read these tales—tales that will shake you from your happy slumber? Are you ready to become a Light Warrior?

Then prepare your heart and your soul and join us. Welcome to the battlefield, dear reader. You are about to become a part of the great MythArc of Mankind.

Current Mytharc Titles include:
Winds of Evil:
Book One of the Laodicea Chronicles

The Armageddon Strain:
Book One of The Countdown

Visit www.mytharc.com for more information! Join the MythArc forum to discuss the books and keep up with the ongoing battle.

ABOUT THE AUTHOR
SHARON K. GILBERT

Born in the rolling hills of southern Indiana to Appalachian parents, Sharon brings a rich heritage to her writing. A childhood spent meandering crooked streams and dancing meadows coupled with a degree in molecular biology and a short career in opera have created a patchwork personality that feels at home with many genres.

Sharon has lived here, there, and everywhere, preferring her native Indiana to all other lands. While living in Indianapolis, Sharon, whose name was then Sharon Ferguson, sang jingles with the likes of Sandi Patty and Steve Greene, through whom she met David Clydesdale, then of Singspiration Music. As a born-again Christian, Sharon happily said yes to a one-year commitment as a featured vocalist with Clydesdale's CCM group, Life Unlimited, touring the continental US, Canada, and the U.K.

Later, as an older student at both the University of Nebraska and Indiana University, Sharon studied human genetics, music, literature, and history, giving her a well-rounded approach to learning and a full quiver for writing.

Sharon K. Gilbert

A lifelong interest in the supernatural and how it might be portrayed in fiction and on film has led Sharon to her current career as a writer of supernatural thrillers. Married to fellow writer Derek P. Gilbert, Sharon is stepmother to a precocious and very gifted teen named Nicole, in addition to acting as assistant keeper to the Gilbert Zoo (three rag-tag rescue dogs named Murphy, Belle, and Gretel). The Gilberts live in Manchester, Missouri.

Learn more about Sharon at her website:
http://www.sharonkgilbert.com.

Discover more about the MythArc Fiction series at the MythArc website: http://www.mytharc.com.

EXCERPTS FROM BOOK TWO OF
THE COUNTDOWN
NINE: DARKNESS

Robert Whitecalf glanced up at the full moon. This would be another crazy night. "Nothing like working third shift this time of the month," he said as he turned a small silver key to unlock the drug cabinet. "You'll find out soon enough. So, how you liking it so far?"

Nancy Howard checked her lipstick in the small mirror that hung on a nail just over a cracked porcelain sink. "It's okay. Quieter than I figured."

Whitecalf began loading up two trays on a stainless steel cart with miniature paper cups, each one labeled with a patient's name and room number. "Yeah, well, it won't stay quiet for long. Here, take this tray. Make Mrs. Olson your last stop. She's probably reading, so she'll complain that you've interrupted her."

"Mrs. Olson's blind, isn't she? She got a Braille copy?"

Whitecalf laughed. "No, she just pretends she's reading. Tell her it's lights out in half an hour. No later."

"Lights out? Doesn't she keep her room dark all the time?"

"Tell her lights out anyway. She likes to think she can still see. I guess I would, too, if cancer had eaten up both my eyes."

"Nice mental picture, Robert," Howard answered with a slight shiver. She took the dull silver tray and headed toward the east wing. Keying herself through the metal security door, she quickly closed it behind her, making sure it had locked. "Ok, folks! Come get your goodies!" she called into the dim corridor. "Mrs. Nelson, you're first," she continued, turning into the first room on the right.

Nedra Nelson had lived in Oldham Mental Hospital since just before her thirteenth birthday, when she'd set her parents on fire for not baking her a chocolate cake. Nancy found her sitting near the darkened window, staring at the pale round orb in the midnight sky.

"It's gonna rain," Nedra murmured. "Gonna rain dark."

"Sure it is," Nancy answered. "Here you go, sweetie. Take this and you'll have a real nice nap."

Nedra traced a circle in the condensation on the window. "Cold," she whispered. "Cold moon. Cold sun. Rain dark."

"Yeah, yeah," Nancy replied mechanically, pouring a cup of water from the pitcher. "Take these, Nedra. They're candy."

Nelson glanced back over her shoulder and stared at Howard. "Candy? Like chocolate?"

"Sure, like chocolate."

The wrinkled crone took the tablets and washed them down with the tepid water. "Yuck!" she spit back. "Not chocolate!"

"Sorry, Nedra. I'll get you some chocolate tomorrow. Now go to sleep."

"Not tomorrow," Nelson said sadly. "Nothing tomorrow. Rain. Dark." She turned back to the window and continued drawing on the slick pane.

Shrugging, Howard slipped back into the hallway and locked the door behind her. She continued with each room, dispensing the proper medications and making small talk with the inmates. *This isn't so bad. Once I get used to the odd hours, this job will be a snap! Maybe losing my job at General wasn't so bad after all. Bunch of self-righteous liars!*

The last room belonged to Letitia Olson, a fifty-something woman with over-bleached hair and inch-long black roots. The cramped room always smelled like mildew and roses.

"Mrs. Olson?" Nancy called as she entered the dark room. "Ready for your pills?"

In the far corner of the room, a shadow moved. Two silhouette hands pantomimed the turn of a page. "I'm reading," a voice crackled.

"I know, but it's time for your pills. Don't you want to have a good night's sleep?"

"Never sleep anymore. Don't care. I want to read my book."

"Well, you take these two little pills, and I'll let you read for a while longer. How's that?"

An arthritic hand dropped the white pills onto a dark tongue and the woman smacked her lips.

"I'll see you in the morning," Nancy said.

The woman's hands moved as if closing a book, and she set the invisible novel aside. "I doubt it," she muttered, leaning into the faint light that spilled in from the window.

Nancy shuddered as the woman's pale face—a skeletal oval with empty black holes where eyes should be—came into view. "Oh my God!" she exclaimed. "Oh, Mrs. Olson, I'm sorry."

Lettie Olson laughed, her blackened teeth clicking together like grotesque castanets. "Ain't I pretty? Look at me! Look at what God holds in store for you!"

Nancy backed toward the door, her heart pounding in her ears. "Goodnight, Mrs. Olson. I'll see you at breakfast."

"You ain't leavin', dearie! No, siree! You ain't leavin' at all!" the crone cackled as Nancy slammed the door. *She's crazy! Maybe this isn't for me after all. Working with screw jobs.*

Wiping sweat from her brow, Nancy made a mental note to check her makeup before taking a smoke break. That cute intern over on C Ward might be there, and she wanted to make a good impression.

As she reached the security door, she set down the meds tray on the polished marble floor for a moment, and fumbled through her right pocket. *Stupid keys! Where did I put them?*

Behind her, she could hear Mavis Lockhart screaming that the cockroaches were eating her fingers. *Whitecalf's right about the full moon. Lunatics!*

Corey Washington began to sing while Theresa Pennington wailed to her dead father. Barks, howls, and pleas for help joined the lunar symphony, and Nancy clapped her hands over both ears to muffle the terrifying chorus. "Stop it!" she screamed. *Where are those keys? Did I leave them in Olsen's room?*

"That's it," Nancy said aloud. "When she startled me, the keys must have dropped to the floor."

Nancy turned around, intent on retrieving her keys.

She would never make it that far.

As she turned, her heavily painted eyes widened at the shadows moving toward her. Black, stretched tall, and breathing.

"Is someone there?" she whispered tensely, acid rising in her throat. "Robert, is that you?"

Rhythmic breathing. Closer this time. Halfway up the corridor, the inky shadows slowly lengthened toward Nancy's shoes.

"Robert, this is not funny. I can report this!"

Time to pay, a voice echoed in her mind. Time to atone for all those babies you killed, Nancy. All those innocent children!

"That's a lie! It wasn't me! The board agreed! You can't blame me for six crib deaths!"

Six murders, the dark voice crackled as darkness consumed the hallway.

"I didn't do it!" Nancy wailed, and she spun toward the locked door, beating on the shatter-proof glass with both hands. "Help! Help me!"

Who helped those children? No one. Not God, not you. No one. You're going to die, Nancy. Die in darkness. And we will keep you with us—always.

Unwillingly, Nancy slowly turned back toward the Shadows, grown tall and angular now and bearing eyes. The lifeless eyes of dead babies.

Nancy opened her mouth to scream, but nothing came out. Terror had frozen her muscles and her vocal cords. Wispy black fingers reached toward her face—toward her beautifully painted eyes—and Nancy's last thoughts were of the handsome intern. She would never get to have that smoke with him. She would never see him—or anything—again.

Robert Whitecalf whistled as he locked up the office at just past midnight. He closed the door behind him and took two steps. He froze as he took in the scene before him. "Dear God!" he cried. Whitecalf stared, jaws agape, his mind numb.

Scattered throughout the narrow hallway, a jumble of flesh and bone decorated the marble flooring like pale islands in a river of steaming blood. Flies feasted upon the ripped and quivering flesh, laying eggs in noses and open mouths. The twisted mounds barely looked human, but Robert knew nearly every patient lay here, dead or dying, fingernails broken and hands covered in sticky red.

Robert shook his head, willing himself to think clearly. Stepping carefully, he forced himself to look upon the anarchy of death at his feet. The smell nearly overpowered him, but he stumbled into every room, checking for patients. One by one, each room echoed his voice—empty. Finally reaching the end of the hallway, Robert gasped as he recognized a pile of blood and crimson rags.

"Nancy!" he cried, bending down, blood soaking the knees of his white uniform. "Nancy! Can you hear me?"

She lay on her stomach, her carefully arranged dark waves soaked in her blood. He turned her over, but she was dead.

As she fell onto her back, Whitecalf screamed.

Nancy Howard's beautiful dark eyes were gone—replaced with angry red holes that stared at Whitecalf accusingly.

"Dark!" sang Nedra Nelson, who sat a few feet away, her own eyes torn from their sockets. "Rain—dark!"

"Dear God in heaven!" Whitecalf cried out, his shocked brain reeling as tears of anguish ran down his face.

"No God," Nedra said with her final strength. "All dark now. All done. Nedra sleep now. No more chocolate. No more light."

The woman stood up for a moment, shakily feeling her way toward Whitecalf, then fell across Nancy Howard's lifeless body.

Robert, his dark hair turned a freakish white, leaned against the spattered wall, laughter rising from an uneasy stomach. Just before his mind snapped, he noticed someone had written words on the far wall—jagged letters in blood.

DARKNESS SHALL COVER THE LAND.
AND SATAN SHALL RULE AT LAST.

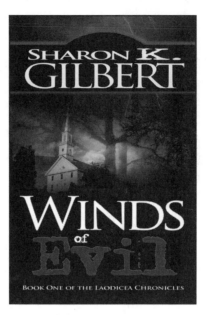

Winds of Evil
Sharon K. Gilbert

What would you do if your town was infested with demons?
When Katherine Adamson returns to her idyllic hometown, everything
has changed. The once peaceful town now has a deep evil boiling under
the surface. Already it's threatening to escape.
Two well-loved high school teens have disappeared, with a running
car and a bloody shoe the only clues to their whereabouts. Strange
lights have appeared over a local farm, leaving behind only
blackened circles. The town's leaders are being blackmailed,
and one has committed suicide.
Katy has returned to settle her aunt's estate, but she finds herself
battling a host of evil she never would have imagined.

ISBN: 0-88368-809-3 • Trade • 304 pages

WHITAKER
HOUSE
www.whitakerhouse.com

www.deepercalling.com